GECKO

by

Dick Tummel

Publishers:
Inspiring Publishers
PO box 159 Calwell ACT 2905, Australia.
Email: inspiringpublishers@gmail.com

National Library of Australia Cataloguing-in-Publication entry

Author: Tummel, Dick

Title: **Gecko**/*Dick Tummel.*

ISBN: 9781925346558 (pbk)

Subjects: Spy stories.
        Guerrilla warfare—Fiction.
        Suspense fiction.

Front cover by Ben King Benkingphotographer.com.

Dewey Number: A823.4

For
Angus & Oliver

Prologue

The mountains of China's Chongzuo Prefecture were high and imposing. Heavily forested, their steep formations created narrow valleys for descending streams to feed into the river Yong. Along these waterways, small and remote communities eked out an existence where they could, but Mao Zedong's infamous Great Leap Forward made survival even less likely than it normally was. In an avoidable famine of immense proportion and immeasurable human loss, tens of millions perished and the most populated nation on earth became shrouded in death.

Now, on the outskirts of a small riverside collective in Daxin County, the legacy of one woman's misery was about to begin...

Chapter One

Guangxi Zhuang Autonomous Region. China.
Chongzuo Prefecture
Daxin County
August 2nd 1972

It was late. Hot and humid. Downstream of idle fishing pots, the water glistened in moonlight as tall trees formed a ghostly gauntlet the length of its run. Burdened with odours of stale peanut oil, ginger and fried crabmeat, the darkness hung heavily over the quiet.

Silent and unseen, a small boy crouched hidden in nearby bushes. His face was a study of concentration and his body was sticky with sweat. Dressed in an open threadbare shirt and black pull-on pants that finished just below his knees, he dug his toes into the cool soil and leaned forward in a vain attempt to understand what he was seeing.

Yung Cheng Bao, was ten years old, strong and stocky and an obvious half-caste. Quiet and reclusive, he had no friends and rarely spoke. Throughout the Collective they called him

'Mongoose' due to an ugly stain of white pigment that ran up his neck to the corners of his mouth. The *mao yo* or mongoose, had similar markings, and while not intended as a term of endearment, Cheng Bao took satisfaction in being likened to an animal that was ferocious and cunning. And just like the *mao yo*, Mongoose, was a great deal tougher than he looked.

Willing himself not to blink in case he missed something, he peered intently into the shadows at his mother slumped twenty feet beyond. Wrapped in a tattered shawl, her upper body moved backwards and forwards in slow rhythmic arcs as she rocked his infant sister at the water's edge. His young heart pounded with uncertainty and foreboding.

Isabella Yung gazed lovingly at the little girl suckling at her breast. The subtle blend of her Spanish and Chinese bloodline was clearly visible. Delicately arched eyebrows and long lashes framed wide eyes that opened and closed languidly as she fed. Flawless olive skin ran smoothly over exquisite features heightening the angelic innocence of one so blessed. She was beautiful. Gently placing her index finger into a searching hand, Isabella felt her daughter grasp and squeeze it. A tear welled and rolled down Isabella's cheek.

Fourteen years earlier things had been very different. China had at long last emerged from its revolution and grand plans for its future were unfolding. It was a heady and intoxicating period, especially for the youth, and particularly for Isabella who, while on exchange at the Jesuit mission in Guangzhou, had fallen in love and married. Her beau, the dashing Yung Cheng Da - a promising scholar and heir to Yung Trading - was also swept up in the excitement. Despite the many warning from family and friends, the couple, armed with little more than youthful zeal and idyllic optimism, settled in Daxin County to live a life of happiness farming the land. But it was not to be.

Years of ravaging floods and inevitable famines had taken their toll. And though they'd survived all that nature had thrown at them, they could never escape being of mixed blood. Then, as now, it was racial abuse that defined their existence, and its isolation... the most difficult to endure. Alone, always hungry, and exceedingly poor, the family and their dreams had withered.

It is said in Asia that raising a daughter is like watering the neighbour's garden; a ludicrous notion in the West, but in the East where extreme poverty was endured on a daily basis, it was simply a pragmatic truth. Isabella ached with the burden of her decision.

Knowing their son was frequently attacked and mocked by the other children was heartbreaking and unbearable. She knew he survived only because he was male. A little girl, she reasoned, would not.

Isabella suddenly felt cold. Reaching under her clothing she took a small carving knife and placed it down near a plank of wood. Tenderly stroking at the generous tufts of black hair on her daughter's head, she removed her nipple, swaddled the baby tightly and drew her up to her shoulder to release the trapped pockets of wind.

She had heard about the dying rooms where orphans were left to die without feeding. She knew about the poisons too, but they were not for her daughter. No, her child's fate, she had decided, would be determined only by God. Lifting herself onto her knees, Isabella kissed the little girl softly and held her at arms length.

"Your name is Mae Lin," she proclaimed loudly.

Holding back tears as best she could, she placed the tiny bundle on the plank, crossed herself with the prayer, "E*n el nombre del Padre, y del Hijo, y del Espíritu Santo*," and set her daughter adrift in the current.

"Go with God," she whispered.

Immediately Isabella Yung picked up the knife, placed the tip at the nape of her neck and, with all her strength, forced its sudden entry into her body to the hilt. In her desperation to punish her own guilt through death, she did not hear the piercing cries of anguish from her panicked son hiding in the bushes.

Cheng Da woke with a start. The family home was in near darkness and he sensed the hour was late. The wick in the diesel lamp was almost out and his reading glass had fallen from his lap to the floor. Wondering why Isabella hadn't woken him for bed as she usually did, he rose to the washbasin, doused his head with the refreshing cold water and listened. It was quiet. Unusually so. Ambling to the bedroom he stood in the doorway and called out.

"Isabella?" But there was no answer.

Suddenly the front door burst open and in the entrance stood his son breathing heavily and dripping wet.

Cheng Da's heart skipped a beat. "Cheng Bao, where is your mother?"

With his eyes beseeching, Cheng Bao held out his arms to his father and moved forward. A soft cry came from the sodden bundle he was holding.

"Her name is Mae Lin father. Do not worry, I will take care of her, she is half-caste like me."

Chapter Two

Singapore
July 1980

The dank smell of the basement permeated every pore of her skin as the little girl struggled to hold her weight on a single leg. It had been nearly forty minutes since her punishment had begun and the ache in her muscles made her head faint and her mind giddy. Determined not to fail, she knew her suffering would only worsen if she weakened and stood on both feet. The telltale rice paper wrapped around her right foot would certainly betray her if she did. To keep it away from the moisture, she tucked it carefully behind the knee of her supporting left leg and waited.

The room, blanketed in darkness was eerily quiet except for the loud echo of water falling from overhead pipes. Straining her ears toward the sounds, she listened over her own breathing to the shifting resonance of each drop.

The rainy season had arrived in Singapore and the worn pipes of her uncle's mansion could no longer cope. Yung Mae Lin was now eight. Her body was slight and shapeless.

Through the small ground-level windows the faint luminescence of the outside security light danced on the puddles nearest her feet. Her eyes, in search of something visible latched on to the undulating movement and memories of China flooded back. Inevitably her thoughts returned, as they always did, to the day that remained most vivid. It was her last day at home and she was six.

It was late Spring in Daxin County, the Bush Warbler's sang their periodic three-note song between feeds on fat insects and the earth was beginning to dry and crack. Squatting low to the ground in the sun, little Mae Lin watched entranced as a line of ants carried the remains of a grasshopper to their nest. She marveled at their determination to surmount obstacles and admired their fearless aggression when driven into the ground with a stick.

"Where are you?" Rang a familiar voice.

"Over here," she called, not moving.

Mongoose appeared through the underbrush dressed in his Sunday best and spotted his sister. His manner was unusually curt. "You must come to the house," he said.

"Wait, come and look at this," she replied, still absorbed in her ants.

Reaching down, Mongoose took her arm. "There is no time. Father said you must come now." Whisking her homeward, his long paces caused Mae Lin to skip several times to keep up.

"Why are you walking so fast?" She puffed.

"Uncle Wu is here."

Mae Lin suddenly leant back on her arm and tried to stop their momentum. Unhindered, her much larger brother maintained his speed and his grip. "Come on, don't do that," he said, "they're waiting."

Mae Lin struggled even harder. "I don't want to, don't Cheng Bao, let me go."

Arriving at the rear of the house Mongoose paused and knelt down to deal with his sister's despondence. "Hey," he said gently lifting her chin, "don't worry, you're not going to be eaten." Straightening her hair and brushing the dirt from her knees he playfully poked at her ribs. "Let's face it, there's nothing on these bones worth cooking!"

Mae Lin lashed out with her foot and giggled. Mongoose smiled and gently rubbed her nose with his fist. "Remember, little one, whatever happens, you must respect what our father says. This is very hard for him. Please try and keep face."

Mae Lin tossed her arms around her older brother and buried her head in his neck. Mongoose hugged her reassuringly and held firm. "Ready?" He asked. She nodded and he stood to escort her in.

Cheng Da poured tea into Wu's cup as the children entered to wait politely until directly addressed. Mae Lin, suddenly frightened, moved a shoulder behind her brother and looked on.

Uncle Wu accepted the tea and continued talking as if his new audience didn't exist. Dressed in a beige suit he was slightly shorter than her father but heavier set. His shirt shone brilliant white and his fragrant *eau de toilette* filled the room with the scent of musk. His dark hair, cropped high at the back, was rigidly combed from one side, over his head to the other. His chubby cheeks narrowed upward to thin yellowing eyes obscured at the corners by excess skin drooping down from his lids. Cleanshaven, he had a mole on the left side of his face, which had three thick black hairs growing out from its centre like plumes. Long fingernails glistened as he wrapped and unwrapped his hands nervously on the handle of his black lacquered cane. Preparing for speech he habitually ran his tongue over his lower lip, which left it permanently shiny and wet. When he did speak, his voice was high pitched and his tone sarcastic. To Mae Lin, he looked like a snake that had just shed its skin.

"Can she read?" He asked.

"Not perfectly," said Cheng Da, "but she is very bright and getting better. I have been teaching her."

Wu struggled to read the tattered cover of the only book in sight. The Fundamentals of National Reconstruction by Sun Yat-sen. Raising an unimpressed eyebrow he sighed heavily and looked about the room.

"How can you live in this ... squalor? What on earth possessed an educated man to give up residential *hukou* and become a peasant? What has it achieved? You must have known you could never go back?"

"That is true."

"And now, after years of silence ... years of not knowing if you were alive or dead, you expect your sister and I to take on the responsibilities borne of this rural romp. Really, it is all too much. You have brought shame upon our families with your sordid worship of foreign blood." He looked with conspicuous disdain at Mongoose's discoloured neck, "The results of which are obviously incompatible, don't you think?"

Cheng Da felt the barb but did not show it. "You are right to correct me on my lack of contact. Unfortunately your correspondence seeking news of my health did not reach me to jog my senses. I note however, that my disappearance has not hampered your ambition with my father's estate. I trust you are not wanting?"

At the mention of the estate, Wu's hands flexed uncomfortably over his cane, "No. Thank you. I am indeed well looked after." Concerned, his tongue deposited more saliva on his already saturated lip, "Surely you do not intend to lay claim?"

Cheng Da let the question hang as he sipped his tea. "Pursuance of my right, brother-in-law, is not something I care to consider at this time. It is quite obvious that you are far better suited to my father's trade than his eldest son, and as you so eloquently point out, my needs are few. However, I am not asking for myself. Without assistance, Mae Lin has no future, and as long as I choose to remain here I have nothing to offer. You see my dilemma, do you not?"

Wu carefully brought a handkerchief from his pocket and dabbed softly at his forehead to soak up the sweat. He knew very well where the real dilemma lay and he was clearly trapped. If he took the 'bastard child' as his wife described her, she would make his life hell. If he did not, her brother would claim what was his and they would lose all they had. Looking across at the children he pointed his cane and spoke directly to Mae Lin.

"Come here, child."

With the assistance of Mongoose, Mae Lin stepped forward to be scrutinised by the yellow-eyed snake.

Overwhelmed by the scent of his perfume she felt a sudden pain in her chest. The prod of the cane was intense.

"I see you have kept it dry," Wu said.

Immediately Mae Lin's consciousness returned to the dank basement in Singapore and her uncle's smirking countenance now close to her face. Having just eaten, he still carried the napkin from the dining table in his other hand. Using it to delicately wipe at the corners of his mouth, he straightened himself to speak.

"Your aunt has agreed for you to eat in the kitchen once you've cleaned up. A magnanimous gesture that in my opinion was neither warranted nor deserved. Your physical attack on her friend's daughter was unforgivable and caused considerable embarrassment for us both. Such behaviour, in light of our generosity, is contemptuous. What have you to say for yourself?"

"Uncle, please, she deserved it, she called me Chap Cheng, and said half-castes were not wanted."

Uncle Wu was incredulous. "This is not the backwater of Guangxi!" He exclaimed. "Here in Singapore we do not attack people on a whim... particularly if the recipient of your abuse has merely spoken the truth." He prodded her chest again and licked his lip, "Most unreasonable, don't you think?"

Mae Lin's face betrayed both hurt and immediate defiance. Her uncle, reading the signs, narrowed his eyes and gave warning, "A bough that doesn't bend in the wind will eventually break don't you know." He leaned in and smiled, "Even a Chap Cheng should understand that."

Smugly satisfied, he swung on his heels and walked off. "You may lower your leg," he called. "Staff practice is at nine, don't be late."

The hum of the heavy and wooden seven-foot Bo filled the room as Wu demonstrated consummate skill with the staff. With every movement Mae Lin flinched in anticipation of the coming attack. Armed with a smaller Jo more suited to her size, her lack of confidence caused her feet to shift.

"Feet still," her uncle yelled. "Hold your form and watch the arms. In *Bojitsu*," he added with a majestic sweep, "you cannot allow yourself to be mesmerized by the wood."

Even at half pace Mae Lin struggled to control her fear of being struck. Holding basic position, she tensed as her uncle advanced.

"Now!" He instructed, *"Age uke."*

Mae Lin quickly adopted the vertical defence and her arms reverberated under the force of impact.

"Now!" He called, *"Sokumen uke."*

Hurriedly she moved to defend her side as her undisciplined feet moved together and her body arched.

"Hold your form," her uncle yelled, *"Sokumen uke,"* he repeated, immediately attacking her other side.

Unable to get there in time, her uncle's Bo slid down her soft defence and struck her bottom hand. Instantly, Mae Lin cried out, dropped the Jo and violently shook her wrist for relief. Wu quickly responded and struck the top of her shoulder from above. *"Age uke,"* he yelled. The blow was measured but Mae Lin immediately went to ground holding her arms over her head and whimpered.

Uncle Wu was unmoved. "On your feet."

"I am hurt," she cried.

"Of course you are, you threw away your Jo."

"You hit my hand."

"And now, in addition, you hurt somewhere else! Perhaps next time you will hang on to your defence." Wu prodded her in the side with his Bo, "On your feet or I will strike you again."

Mae Lin stood gingerly and, still sniffling, wiped her eyes with the back of her hand.

"The greater the pain, the greater the lesson." Wu said as he picked up the Jo and offered it back. But it was refused.

"Take it," he ordered

"No"

"I said, take it!"

"I don't want to. It's stupid." She cried.

Wu sighed. "You wouldn't say that if you knew what it was."

"Its a stick." Mae Lin mumbled belligerently still rubbing her eyes.

"Then you are more of a fool than I thought," he countered.

Unperturbed by her recalcitrance, Wu played aimlessly with the wood, as he spoke. "As you know, *Bojitsu* was developed in Okinawa, but it may surprise you to also learn that Okinawa is in many ways like your home in Guangxi ... full of mixed bloods and peasants."

Mae Lin raised defiant eyes to meet her uncle's, and pleased to have her attention, he licked his lip. "Four hundred years ago the conquering samurai Shimazu Lehisa, the daimyo of Satsuma, invaded the southern lands and banned weapons throughout all the Ryukyus. With the peasant farmers unarmed, the Japanese masters reasonably believed there could be no revolt. But you will discover, Mae Lin, just like the samurai, that things are not always as they appear."

Suddenly, Wu let out a blood-curdling scream, and using the Jo, swept Mae Lin from her feet. As soon as her body hit the floor he pounded the end of the staff in a mock killer blow that landed just inches from her cheek. The power of the strike shook the room and, though unharmed, Mae Lin was too frightened to shift.

Satisfied with the effect, Wu withdrew to resume his distance. "Please return to your feet," he requested.

When she had risen, Wu spoke firmly. "Do you know what it is now?"

Mindful of her safety, Mae Lin complied. "A weapon."

"Exactly! " He smiled. "In the right hands it has the power to snap the sword of a samurai into pieces." He rotated the Jo one way, then the other. "And unlike the sword, it is equally formidable at either end. Most impressive don't you think?"

Wu eyed his niece with contemptuous pity and sighed heavily. "And so. Here we are some four centuries later, and another misery-guts peasant stands before me, her unfortunate uncle. Weak and oppressed, she weeps for herself while longing to strike back. Yet right before her eyes is the very thing she so desperately seeks... a weapon."

"A weapon," he added, while admiring the wood, "that at first glance, looks nothing more than a simple stick."

Wu extended his arms, and offered it back.

"It is up to you to decide," he stated. "Stick or weapon? Weakness or strength? Chap Cheng or Ryukyuan?"

Realising the significance of the moment, Mae Lin controlled her loathing and reached out to accept the staff, and in doing so, sealed her fate.

Chapter Three

N.E. Province, Laos.
October 7th 1996.

It was only an hour into the day in The Land of the Million Elephants and already the air was thick and sticky, and the heat stifling. A narrow tributary slowly wound its way through wild and inhospitable jungle as a red-tailed Pipe snake glided easily over its surface looking for prey. Great fallen tree trunks, victims of monsoons past, spanned the embankments as the inexorable vegetation reached out to reclaim the land. In the shadows, clumps of mosquitoes droned noisily over their larvae.

Quickly moving from hiding place to vantage point, a lizard paused briefly on a protruding outcrop of rotting wood. With its throat puffing frantically, it scanned for danger. Suddenly startled, it disappeared.

From the distance came a flotilla of six small dinghies, each black and dull and emerging one behind the other. With oars carefully placed and drawn they made silent and purposeful progress upstream. Aboard were twenty-four men, all soldiers, all camouflaged, all heavily armed.

These were not regular soldiers. Assorted kit and styles blended with an array of customised weaponry that defined subtle and individual preferences for the kill. All choices that elite men of Special Forces were inclined to make.

Australian SAS Major John Landau, code-named Gecko, sat at the bow of the lead boat. Tall and athletic, his high cheek-bones were accentuated by the shadow of a two-day growth. In relative comfort, his cool eyes were vigilant and his mind relaxed. While afforded the opportunity, he contemplated the coming mission, the men he accompanied and their mission commander.

Tall, with blonde hair cut close to his scalp, the dignified major from the highly rated Russian Spetsnaz was known only as Boris. Sixteen of the soldiers here were Russian; this was their party and their war. Apart from himself, Risso and six Laotian commandos, everything about this mission was Russian.

It was not surprising, thought John, that Boris played his cards close to his chest... they were, after all, joined from camps that were diametrically opposed. But it was of concern that neither he nor Risso were involved in the planning and only Russian Intelligence had been used. Nevertheless, he liked Boris and his soldiers. It always followed that men of a certain ilk respected similar qualities in others.

Each was aware that while they fought together today, it was highly probable that tomorrow might see them opposing. Even during this joint incursion, their respective countries were no doubt plotting against one another on various fronts. It was an irony of the profession that never sat well with John.

Up until a week ago he had known little about the Russian involvement in Indo China. There were strong rumours that the alliance between the government of Laos and the Kremlin, via Vietnam, was embroiled in ethnic cleansing. A charge often repeated by human rights advocates, but vehemently denied by the accused.

Since the end of the Vietnam War and the fall of Cambodia's Pol Pot, Russian political manoeuvring in the region required more than economic aid alone. Now, military assistance was needed to crush pockets of resistance against the incumbent parties. Some pockets had proven more difficult than others, and it seemed, none were more difficult than the area they were now entering.

Warlord Xiang's hold on the N.E. Province had proven impossible to dislodge. His highly effective guerrillas had inflicted some devastating defeats on all comers, and in particular, Russian trained Vietnamese insurgent teams stationed in Laos. Not content simply to defend, the guerrillas were now beginning to conquer.

Politically aware, the ambitious Xiang had acquired covert assistance from terrorist organisations from around the world. This, and the very public shooting down of a Russian YAK-24, was the final precursor to a call for help from Force Delta: The West's pre-eminent covert anti terrorism and insurgency group. Their mission was an intelligence gathering reconnaissance better known as a 'Search and Capture' and John and Risso were there to advise.

Two boats astern sat US Ranger Major Anthony Griswald, code-named Risso. A lanky Texan, with a distinctive drawl and mischievous humour, and his best friend.

The pair had been inseparable since being assigned to Force Delta four years earlier. The highly skilled Ranger was the first man John had met who could cough without making a sound, and only the second he could trust with his life. He was a complete soldier and ideally suited to his line of work.

Catching John's gaze, Risso gave a laconic smile and raised his eyebrows mockingly toward the rest of the group.

The sound of crackling headsets broke the silence. In his native tongue, a huge Russian sergeant boomed down the line.

"Landing one hundred metres."

"Good," said Boris. "I'll be much happier out of this floating bathtub. Keep an eye on the visitors for me, Mikhaiel, we don't want them damaged."

The sergeant grinned widely, "Ha! Now there's a problem I don't need... watching Western arses!"

"In that case," Risso responded, "You and your perverted Bolshevik mates should watch your own arses and keep your filthy red mother-fucking communist eyes off mine. Thankyou and God bless America."

The banter pleased the whole group and momentarily their mood relaxed. John pulled them back.

"Mind on the job gentlemen." He pointed to a likely landing, "What about here Commander?"

"Excellent!" Replied Boris, "Let's get wet."

In unison they leapt from the dinghies and secured them to the bank. Then with weapons held high they hugged the shoreline and waded upstream.

Closer to the nearby foothills the vegetation expanded in volume and became more defined. Huge trees soared a hundred feet into the sky ... their thick canopy creating the perfect environment for the plush undergrowth below. Like a land of make-believe, everything was larger: the insects, the leaves, and the enormous roots along the ground. With the cooler air came the damp scent of rotting humus.

At a small clearing on the water's edge, a lone forward scout crouched in hiding with his weapon ready. As droplets of water trickled down his blackened face, he remained deathly still as his eyes searched for movement and his ears strained to detect sound. Slowly he unfolded the butt of his AK-105 and lowered it into the water. With eyes still trained ahead, he reached for his blade and tapped the weapon's muzzle three times.

Behind him, the heads of his comrades immediately broke the water's surface. With practiced precision they emerged above the waterline with their weapons arcing through all directions. In moments, they were ashore and out of sight.

Two hours later the squad had advanced 700 metres into the jungle. In rough extended line the men made careful progress toward their target. Now, using only hand signals, each man concentrated on the slow walk: short steps, toes up, the outside of the ball of the foot first, then all the ball, then heel, then weight. Each patiently avoided branches and cracking twigs. With their senses on high alert, they all continually scanned the undergrowth and canopy for an enemy lying in wait.

The sergeant dodged and weaved with the agility of a man half his size. He was enjoying himself. His rising adrenaline fuelled by the tension of the moment and his heightened anticipation. Few men, he thought, could understand the euphoria of putting your life on the line. It was the ultimate test of a man and in his opinion, a test to be savoured.

Having successfully passed a decaying bough, the big man rounded upon Risso ten metres to his right. Despite his rhetoric, the veteran knew good men when he saw them and the two Westerners were undoubtedly good. Risso, aware of the camaraderie gave him a pronounced sassy look and Mikhaiel responded in pantomime with a blown kiss. Smiling, the sergeant placed his next step ... suddenly, there was an audible 'snap'.

Instantly both men stopped. Risso quickly wheeled his head about as the sergeant deftly raised a hand to indicate he should stay where he was. Stoically the big man remained still. Forcing himself to concentrate, he replayed the sound over and over in his mind. Unable to draw on anything in his memory he cast a quizzical eye toward Risso who apologetically shook his head ... it was nothing he recognised either.

Careful not to adjust his weight, the Russian unsheathed a knife and delicately leaned down to probe the earth beneath his foot. Risso waited. Unable to find anything, the sergeant stood, took a deep breath and slowly, very slowly, lifted his leg. Nothing.

He expelled air in relief and nodded the 'all clear' to Risso who, equally relieved, nodded back. Watching the American move on, Mikhaiel took a moment to compose himself and wipe the sweat from his face. Satisfied and ready to continue, he motioned forward ...

It is unlikely he heard or felt anything from then on. Not the spike or the whoosh it caused as it sprang violently from the ground, or the thud it made as it plunged powerfully into his chest. Death was instant.

Risso immediately raised the alarm. "Booby Traps!" He whispered over the radio.

Everybody stopped. The warning, timely for all except one. Unfortunately a foot already lifted could not be replaced. Slashed by a vicious horizontal blade the victim's severed torso lay quietly twitching beside his bowel and legs.

"Casualties?" Requested Boris.

"One down. Mikhaiel, dead," said Risso.

"One here. Alex, also dead," said another.

Boris was calm. His men had been well trained. "Hold and cover," he instructed.

In unison the soldiers clicked safeties off and postured down.

"Ivan?" Said Boris.

"Yes Commander."

"You see anything?"

The forward scout had stopped thirty metres ahead of his party. His senses strained for anything unusual. Everything was quiet.

"No, nothing!"

The silence was palpable. The men aware that if their sergeant didn't see a trap, then it was just as likely they wouldn't either.

Boris quietly continued, "Charlie?"

"Commander?"

"Anything happening out back?"

The man at the rear was thirty metres behind the main group and three hundred metres from the rendezvous point: where they would all gather should anything go wrong. Like the scout, he saw nothing.

"Nothing at all."

John, fifty metres deep into the right flank squatted silent and alert. His eyes searched for signs of life. Nothing. Aware of something in the wind but unable to place it, he held his weapon with soft hands. His breathing was steady.

Boris addressed his troops. "It looks like we've stumbled onto an unmanned perimeter defence and a good one. Our enemy has talent so take that in. Intelligence insists this backdoor is wide open so we'll proceed. We'll give it ninety minutes just to be certain it is what we think it is. Ivan, stay on your toes in case we woke somebody."

"Roger."

"And everyone," Boris warned, "Remember the rule."

They all knew the rule the commander referred to. It was the rule of 'No Assistance'. A clever enemy would cover a trap with others. One man caught would invariably attract others to his aid, and this increased the potential for more victims. The rule saved lives, nobody doubted that, but few liked it. Having to walk passed a suffering comrade who was not yet dead, inevitably brought most men undone. If it didn't cause a mistake on the day, then later, the memory surely would.

For the moment however it was silence, patience and waiting ... all valued components of a commando's arsenal.

This was what set Special Forces apart. Years of dedicated training and psychological profiling to find elite men capable of performing at the edge of endurance. Men able to hold still for hours at a time, regardless of posture, or the weight of weapons and kit. Resisting itches, cramps, tickles or coughs. Controlling body and mind as well as fears and urges. Always alert and ready to strike at a moments notice.

Opposed to conventional theories of warfare, these men avoided noise at all cost, even when under attack. Silence was a weapon that gave the enemy no information. It unsettled them. In heavy jungle, if a man held his nerve long enough, his effect could be devastating.

Such was the theory being played out here. Patiently they waited, silently observing and listening. If an enemy did lie in wait, this would test his resolve. Not knowing the effect of his traps would sorely drive his curiosity to take a closer look. An hour passed. Nothing moved, nothing happened.

Risso waited patiently with his custom-built assault weapon pressed neatly against his shoulder. The lifeless and inert body of Mikhaiel, caught mid stride, was still visible from his position. The uncomfortable sound of his dripping blood had now thankfully ceased as death had run its course. Risso regretted not knowing him better, but he didn't dwell on it. Dead was dead. He knew the sergeant would have agreed.

Instead, his thoughts fell to his friend and the responsibility of being best man at his coming wedding. Since their joint induction into Force Delta, John had been talking about Rachel, in fact, she was all he ever talked about. Risso warmed at the thought of a union that was obviously meant. Rachel was John's counterweight and she gave him balance in a life that was ugly and confronting. It was a heavy burden placed upon men asked to visit the places he and John had seen and to do the things that they did. He shuddered at the thought of what John would be like without her. No man, before or since had been as efficient in the art of combat as John, and Risso was fully aware that if anything ever opened the door to Gecko's 'dark side', there would be no one to stop him.

Ninety minutes passed without incident. The radio sprang to life.

"Ivan?" Boris queried.

"Clear."

"Charlie?"

"Clear."

"Let's move."

Content they had eliminated all possible risk, the men clicked safeties back on and resumed their mission. John didn't move. Something was not right. On the other flank, Risso's alarm-bells were also ringing.

High above and unseen, a heavy ten-foot wooden spike descended silently. Building momentum, it swung through its lethal arc toward a soldier who had no idea it was coming. The force of impact picked him up mid-torso and drove him backwards, spearing him onto a tree. The air was immediately filled with the chilling screams of the impaled man as he writhed in agony. Unnerved, two Laotian commandos from either side of him rushed to his aide. Both men were instantly killed by spikes lying in wait for their error. The screams continued unabated. Everyone was in desperate search of an enemy, but they could see nothing.

Risso's soft voice came over the radio, "Gecko?"

"Yeah I feel it," John responded.

An arrow suddenly slammed into the screaming man's heart and ended his torment. A sinister message came with the quiet. The enemy had finally arrived.

Boris had been in fire-fights many times and the familiar rise of tension quickened his pulse. But this was different. His body became cold with the realisation that he and his men had been outplayed on a field in which they should have had no equal. They were in big trouble and he knew it.

As did John. The fact that they had not sensed an enemy building could mean only one thing. Clearing his mind, he prepared for battle and spoke softly into his mouthpiece. "They're among us," he said.

"Pull back," Boris commanded.

But it was too late. From everywhere guerrillas appeared from hiding. With blood curdling screams they hacked at falling bodies with machetes and thrashing knives.

"Ambush." Risso called, "It's a fucking trap."

Now with an enemy to engage the Special Forces could at last fight. Automatic weapons spat lead from everywhere. Exchanges of small arms fire were joined by the heavy rhythmic volleys of machine guns. Overhead, the whistle of mortar rounds fell to explode behind them and cut off hope of escape. It was chaotic and soon apparent that they were fatally undermanned and outgunned. With the air thick with cordite, the battle raged and intensified as men from both sides were killed.

Boris, bleeding from a side wound, bravely held his ground until the weight of numbers surging toward him quickly became too much. Struggling to change his magazine in time, a huge cudgel wielding giant attacked him just moments before he could release the bolt. The Commander fell where he stood.

John was besieged from everywhere as the enemy attacked in waves. Calm and steady in the hail of bullets, he minimised his own target area and returned bursts into their centre mass. Seizing his opportunities to move, he ran left and fired. He then changed direction right and fired again, ... one moment he was withdrawing and the very next he was attacking. Highly accurate with instinctive firing from either shoulder or hip, John was Force Delta and knew exactly how to counter-punch with effect.

His rapid movement and deadly purpose cut a wedge of carnage into the enemy line. One attacker fell, then another and another and more followed. Backwards and forward he moved, traversing left and right. Hidden or open, he was slick and efficient. Deceptively mobile, then suddenly still ... brutal and unpredictable. But the numbers were incredible as victorious guerrillas from other parts of the battle swelled the odds. Again and again they came through the jungle until he was almost overrun.

Elusive and courageous John ran faster, dodging and weaving until suddenly he triggered a trap. His heightened awareness and sideways movement assisted the speed of his reaction as he barely avoided the spike. But the surprising velocity of the attack wrenched the weapon from his grasp. Immediately vulnerable and drawing fire, he rolled to regain balance and threw a grenade to mask his escape.

Armed or unarmed John remained lethal, and in this environment he excelled far beyond others. Quickly diverting into the path of two guerrillas he moved like lightning with both hand and knife. With blinding speed he severed the carotid artery of one man and left the other with a broken neck. Grabbing the dead man's prized AK and pouches he quickly reloaded, cocked and fired just in time to defend against certain death. Pursued but now re-armed he suddenly wheeled around to movement on his left flank.

Risso burst through the undergrowth in full flight from an enemy in hot pursuit. Quickly spotting his partner he rolled clear of the firing line and John cut them down.

"Rendezvous compromised," Risso said quickly as they both opened fire on an enemy now on two fronts. Using cover and movement they edged sideways as fast as they could. It was relentless! With practiced teamwork and alert to diminishing ammunition the two, both agile and accurate, inflicted enormous casualties ... yet still they came. More and more, again and again. From empty rifles to pistols they used everything they had until done. When that time came, the two professionals had only one choice.

"I'll take the gorge," said John.

"I'll take the river," Risso replied.

Immediately they parted. Risso one way, and John the other.

With ears ringing and bullets flying past his head, John zig-zagged rapidly forward. Carefully he concentrated on holding his feet and avoiding hazards that would slow him down. Forcing his way through small branches and undergrowth that tore at his skin, he drove himself on. Exhausted and pursued relentlessly, he drew on all his reserves to keep up momentum. Spotting the edge of the ridge top and hearing the approach of an incoming shell, he pushed himself to close the gap between freedom and imminent death. Arriving with his lungs screaming and his heart pounding, he blindly leapt into the void beneath. Behind him, the ground exploded with ear-shattering force.

Clouded from the percussion, John free-fell into the canopy of the gorge below. The first impact against the upper branches violently twisted his body sideways, knocking the remaining air from his lungs. The second tossed him backwards into smaller branches that ripped savagely at his body as inertia and gravity sucked him down. Desperately, he held out his arms clutching at anything to stem the acceleration. Lacerated and bleeding, he crashed heavily earthward as his body bounced from branch to branch until abruptly and barely alive, he burst into nothingness and plummeted.

Much has been written of the time spent between leaving consciousness and approaching death. It is impossible to prove scientifically, yet those who have returned from the brink all describe the great light and the peacefulness experienced as they witnessed replays of significant moments in life.

Hit by the enormity of silence and sudden peace, John floated aimlessly in the absence of time as his mind closed down his body to embrace the sanctuary of infinite space.

Clear images of his mother, his childhood, and his life passed unhindered as he passively looked on. The serenity comforting, until suddenly something out of place took hold. With a rush, a cold and menacing perversity washed over him as his head filled with the lyrics of a nursery rhyme growing in intensity with the wind.

The tune of *'This little Piggy"* became louder as John was drawn to surreal visions of schoolgirls singing. Stark, raw and colourless, they danced around another girl who was crying. Holding sticks, they beat and teased her to the rhythm of the rhyme ... *"This little cow eats grass,"* they sang, *"This little cow eats hay. This little cow drinks water. This little cow runs away. This little cow does nothing. Except lie down each day ... We'll whip her. We'll whip her. We'll ..."*

John hit the upper bushes and vines of the underbrush with immense force. Rolling and crashing, he finally, heavily and painfully, was still.

Lying flat on his back and unable to move, the distant lyrics trailed from his head. The sun was shining and the light warmed his face. He heard a girl giggling ... it was strange, mischievous and evil. Opening his eyes he squinted into the sun and saw the outline of a woman standing over him in a coolie's hat. Unable to react to the warning signs of a strike, he braced for a blow that brought sharp pain and immediate darkness.

Chapter Four

Bath, England.
April 26th 2000.

Harold Lassiter sat at his breakfast table with his morning paper. His arms were fully extended and the large copy of The Times obscured him from view. Parked outside his Tudor cottage, a mini cab waited with its engine running. The small lane where it sat, was cobbled and leafy.

In the kitchen, Harold's wife, Penny, spoke across the counter that separated them.

"Well I don't understand it at all, quite frankly," Penny said.

She placed hot toast on a plate and began to apply butter and marmalade. Hearing no response, she looked up at the silent paper.

"Harold?"

"Yes dear?"

"I said I don't understand why anyone would bother to fly half way round the world for a blinking toy. Business trip or not."

Harold lowered the paper revealing his greying temples and distinguished features. A man in his late fifties, he wore a fresh white shirt with gold armlets and a striped blue and yellow silk tie. His eyes, slightly magnified behind horn-rimmed glasses, gave evidence that his feelings were hurt.

"A 1912 working model of a Harrington Steam Locomotive is hardly a toy Penny. It's a priceless example of mans ingenuity in his quest to harness the power of steam. It stands as a reminder to us all. A monument to progress and a unique era of Industrialisation. The Harrington is one of a kind!"

"Oh for goodness sake Harold it's ten inches long!" She said passing his toast.

"Which, my dear, is entirely the point!" He said taking it. "Not only is every detail precisely engineered, the boiler delivers exactly the same psi as the original. A rare find indeed wouldn't you say?"

Penny sighed in surrender. Her husband was, and always would be completely obsessed about the most absurd things. Feeling the onset of another flush she put her palms against her glowing cheeks and reached across the counter for her pills. Still in her dressing gown she flicked her head back and swallowed a tablet with her tea.

Harold looked up from his toast and took in the scene.

"I'm sorry I'll miss your sister," he said.

"Yes well, it can't be helped I suppose. How long will you be in Jakarta?"

"The conference finishes on Tuesday but the company have asked if I might oversee a claim involving a shipment of soy beans while I'm there. It's a particularly interesting claim too, International Law as you know only allows for ..."

"Don't dear," she said cutting him off. "Remember the plane. If you start explaining insurance to me you'll never leave the house." She moved around to help with his jacket. "Just promise you'll be back for the Gordon's dinner party."

"When is it?" He asked.

"For the fifth time it's Saturday," Penny said whilst brushing lint from his shoulders and correcting his tie. "Your memory is getting worse and worse. God knows what you're going to be like when you're seventy."

"Defensive memory loss has nothing to do with age, Penny, it's about survival. The thought of sharing dried mutilated beef with escapees from Billy Butlin's is enough to shut any mind down. Don't we know anybody that can at least cook?"

"We've already accepted and I'm looking forward to it."

"Then I wouldn't miss it for the world," he said draining his cup, patting her bottom and pecking her cheek, "Take care of yourself. "

"I will dear, safe trip." She replied.

"I'll call when I've landed."

She watched him collect the bag by the door and head off. Then with a sudden memory, "Oh Harold" she called after him, "You won't forget my perfume will you?"

"Which one is it again?" He yelled.

Penny sighed. Twice a year for the past twenty-four, he had been buying the same thing. "Youth-Dew," she yelled back.

He waved, the cab departed and Penny closed the door.

Chapter Five

Jakarta, Indonesia.
April 27th 2000.

Standing on the patio of a penthouse apartment, a couple enjoyed the quiet night air of a tropical climate. Dressed in eveningwear they were having a nightcap before turning in. Looking over the railing they lazily sipped gin slings and took in the serene beauty of Jakarta by night. Forty-eight stories below, the bustle of a city that seldom slept, added to the ambience of their birds-eye view. Imperceptibly at first, a glass resting against the railing began to rattle to tiny vibrations. As it grew in volume the couple looked at each other perplexed. Suddenly the sky exploded with incredible noise as two helicopters screamed passed at full throttle. Clearing the building by the smallest of margins, their arrival was staggeringly quick and their departure was even quicker.

The two unmarked Sikorsky Black Hawks flew close together banking and twisting at speeds in excess of 140 knots. The throb of their powerful twin turbines was enhanced by the acoustics as they disappeared into the high-rise canyons of the city proper. Each fitted with external stores supports, they carried a payload of guns and missiles sufficient to ward off any challenge. The presence of detachable fuel tanks and external jamming antennae indicated a long-range mission of both expense and significant purpose.

Inside, teams of men wearing white overalls and surgical gloves sat patiently waiting. Members of MI6's 'Cleaning Unit' they were on loan to the CIA to attend a target of opportunity.

On the thirty-second floor of the Royal Orchard Hotel Jakarta, Vladamir Dravich reclined on the king size bed of his palatial suite. Wearing only a towel, he lay with his hands behind his head feeling decidedly content. Life was good. For once, a career promotion had delivered benefits that lived up to the promises given by his superiors. As the newly appointed Head of Field Operations in S. E. Asia, his long service to the former KGB and now the Foreign Intelligence Service or SVR, finally meant he could enjoy life a little. Not a bad effort, he thought, for the son of a Slavic immigrant.

Looking about at the opulence of his surroundings, he remembered the struggle it took to get here. His time in the field had been tough and he had served with distinction in difficult times. Wounded twice in operations, he had received five separate citations, and most recently, a Distinguished Employee Security Badge had been presented by the Chairman himself. A man for the men, he looked forward to making a difference before retiring to the Black Sea.

The opening of the door to the adjoining bedroom stole Vladamir's undivided attention as a magnificently endowed high-class hooker seductively walked in.

A gift arranged by his predecessor, they had both joked that his first official shagging in the job should at least be on his terms and enjoyable.

The young blonde, dressed in a brief chemise and nothing else, carried a large platter of fruit and a smile. Eager to begin, Dravich lifted himself onto an elbow in anticipation. Enthralled, his eyes gravitated to her sheer top as her nubile breasts undulated and enticed with each stride of her flawless legs. Nearing him, she paused to allow the scent of her perfume to intoxicate and excite. Then, placing the fruit in the middle of the bed, she playfully and provocatively moved toward him.

Immediately outside the double doors of the master bedroom, five bodyguards sat in various positions of relaxation about the main room. Dressed in compulsory dark suits, they placated their boredom with newspapers, magazines and low volume news bulletins on CNN.

Disturbed by a knock but expecting it, the pair closest to the door rose to answer. Looking through the spy hole the smaller of the men nodded his assent to the other, who in turn, cracked open the door for a second look. Seeing familiar faces and no change to the routine, he opened it fully and allowed two maids to enter with the meals trolley and fresh towels. Unremarkable in appearance, the frumpy women in their forties, drew scant attention from men more interested in younger bodies and smaller hips. While the trolley was off-loaded, the taller man followed the towel-carrying maid to the bathroom as a matter of course.

Thundering into position on top of their target building. The Black Hawk's hydraulics bounced softly down as their weight settled them to a stop. Immediately, the men in white disembarked on the run. With military precision they streamed forward carrying bags and equipment to descend stairs to the floors underneath. Following briskly was a man dressed in a clinical white coat and shiny black shoes. With one hand he carried a medical bag, while with the other, he wheeled a portable light.

Now sitting astride Dravich, the flirtatious blonde picked up a large plum and bit into it with overt eroticism. The juice slid down her chin and dripped onto his chest. He smiled. She took another plum and placed it into his mouth. Playfully she motioned for him to open wider. Liking the game he complied.

Suddenly her eyes darkened. With vicious speed and a short sharp metallic click, six small steel barbs - three up and three down - burst from the plum and snapped into the flesh around his mouth sealing it open around the fruit.

Reacting to the assault Dravich grabbed desperately for her throat but her slick operation of the stun gun secreted beneath the tray quickly rendered him impotent.

In the bathroom, the towel-lady swung around with a silenced weapon and rapidly sent three rounds into the man who had followed. Showing surprising speed she raced back to the main room and with deadly accuracy dropped two more. Her companion now armed in a similar fashion, took care of the others. They were professionals and it was over in seconds.

Quickly, one went through to the bedroom as the other opened the main door. Standing in wait at the doorway was the clinically dressed man with his bag. From behind him the cleaners began filing in. The maid took the light from his grasp and led the way to the master bedroom.

Inside, Dravich was held seated and dazed on a chair. As the man entered, he took in the room and nodded.

"Mr Dravich."

Vladamir, still with his mouth around the plum, watched intently as the unfamiliar man calmly placed his bag on a nearby table, snapped it open and handed the blond girl a tourniquet.

'Left arm please." He said smiling at her state of dress.

As the light was positioned and switched on, he pulled a syringe from the bag, attached a needle and inserted it into a vial. "Vladamir, can you hear me?" He asked.

Vladamir nodded.

"Good. I'm sure you appreciate that if we meant you harm you would already be dead."

Again, Vladamir nodded.

"I am a dentist." Removing the syringe from the vial and squirting a stream into the air, the dentist looked directly at Vladamir. "I assume you know what happens next."

Vladamir's eyes went to the syringe.

"Just an anaesthetic."

Dravich considered his options, and signaled consent.

The cleaners in the next room worked quietly and efficiently. The bodies, now bagged, were being taken to the choppers and the cleanup had begun in earnest. On the spot analysis of materials and mixing of chemicals ensured nothing was left to chance.

The food trays, glasses, towels, bins, even the 'S' bends of the plumbing were removed and cleaned. Plaster was mixed and dried to cover holes. Paint was chemically aged and applied, while tiles were re-glazed and blood spattered grout was replaced.

In the bedroom the dentist worked on a now unconscious Dravich. Removing the plum but leaving the spikes in place, he began delving inside Vladamir's mouth. Moving backwards and forwards from his bag he talked absentmindedly to those looking on.

"Agents with access to sensitive information are now required to carry emergency suicide tablets secreted somewhere, I'm told, in the teeth." Spotting something of interest he paused for a closer look. Momentarily preoccupied, he reached into his bag and searched for the next instrument of choice. "No doubt," he resumed, "to avoid embarrassing fat government officials. Hardly seems fair when you think about it..."

A suited man in horn-rimmed glasses arrived in the doorway as the dentist extracted a tiny capsule and held it into the light. "Cyanide."

Turning to the new arrival he relayed the news, "He's clean. Give me a minute and he's all yours"

Harold Lassiter nodded.

Chapter Six

Bangkok, Thailand.
April 28th 2000

The following morning Harold sat across the desk of Walter A. Emerson, CIA's Regional Director of Operations in Asia. His office was a grand affair with a large mahogany desk running adjacent to huge windows that overlooked the court-yard of the American Embassy in Bangkok. The wall behind him was emblazoned with the eagle and shield emblem of the agency sitting between two perfectly positioned flags bearing the Stars and Stripes. A relatively young man for his position, Walter Emerson was highly regarded.

"There were no problems?" He asked.

"None whatsoever," answered Harold. "The entire operation was complete in an hour and a half."

"Including the clean?"

"Yes. The decision to use ammunition of reduced powder and muzzle velocity proved correct. There were only two through-rounds and therefore less damage. It saved a lot of time."

"Excellent."

For a moment the two men sat looking at each other in thought. Emerson smiled and leaned forward to push a button on his intercom, "Margaret?" He called.

The speaker sprang to life, "Yes sir."

"Has that package arrived for Mr Lassiter?"

"Yes sir." She replied.

"Bring it in would you."

Immediately the door opened and Margaret, Emerson's personal assistant, walked in. An elderly lady with elegant dress and sparkling eyes, she smiled maternally at the men in the room and handed Harold a small box.

"Thankyou Margaret," Harold said pleasantly.

"You're welcome Mr Lassiter."

Emerson nodded, granting her leave.

Harold opened the package to reveal the 'Harrington Steam Locomotive'. Turning it upside down he located the serial number and checked it against a note from his pocket. Holding it up he briefly admired the workmanship before replacing it in the box. Amongst the packaging paper he noticed a bottle of Estee Lauder 'Youth - Dew' with a price tag from a Jakarta emporium. He looked up into Emerson's cool gaze.

"All there?" He asked.

"Thank you, yes. I'm sorry to have troubled you," Harold said, placing the box to his side.

"Not at all," Emerson insisted.

The CIA man's fingers softly drummed the top of the manila folder on his desk. "Any idea why I've requested your services?" He asked.

Harold smiled, "I assume it has something to do with last night's target. But other than that, anything else would be pure conjecture. Limited entirely by a mix of probability and facts."

Emerson leaned back in his chair and placed his fingers together in front of his chest. "Please continue," he said.

Harold knew he was being evaluated. Working with another agency was always difficult because of secrecy and trust and this was his opportunity to dispel doubts. If he were frank, then Emerson would be frank in return.

"I am aware of three elements," he began.

"Three?" Asked Emerson.

"The first is you I'm afraid. I begin by asking myself why the CIA would risk it. Vladamir has hardly been in his new position long enough to warrant an exercise of this nature for information alone. So I suspect that his real worth is in his value to somebody else. Without testing the waters of our transatlantic alliance, I respectfully suggest that to request my services is one thing, but to have that request granted, is entirely another thing.

Since the nature of our business is to keep secrets from each other as well as everybody else, I can only speculate that this therefore concerns both of us in some way. I am not aware of any existing covert operation between us so my instincts are pointing me toward something military."

Emerson raised an eyebrow. "Based on?"

"The second element. Vladamir Dravich is a highly decorated SVR agent who spent many years building a formidable anti-terror network in and around Chechnya. In 1994 information gained by him led to the timely thwarting of an assassination attempt on the life of Colonel Alexander Sashenka Kastinov." Harold rose to look at the view beyond the windows. "That Colonel is now General Kastinov, commander of the Russian Forces in Indo China, which by coincidence," Harold paused to face Emerson, "is just north of here, is it not?"

Emerson smiled.

"So I would hazard a guess and say that you want to use Vladamir Dravich to force a favour from the Russians who are where we are not. To aid a military project, of which I know nothing about, but involves both the U.S. and Britain."

"You mentioned risk?"

"There are several. One is that you invite retaliatory kidnappings of your own people. Two, is in convincing the other party that the goods are undamaged and worth retrieval. In either event, it will require a good deal of diplomacy and a very good liaison. This, I gather, is why you want the third element."

"Which is?"

"Me."

Emerson knew he had the right man, "Please take a seat Harold and allow me to fill you in." He slid the manila folder across the desk.

Sitting opposite, Harold picked it up. On the front in bold letters it read: '*For your eyes-only*'. Harold looked to Emerson for confirmation he could go ahead.

"Open it," said Emerson. Harold did. It read:

Operation Harvest-Moon.
Agent Exchange.
Allied Coalition US/Brit/Aust.
Anti Terrorism and Insurgency Unit.
Force Delta: Missing In Action.

Advancing to the following pages, Harold Lassiter found himself looking at the smiling face of John Landau. Underneath was written:

Gecko.
MIA 1996.

Chapter Seven

Gulf of Thailand 1990.

Cheng Bao stood on the deck conspicuously struggling with his lack of sea legs and the vessel's incessant movement from side to side. Tightening his jacket against the night wind, he checked and adjusted the cluster of throwing knives he kept hidden in the small of his back. From his pocket he pulled a copy of the Singapore Times given to him by a Thai fisherman that morning.

He had grown since Daxin County. His body was now full and his shoulders were broad and strong. Drooped round his mouth a sparse moustache neatly framed his white chin. No longer a farm hand, Mongoose looked like the warrior he had become. Tough and uncompromising, he had found his place amongst men recruited to fight for the Laotian warlord known as Xiang.

At last in an environment where he was treated like any other, he revelled in the camaraderie that came with a common cause. His diligent approach to duties earned him respect and privilege within the tight-knit group of men, and this mission was an example of the trust placed in him by senior members of the inner council. Steadying himself against the handrail, Mongoose acknowledged the smile from the Vietnamese pilot who attended the wheel. Around them, the other boats in the fleet rose and dipped with the ocean's swell.

Small and innocuous, the group of fishing vessels trawled slowly northwards while maintaining visual contact with the shore. Spread in typical formation, they looked like any other fishing fleet in search of a shoal. Hidden beneath the waterline however, twin propellers powered by huge diesel engines belied the truth as their vast submerged hulls were filled to the gunnels with ammunition, high explosives and arms.

The shipment had been sent from Karachi via the Indian Ocean on a Panamanian vessel bound for Singapore. Due to its importance, the entire operation had been meticulously planned. Loaded as deck cargo the airtight containers were fitted with marine archiving GPS and ultrasonic transmitters. As the ship approached the Straits of Malacca the containers were deliberately jettisoned into the sea. From the shipping lanes they floated with the seasonal northwest current, which at this time of year, moved at almost a metre per second. From Malaysia's west coast, pirates based in the old Portuguese fishing settlement of Melaka, would then, under the cover of darkness, locate the containers and cut into them from above.

Once emptied, the containers were scuttled to the ocean floor thereby completing the initial phase of the maritime ruse. On arrival in Singapore the ship's log would account for the missing containers as lost at sea. An insurance claim by the originators for a high and fictitious value would eventually reimburse transportation costs and bring neat closure to the paperwork trail.

Fully laden, the pirates sailed north under darkness to the Andaman Sea through the Mergui Archipelago to the west coast of Burma. With the assistance of co-conspirators from the local Myanmar junta, the arms were driven east across the mountains into Thailand's Prachuap Khiri Khan Province and despatched to Vietnamese fishing vessels waiting in the South China Sea. Joined here by Mongoose and his passenger, they headed across the Gulf of Thailand toward Cambodia and Vietnam. If they could safely pass through the Mekong Delta, it was only a matter of days to their eventual destination in Laos.

Mongoose passed the paper to his sister. "You are famous," he said.

Mae Lin, lost in thought, struggled to hear above the wind and the sea. "What?" She asked.

"You're famous," he repeated raising his voice, "Look ... the front page," Mongoose pointed, "down the bottom. Here."

The article told of a large house razed by fire and the grisly discovery by police of its owner's dismembered bodies in the ashes. Fears were held for the safety of their missing stepdaughter. One of the deceased was believed to be Mr Wu Choy, chairman of Yung Trading, a large multinational export company with offices throughout the Malay peninsular, China, India and the Philippines. A company spokesman suggested Mr Choy's recent comments to the International Maritime Organisation's (IMO) piracy committee might have contributed to his horrific death. As a member of Singapore's delegation to the committee, Mr Choy had pleaded for international support of armed coast guards as the only way to quell the rise of piracy in the region. Death threats from organised crime syndicates had followed. The police were continuing their investigation.

"Did you know about the death threats?" Mongoose asked.

"No," Mae Lin answered as she passed the paper back.

Mongoose shrugged and tossed it into the sea. Mae Lin gently tucked herself under her brother's protective arm and the two watched as it disappeared.

It was her eighteenth birthday and the year of the horse. The horse was a lover of freedom. Her aunt had spitefully maintained that Mae Lin's birth held little cause for celebration... particularly as her niece was born in the year of the rat and the rat was known to be devious, psychotic and cunning. Not even she, with all her bigotry and hate could have imagined how close she was to the truth. Had a scholar read the signs, it would have been noted that the combination of both horse and rat did not bode well.

Throughout her upbringing in Singapore, Mae Lin had endured an unnatural amount of abuse. From day one, her schooling proved a minefield of bullying and exclusion. Tearful and alone, her surrogate family gave no respite to the enormous anguish she felt. Her aunt, cold and aloof, took great delight in holding her up for ridicule in front of friends. Her sadistic uncle, devised punishments that progressively grew more extreme and perverse. Yet despite this, and them, Mae Lin had survived.

Withdrawn and reclusive she drew on the lesson of the staff: Striving to become the weapon that looked no more than a simple stick.

Her devotion to Bojitsu gave her the strength to absorb the taunts. As she grew, so did her power. From absorption she learnt deflection. From deflection she leant manipulation. From manipulation she learnt attack. Always a pretty girl with a disarming smile, her rapidly developing beauty soon formed the platform of her assaults.

Her greatest victim was none other than her master and chief tormentor, Uncle Wu.

As the most dominant figure in her life, Mae Lin had many opportunities to study her uncle and feel first-hand the swing of his outrageous moods. His anger often led to the most preposterous outcomes and his punishments bordered on the absurd. Yet his emotion was not as one-dimensional as she first thought. Slowly it dawned upon her that her uncle's need for his niece, and her punishments, had taken on an importance of its own.

In adolescence, her movement of the staff was elegant and self-assured. For hours, Uncle Wu would call instructions from the sidelines while studiously watching her form. Her talent was obvious. Her beauty and grace dominant. Her power deceptive. As she developed so did Uncle Wu's attentiveness. So preoccupied did he become that soon Mae Lin felt the rise in acidity from her aunt. At last, an opening had presented itself. Mae Lin revelled in her long awaited chance at revenge.

A childish giggle, an open blouse, a compliment or a timely smile, often brought Mae Lin reward. Carefully, she manufactured tension to later ease it with a deed or word. As the silent gap widened between husband and wife, her uncle grew more dependent on his time spent with her. The seed sown, the ruin of her nemesis had begun. But as fate would have it, it would never reach its conclusion.

Her father had correctly foreseen his daughter's ability to learn. Mae Lin's A levels had been a resounding success and tertiary study seemed a fait accompli.

Since twelve, Mae Lin had supplemented her Bojitsu with Shotokan, the original art of karate-do. So impressive were her results that Uncle Wu funded private tuition. At eighteen she had mastered many of the rigid Katas and had already begun advanced learning. Her sensei's dojo was not far from home and she often walked the small distance there and back. Mae Lin's most recent visit would be her last.

It was night and although not late, the streets were quiet. The moon was out and the neon lanterns created pools of light between the evergreen Angsana's that lined the verge. On her way home and unconsciously stepping around the fallen seedpods that lay in clusters at the base of each tree, Mae Lin became aware of being watched and felt a presence in the shadows ahead.

Without breaking stride she continued forward until the outline of a male figure appeared and moved toward her. Mae Lin instantly adopted an attacking stance that halted his progress.

"I wonder," said the mellow voice from the shadows, "Who would teach a skinny peasant girl the art of open hand? Especially one as pretty as her mother."

Her heart skipped a beat. She dared not believe it. Mae Lin had heard nothing of her family since leaving China. Yet the voice was so entrenched in her memory that she was immediately drawn. Although she could not see his face, his brazen swagger and the cocky angle of his head made her wonder if it was really true. "Cheng Bao?" She asked.

As he stepped into the light, the white chin was unmistakable. "I thought for a moment that you had forgotten me," he said smiling.

Mae Lin squealed and launched herself at her brother throwing her arms around him. Lost in a wave of emotion she held on as tightly as she could.

"It is a little late, but happy birthday," he said quietly while holding her with equal strength. Mae Lin remained buried into him and her body silently shook.

Prising her off with "Let me look at you," Mongoose held his sister at arms length. Casting his eyes over her feminine shape, he offered apologetically, "Well I have obviously been given all the good looks." Then with a sincere lift of his eyebrows he added a heartfelt, "So sorry," and kissed her cheek.

Mae Lin smiled as she attempted to take in all his changes. Unused to the scrutiny his face broke into a nervous grin.

"Oh, you have lost a tooth," she noticed. Gently she took his cheek in her palm to support her concern. He was seldom treated to such warmth and she felt his awkwardness. 'It's all right, Cheng Boa, a sister is allowed to touch. I daresay we are both long overdue. How is father?"

Mongoose took Mae Lin's hand from his face and his eyes saddened. "What is it?" She asked.

"You don't know?"

Mae Lin tensed and shook her head.

"Father is dead."

"What?" Mae Lin's face went white. "When?"

"Six years ago."

"Six years ago!" She struggled to come to terms with the news, "But how can that be?"

"Didn't you get the letters?" Mongoose asked. "I wrote many times."

The shock hit her. "But that's not true, I am the only one who wrote," she said. "Years and years of letters and nothing ever came back." She thumped her brother firmly in the chest and he recoiled in confusion at her reaction. "Only last week I sent news of my A levels hoping he'd be proud." With both hands she banged into him again and again. "Surely you must have seen something?"

Mongoose grabbed at her flailing arms, "I saw nothing," he said.

"But my life ..." she screamed, "All those years of my rotten life ... how can you not know what I've endured? How can you not?" Finally with strength, Mongoose controlled her arms and drew her to him.

"I swear on our parents grave, Mae Lin, I saw nothing."

Mae Lin collapsed with the weight of so many years of absence from her own blood. "You don't understand. It was all I had," she sobbed. "Knowing that you both knew ... was all I ever had." Completely shaken Mae Lin began to weep.

Throughout all her unspeakable suffering and incredible loneliness, the letters she wrote to her family reinforced in her that she belonged, and that somewhere, somebody loved her for who she was, and didn't loathe her for who she was not. Knowing that they knew what she was going through, that she was keeping face, and that she was making the most of an opportunity that cost so much.. meant everything to Mae Lin. It was in her letters she revealed her dreams, her aspirations and her innermost thoughts. They were her sanctuary and her strength... to find out at eighteen that not a single word had reached home since she was six, simply cut out her heart and left a hole that couldn't be filled in.

Mongoose held his sister for more than an hour. Gently he stroked her hair and gave comfort. Finally and wearily, Mae Lin stood under her own power. "I'm sorry," she whispered.

"It is fine," he shrugged.

Mae Lin stretched her back and shook her head. "The last memory I had was of you holding me as I cried. So long ago."

Mongoose nodded apologetically as his sister walked several paces from him to take stock and some deep breaths. When she returned, she was stronger and resolute. "Tell me," she asked softly, "What happened?"

Together the two walked and talked for hours as Mongoose recalled the events leading up to Cheng Da's death.

Four years after her departure, he had taken ill. At first it was just a cough and typically their father had opted to work through it. As it spread through his chest, his breathing became more difficult and he was always tired. In the ensuing months it spread further... he lost his appetite and struggled to eat. Finally, weak with fever, the sickness took over and he became bedridden. Mongoose pleaded with local doctors but as there was no money, none bothered to attend. Together they tried concocting herbal remedies, but to no avail. By the following summer Cheng Da had become so fragile that he could no longer raise his head. Constantly he wandered in and out of fever and began at times to soil the bed. Frightened for his father's life, Cheng Bao took it upon himself to write Uncle Wu for help ... but none came. Again and again he wrote, yet heard nothing. By winter the struggle was over, and their father quietly faded and died.

Mongoose buried him next to their mother at the back of their plot. With no reason to stay, he had left Guangxi to find his place and perhaps his sister. And so, six years later, here he was.

"Did he speak of me?" She asked.

"Often. He felt responsible and said letting you go was the hardest thing he ever did. But he knew it was what our mother had wanted, and he acted out of respect for her. He thought you didn't write because you were angry with him." Mongoose looked at his sister, "If it means anything, were he here today, he would be proud."

"You miss him don't you?"

"Yes."

"Are you your father's son?"

"He taught me many things. But our father was a kind and tolerant man, and there are many who would say those virtues passed me by."

"I wouldn't." She confided.

"You are blood." He countered.

"Did you find your place?"

"I believe I have," he answered.

Deep in thought, they continued walking. As the streets narrowed, their footsteps began to resonate and echo. "How many letters did you write?" He ventured.

"Many," she said.

"I'm guessing you didn't forget where we lived?"

Mae Lin shook her head, "I sent them through Yung Trading, as I was advised." Mai Lin's eyes narrowed. "Who did you address your letters to?"

"Uncle Wu. Father insisted it was more polite."

They walked in silence for another block and Mongoose could sense her mood darkening. Suddenly she turned. "Come on," she said, "we have business to attend to."

Mongoose had never seen this side of his sister, but it felt familiar and instinct told him that their blood ran much deeper than he first thought. Her stride lengthened and the power she exuded had menace. "I take it you mean family business," he said.

Mae Lin's demeanour was like ice, "I suspect, my brother, that today of all days, our father's memory deserves a peasant rebellion that severs the head of the ruling class." Her lip curled and she raised an eyebrow, "Don't you think?"

Chapter Eight

N.E. Province, Laos.
March 12th 1998.

In the darkness, eyes blinked. Fearful and uncertain, they were the empty and tormented eyes of men searching in hope of an end. Freedom or death, whichever came mercifully first.

Incarcerated in a series of rectangular holes cut into the side of a dirt wall, they lay barely able to move. Too small to allow full extension of their limbs, the shallow holes resembled small coffins, and stacked three high, they covered the distance of the entire wall. Held behind bars locked from the outside, their faces pressed against the metal in a desperate bid to escape claustrophobia and the stench. Their hands and feet were shackled with chains. Wearing nothing more than rags or loincloths they suffered sickness and injury beyond anything one could imagine. Captured and imprisoned, they were all that remained of failed raids on the territories of the infamous warlord Xiang.

Lit dimly by the light from a nearby flame, John Landau pressed his face to the bars of his cage and listened. He heard men laughing in the distance ... they were gathering and he wondered what horrors the night would bring.

In an effort to control the growing dread, he forced himself to think like a soldier. It was a practice that brought him a degree of separation from the reality of where he was. This and his memories were all he had left. Anything he saw, anything he heard, smelled or tasted ... any information at all formed the basis of his Intelligence gathering. As he tried to paint a military picture and an overview of his situation, he knew that if his mind succumbed to desperation, he would lose. The enemy owned him physically, if he let them have his mind, he would most certainly die.

There were gaps in his memory, but to the best of his ability he figured that he'd been captive for around two years. Since the ambush he had been moved three times to different camps. Each move taking him further north and higher into the mountains. Each camp, progressively bigger and more entrenched. The camp he occupied now, was by far the biggest and most impressive. With wells and water wheels and elaborate camouflage, this was the home of an enemy that had no intention of moving.

As he went through his thought processes John flexed and relaxed his muscles. It was his routine. Whatever he could do he did to maintain a regimen of conditioning. He was losing body mass and he took every opportunity to delay the physical decline. The distance between his body and the roof of his cage was only a matter of inches, but he used it. Creating short versions of push-ups, he varied the arms and fingers that he worked on in order to gain the greatest result. He spent hours pushing his legs against the walls and rotating joints. He visualised body movements and extensions, playing out defensive and attacking combinations in his head. Aware of the breaks in his bones from beatings, and the weakness he felt from sickness and lack of nutrition, he knew his mind was the key to placing survival above anything else ... his body simply had to keep up.

Anywhere he was, he looked for positives. In the previous camp his cell was a hole in the ground ... so narrow, that he could not take the weight from his legs. But the bars on top of the hole allowed him to exercise his arms, which in turn relieved the ache in his other limbs. He used dead sticks to chew on and clean his teeth. Hiding the small pieces of wood under his tongue was one of many small victories that motivated him to seek more.

Used sometimes for labour during the day, those strong enough to participate received better food. Regardless of how often he was beaten, John always worked. Food meant strength, and it was strength that was needed to survive the nights.

Hearing the sound of them coming, he pulled his face from the bars and waited.

Deeper into the camp proper, a fifty-inch plasma television sprang to life with satellite images beamed from the other side of the world. In brilliant colour, Las Vegas dancing girls went through dazzling twirls and high kicks as a superimposed graphic appeared over the screen: Direct from Mandalay Bay, Las Vegas: We present on pay-per-view: Ultimate Fighting.

Comfortably sitting in front of the set, Warlord Xiang, commander of the most feared guerrilla army in Laos, was watching. This was his favourite broadcast. Positioned as close as his eyesight permitted, he sat glued to the pictures of men fighting before well-heeled Americans out on the town. Through round bifocals his compassionless eyes consumed every detail of the extravagant display.

In his early fifties, Xiang, when standing, stood less than five foot ten. Physically, he was a strong and stocky man with wide shoulders and solid legs. Dressed in a mix of Chinese and Russian military clothing, he wore a single bandolier of nine millimetre rounds draped diagonally across his chest. Strapped to his thigh was the latest micro Uzi sent to him by a Syrian arms dealer via Pakistan and Phnom Penh. His hair, heavily clipped at the sides, hung in matted strands over his shoulders. Scarred and pock marked under his chin, his complexion betrayed Mongolian ancestry that dated as far back as Kublai Khan's military domination of the Mekong and the Mon-Khmer.

Draining the contents of a small cup held in a gnarled hand, he expelled a satisfied sigh from a mouth full of yellow and black teeth. Without shifting his gaze, he extended his arm and signalled his desire for more.

On hand to acquiesce was his concubine and trusted lieutenant, Yung Mae Lin. Sitting on cushions at his feet she reached for the pot containing the spirit from indica rice. Her beauty was breathtaking.

Now twenty-six, she had blossomed into womanhood. Wearing black fatigues her straight posture and assured movements were indicative of a confident female in her prime. Sparkling wide eyes and delicate cheekbones accentuated full lips and a youthful smile. Her long black hair, neatly plaited down her back, was secured by a metal bauble covered in sinister spikes.

Having replenished Xiang's cup, Mae Lin returned her attention to the broadcast. As she did so, the cameras zoomed in to a close shot of a man being held down and punched repeatedly in the face. The crowd of Americans stood to applaud.

Banging his cup down, Xiang came to his feet and issued the awaited edict. His voice was harsh and guttural. "I am ready," he stated.

Chapter Nine

Striding out into the open, Xiang breathed it all in. He was the warlord, the man most feared, and these were his headquarters. Before him, a large group of men had gathered in anticipation. Acknowledging those that made way, Xiang headed enthusiastically toward his very own Chamber of Fights.

Filing in behind him, Mae Lin confirmed the go-ahead. "Inform Mongoose," she called. A cheer rang out and the mob eagerly followed.

The Chamber of Fights was an enclosed dirt floor of fifteen square paces. Lit entirely by torches and with little ventilation, it's close atmosphere promoted the stench of sweat and fear. On one side was a raised dais with chairs and some scattered cushion and it was here that Xiang took prime position with Mae Lin again at his feet. His soldiers, squeezed in ten deep around the chamber, began the rhythmic chant for a fight.

With torches held high, Mongoose led his guerrillas down to the cells. The prisoners, swept with fear, cowered away from the openings in an effort to avoid being chosen. With no particular preference, Mongoose randomly selected his quota. Violently, the guerrillas dragged, beat and pushed the unfortunate victims toward misery and probable death. This night, John Landau stood among them.

The fighting had begun. Two men, shackled at the feet, were battling each other to the limit of their weak condition. They were exhausted and blood flowed freely from their wounds. The crowd quietly looked on as the least competent fighter now lay huddled under his opponent with his hands wrapped defensively around his head and his eyes shut to exclude the horror. The other, though in ascendancy, whimpered while beating him with ineffectual blows from arms now devoid of strength. Mae Lin, transfixed by the situation suddenly and without emotion yelled, "Tobacqui Khan! The hammer."

Immediately the crowd came to life and roared. The man on top looked confused and began to panic. Uncontrollably weeping, he beat the other quicker and with more desperation. Out of sight of the fighters a heavy cudgel was lifted and carried toward the action. The crowd were laughing. Mae Lin's eyes were wide with anticipation as she excitedly held her breath.

Totally confused and exhausted the man stopped and tried to focus on what was happening. With the dirt and bloody sweat running into his eyes he struggled to see clearly. Looking at the smiling faces in the crowd he attempted to smile with them. In the increasing laughter his eyes found Mae Lin. There was something in her eyes that he couldn't figure. Suddenly aware, he turned into a sickening blow that pulverised his skull and face.

A roar of approval came over the chamber as the crowd voiced their appreciation. Mae Lin raised her hand to her mouth to hold a squeal of delight.

Outside and adjacent to the chamber, the rest of the unfortunates waited under guard in the holding area. Hearing the roar of the crowd they knew that somebody had just died and that their own turn drew nearer. Some began to pray.

John looked across at the men sitting opposite him. He scanned their faces and tried not to be affected by their emotion. He had been here many times before and in order to hold his sanity he knew he must keep his military mind alert and think like a soldier, not like a man.

Suddenly his gaze diverted back to the dangling dog tags of one man in particular. There was something familiar about them that drew him to them. His heart skipped a beat. As the man shifted his hunched position the tags spun outwards and in the highlight from a burning flame, the name 'Risso' was clearly written.

John's eyes snapped up as their owner groaned and slowly lifted his head backwards to rest against the wall behind. His eyes were closed, but John immediately recognised his friend and was nearly overwhelmed with emotion. He had always assumed Risso had made it back, and the joy of seeing him was quickly replaced with sadness for him suffering the same fate. Tears welled uncontrollably as John could see that his closest friend in the world was thin, weak with fever and barely clinging to life. Showing the scars of many beatings, Risso's bruised skin was covered in open sores and his face was pale.

"What are you two looking at?" Called a voice from the past.

It was June 8 1992 and John and Risso had been caught ogling the female soldiers working-out in the adjoining gym. They quickly spun around and looked innocent.

"Come here Landau and bring Griswald with you," yelled Colonel Masterson.

In the gym proper, the twenty newly arrived 'group of hopefuls' the colonel was teaching were going through the parry and thrust of unarmed combat drills. As was the rule in the gym, everyone was dressed in fatigues and T-shirts, except of course, Masterson, who typically wore his braces over the top. He was their boss, teacher, father and mother all rolled into one.

The pair joined him as he walked the group. Watching and correcting, he yelled commands that were dutifully echoed.

"We've come a long way, haven't we?" He said.

Risso rotated his finger around his temple to imply insanity. Masterson turned his head to look directly at Risso. "Haven't we?" He repeated.

"Yes sir," said Risso.

Masterson smiled and continued. "Well I can't do any more with either of you. I don't have any more to teach." He issued another loud instruction and the group quickly organised themselves into one on one. Satisfied, Masterson gave a sharp order and they began the drill. He looked to his two men.

"So you're both out of here and on active service."

"That's it?" Said John.

"That's it."

"We're done?" Asked Risso.

Masterson calmly avoided an errant blow from within the group and smoothly despatched the culprit.

"Yep, you're done" He extended his hand to each, "Remember the code and make me proud."

"Will we see you again?" Asked John.

"If it involves beer and seafood," he said smiling, "Now git, go on!" Masterson returned to his class before calling one last instruction.

"You two boys look out for each other. You hear? Always!"

In the torchlight, Risso's eyes slowly opened on the man staring at him, and, for a long while, struggled with any recognition at all. Suddenly realising who it was, his head straightened and in a moment of impulse he lurched joyously forward. Alarmed, John immediately warned against it by shaking his head. Risso, alerted to the guards, quickly altered his movement and covered his actions with a show of discomfort in his seat. After a period of diverted eyes they again looked at each other when it was safe. Sick as he was, Risso tried to smile.

Always an attentive guard, Mongoose did not fail to notice.

Xiang, enjoying the moment in the chamber, tossed a pistol within reach of the man still cowering and hugging the ground. The crowd cheered as the petrified man eyed the gun through the gaps in his fingers. The tension of his decision enthralled the audience and brought a hush. Mustering all his strength he threw himself toward it and quickly turned to point the weapon at the gigantic barbarian now standing over him. Armed with the cudgel, the huge Maori with a warrior face exuded a lust for blood. Dressed in a distinctive sleeveless top with a large scar that extended upwards from his left armpit, his enormous arms were spattered with the residue of his most recent kill. The same man responsible for the demise of Boris, Tobacqui Khan stood ready to strike.

Looking about pathetically the doomed man smiled and began laughing through his bloodied mouth. Defiantly he raised the gun to his temple and pulled the trigger. Nothing happened. Panicked he pulled again, and again, nothing occurred.

The crowd burst into laughter. Mae Lin was beside herself. The cudgel fell to huge 'oohs' from the crowd and spontaneous applause. Mae Lin turned to Xiang, placed her hand on his groin and smiled up at him. He nodded his approval and feeling peckish, summoned food.

Aware of the bodies being dragged from the chamber, Mongoose rose and slowly began his walk along the prisoners. Enjoying the theatre of his own swagger, he basked in their fear and loathing. Stopping at John he pointed, and in response, John stood and waited.

Walking a little further Mongoose stopped and looked back at John whose eyes remained emotionless and steady. Smirking, Mongoose kept his eyes on John and picked Risso.

John immediately reacted and grabbed at Mongoose, "No not him," he pleaded.

The other guards were quick to rush in and restrain his efforts. Frantically John pointed to others in the group, his voice rising in level with his demands.

"What about him ... or him ... why fucking him you filthy fucking bastard ... he's sick ... fuck you ... fuck you."

Mongoose wielded his stick and applied some punishing blows. Eventually subdued, the two were dragged into the chamber. John, bleeding about the head had several guards still hanging on to him. The crowd were expectant.

Mongoose acknowledged his sister and looked to Xiang for instruction. Absent-mindedly licking the dripping fat from his fingers, Xiang momentarily stopped eating his barbecued pork and took in the scene. Reaching down beside his chair he unsheathed a Japanese short sword and tossed it point first into the chamber.

"Untie them Mongoose," he instructed, and returned his attention to his food.

The crowd muttered enthusiastically as Mongoose smiled at John who was still held back by his arms. Grabbing his right arm, Mongoose undid the manacle. John offered no resistance and allowed his arm to lower by his side as he watched his friend fight delirium and try to come to terms with where he was. Moving to John's other side, Mongoose reached for the left manacle and undid it. In an instant John grabbed Mongoose's hair with his left hand and moving his right hand like lightning, speared two fingers deep into the soft flesh just below the Adams Apple. In complete shock, Mongoose dropped the manacle and grabbed for the wound and John's hand that remained in it.

Mae Lin stunned, let out an audible gasp.

Amidst the sound of expelling air and the inability of the other guards to pull his hand away, John with steel eyes locked firmly on Mongoose, clenched and pulled down with all his strength to reveal a bloodied and broken windpipe. Eventually, under the weight of guards he was subdued and held face down against the floor alongside his victim.

Mae Lin leapt up and rushed to her brother as the last gurgle of breath escaped his wound. Grasping for his hand she watched helplessly as his life faded.

The sudden flash of a clear blue sky, a cool breeze and the freedom of carelessness swept her back to the small clearing beyond their property in the woods. A moment not thought of for many years. In their own secret garden the two children lay on their backs stretched out like stars and aimlessly watched the clouds create shapes above them. The tips of their fingers touched lightly as little Mae Lin turned her head from the brightness above to observe her sole friend and protector.

"Cheng Bao?"

"Yes."

"Why is your chin white?" She asked.

"Mother said it is God's hand holding my face to the sun." He said.

Mae Lin raised herself onto an elbow and craned her head around her brother searching for God's hand. "Where?" She asked.

"You can't see it."

"Why not?"

Cheng Bao looked at his sister. "Because it's just a story," he said.

Just a story, she thought... his life gone, Mae Lin gently closed her brother's eyes.

The chamber, filled with the shock of a sudden loss, grew anxious in the knowledge of the coming fury. Mae Lin turned to Xiang with pleading eyes. With his assent she took to her feet and readied.

Under applause from the crowd Mae Lin signalled the guards to release John as her brother's body was carefully carried out. Motioning to Xiang ... he threw her Bo. Willing to accept his fate in place of his partner, John rose to his feet as she began her artistic preparation. Exhibiting years of skill, the chamber was dominated by the hum of the staff as it travelled its lethal arc.

John braced himself as Mae Lin calculated her approach and swung a blow that deliberately missed him by the breadth of a single hair. John did not react. With more intensity she swung two more and still he kept his nerve. Suddenly a real blow and John reacted, blocking it with an obvious ability that betrayed his skill. Mae Lin's eyes gleamed with satisfaction at the resistance. The crowd likewise found their voice. Swiftly she launched a multiple strike that broke through his defences and brought the two of them together and face-to-face. John aware of her now as the girl in the coolie hat, was besieged by the enormous weight of her venom.

Unexpectedly Mae Lin flicked her plait and the spikes of the bauble spun around to open a punishing wound on his face. He reeled back and the crowd erupted with generous applause.

Launching immediately into attacks with precise intent, each flurry ended in a damaging blow and majestic movement. John with feet still shackled, tried his best to defend himself but he was outgunned, soon exhausted and clearly condemned. With increasing severity, his bones were cracked and his muscles torn as he was beaten and pummelled to his knees. Whereupon, Mae Lin unleashed a gut wrenching bout of brutal blows that left him anticipating imminent death.

Pausing with the head and arm movement of a ballerina, Mae Lin eyed her quarry. Her breathing was powerful and she was enjoying her revenge. Lowering the staff she dropped her weapon in favour of the other that now stood close at hand. In lewd fashion, she bit her bottom lip and raised the short sword over her head. The crowd was silent. With exaggerated movement Mae Lin closed the distance between them and hovering provocatively, she readied to seal his fate.

A faint whimper broke the spell. Mae Lin wheeled her head to see Risso slumped and crying. Overcome with emotion he was weeping for his friend.

Mae Lin went to him and spoke with compassion.

"It's ok ... shhh! He is your friend isn't he?"

Risso nodded and sobbed more. Mae Lin placed her hand upon his cheek and allowed his head to fall gently on her shoulder.

"Come on ... let it out. It's almost over. Shhh ... shhh."

Lost in the horror of the moment Risso, sick and delirious with fever, let his body melt into the sudden sanctuary of a shoulder on which to cry.

"Shhh," whispered Mae Lin.

Suddenly Risso's eyes bulged and his entire body stiffened.

Mae Lin let out a little giggle. The chamber, now aware of the sound of tearing flesh, watched as the blade of the short sword slowly broke through the rags on Risso's back. As it reached it's full extent blood began to trickle from the corner of Risso's mouth.

Mae Lin's eyes glowed with enormous delight as the blade began to cut upwards until, with an encouraging lift of her eyebrows, it lurched to a distinctive 'crack' ... and so continued through each remaining rib toward the shoulder blade, and finally out.

Risso, already dead, fell down her body to the floor.

A long, low and beseeching cry of immense anguish escaped John's lips as he lay inert, powerless and completely devastated.

With speed and perfect balance, Mae Lin swung the sword to point directly at him and in so doing, flicked a trace of Risso's blood onto his face. Their eyes locked. Her voice was calm and controlled but laced with poison.

"Blood, for blood," she said unblinking. "Welcome to hell."

A chill went through John as her lips curled into a childlike smile.

Spinning to the crowd Mae Lin raised her sword high to rapturous applause as John was dragged from the chamber. His body in agony, and his memory burning with the final and lasting image of his friend.

Chapter Ten

The soft blue hue of morning broke over the dark shadows of a jungle still trapped in the receding night. On the horizon a huge flock of bats flew into oblivion as the distant calls of a barking deer faded into the quiet.

Silhouetted against the light, John hung suspended on a rope several metres above the ground. Bound by his wrists his head fell awkwardly forward of his straining shoulders. The silence broken only by the creak of stretching rope, as he swayed slowly in the gentle wind.

Bruised and swollen, his breathing shallow and barely perceptible, John sought solace in his unconsciousness and the enduring memories of his life.

It was Spring 1996: The white sands of the Northern New South Wales beach arced gently around the secluded cove that had been the Robert's family holiday destination for as long as John could remember. Their cottage, overlooking the vastness of the Pacific, was the only building visible from the shoreline. Its bright-corrugated roof gleamed like a beacon in the afternoon sun.

John and Rachel walked their horses in the shallows of broken waves. They were laughing and kicking up the water. Rachel beautiful and smiling with her red hair flashing at every turn. It was a happy day and they were deeply in love.

"Hey look!" She said, stopping and throwing John the reins of her horse. She rushed over to pick up a seashell lying in the sand.

John paused to look at her head down, arse up position.

"It's a girl thing isn't it?" He asked.

"What's that?" She answered.

"Picking up things on the beach."

She stood and returned to him with the large conical shell.

"Don't be so male, they're pretty. Look, listen," she put it to his ear.

"Anything?" She asked.

John listened and raised a surprised eyebrow.

"What is it?"

"South Sydney are up against St George."

Rachel pulled the shell away smiling and hugged into him, "Big idiot."

John wrapped his arm around her and they continued their walk, enjoying the moment.

He loved Rachel being in his arms. It was the most comforting feeling he'd ever known. The smell and feel of her, and the way she moulded so easily into him. He'd always loved her. From the moment they'd met, he'd never once doubted they'd be together. Everything she did was perfect. Always strong, always attentive and caring, always saying the right things to match his thoughts. They had never talked about being a couple, it just happened.

"It's a beautiful day," she said.

"Sure is."

"I love you, you know that don't you?"

"That's lucky when you think about it," he offered.

"Why?"

"Well if you didn't then it would be fairly awkward, me loving you back. Wouldn't it?"

"Yes, I suppose it would be ... " Rachel's sentence was interrupted as John's horse snorted and used its nose to push him forward. Rachel laughed.

John looked back and talked to his horse. He turned to Rachel; "Flicka thinks I should do it here."

"Do what? And who's Flicka?"

"The horse."

"Her name's Chelsea."

John cleared his throat. "Rache?"

"Yes."

Taking her hand John knelt with his knee in the water. Rachel's heart skipped a beat.

"Rachel Roberts, I love you more than anything in the world. Everything that is good and beautiful in my life is due to you. I can't promise anymore than what I have at this moment, but I can promise I will love you forever. "

He produced a ring with a centre blue sapphire circled with diamonds. Rachel gasped. John reached for her left hand holding the reins but Rachel was in a bubble and could barely move.

"Rache?"

"Hmm"

"Let go of Flicka's friend."

She did and he slipped the ring over her finger.

"Will you marry me?" He asked.

Rachel knelt with him, "Oh John it's beautiful." And through tears of happiness whispered, "Yes."

That night in their cabin the newly engaged couple lay in an old enamel bath full of bubbles. A bottle of red wine and two glasses sat within easy reach and one of John's feet dangled carelessly out. Rachel, lying with her back to John's front rested her head in the crook of his arm and played with her future name. "Mrs Rachel Landau. Mr and Mrs Landau," and with noted importance, "Lord and Lady Landau."

"Hey, steady."

She giggled. "I wish this day would last forever," she mused.

"We'd get a bit wrinkly."

Rachel snuggled in. "Do you have to go away John?" She asked. "When you're here, everything's so complete."

He stroked her hair gently. "We're never really apart, you know that."

"I know. Do you know why?"

"Why?"

"Because we're soul mates. We have been ..." she offered cheekily, "ever since you showed me yours behind Mrs Pringles garden shed."

"Ah the old shed. Now there's a blast from the past!" He laughed.

"You remember?"

"I do. But you showed me yours first."

"I did not," Rachel said affronted.

"Yes you did... you couldn't wait to snap me up."

"John Landau, I was seven."

"A hot seven too as I recall. Skinny, but definitely hot." He kissed her head.

She laughed. Extending her soapy arm and looking at her ring, Rachel put on her airs and graces and loudly announced her arrival at the ball, "Her Royal Highness Princess Landau." She squealed as John dumped bubbles on her head.

The rumbling approach of distant rain slowly built in intensity as the force of the heavy drops pounded the vegetation. Guerrillas nearby ran for shelter. With increasing volume the camp was suddenly swamped by rolling sheets of water as the rain swept in.

John remained hanging. The dried blood of his wounds slowly moved downwards and turned the flow of rivulets on his body a dark pink.

A short distance away, two guerrillas squatted under a humpy. Eating rice from small bowls with their fingers, they watched the suspended prisoner through the rain. The older of the two paused to make an observation. "That one should have gone long ago."

"True," said the other wiping his chin.

"Something holds him."

The younger man contemplated this as the rain became heavier. He raised his voice to compete. "Perhaps," he added subjectively "he's not done with this life yet."

"Perhaps." They both nodded in agreement and continued their meal.

In the back garden of the family home Rachel's brother Daniel went through his fight warm-ups with John. Since the death of Daniel's mother five years earlier John had filled the void in his life. He was a good kid and John enjoyed having him as part of his extended family. Daniel had taken like a duck to water to the disciplines required of a combat disciple, and at sixteen, the majestic sweeps of movement and balance showed a firm knowledge of the art. Daniel hung on every word from his teacher as he tried desperately to mimic even the smallest nuance. He loved it. His blonde hair bounced dramatically with each effort and his taut body glistened with sweat.

At the rear of the garden, Edward, Rachel's dad, practiced his golf swing on an old elasticised driving tool. A naturally ungifted golfer, Edward was determined to improve. The redness in his face betrayed his frustration and the unlikely success of the session.

Close to lunchtime, Rachel appeared from the back door carrying plates and cutlery for the outside table. It was a sunny day and her mood matched the sparkle of her new ring.

Looking up at the men in her life, she sighed contentedly and announced, "Lunch in ten minutes." And then to her father who, in the process of his final hip wiggle, was about to swing. "Dad!" She yelled, "Where do you keep those yellow napkins Mum used?"

Edward's follow-through resembled something out of a ballet and the ball veered acutely to the right. "Bugger." He looked up at his daughter and then back at the ball.

"Third drawer," he shouted annoyed.

John and Rachel shared a smile.

"Come on Daniel," John sat crossed-legged on the ground and motioned for the young man to join him.

As he did, John began his lesson, "How is school?"

Daniel sat still puffing and brushed the hair from his eyes, "It's okay. But I'd rather train."

John looked at his young charge, "What's your hurry?"

"I want to be good."

"And you will be, but to rush is not the answer Daniel," he smiled as the young boy corrected his knees to mirror his own. "What are you training for?"

"I want to be like you."

"Two of me! Doesn't your own family gene hold any value?"

Daniel thought for a moment, "Yes, of course."

"Well then, let me be me and you concentrate on being you." John waited for this to sink in, "Why do we train?"

The young man replied quickly with an answer he knew, "For strength and discipline."

"Where is the centre of our strength?"

Daniel touched his chest with his fist, "Within."

"Our power comes in many guises. Strength, flexibility, awareness and discipline are all good things... but it is knowledge that gives us the wisdom to use them. Training and school is a good balance, Daniel, grow in as many directions as you can, it all adds to who we are."

Daniel acknowledged his understanding with a nod of the head.

John continued in a lighter vein, "Reading is a good exercise."

"It is? Good for what?"

"For the eyes. I shall test you next time."

"Test me?"

"Of course. I know you have strong arms and legs but perhaps you've been neglecting the muscles that control your sight? What's the use of good defence if you can't see an attack in time to use it?"

John raised his hand and moved it up and down and side-to-side in front of his own face. While he spoke his eyes followed, "Side to side, up and down. Work on extending your peripherals. The stronger the muscle the greater the speed."

Daniel worked the test for himself, "Side to side. Up and down."

"Head still," corrected John.

Edward who had been cracking the golf ball had teed up another, but this time the elastic gave way when he hit. Flying off with a typical slice it headed straight for John. He hadn't time for a warning.

"Side to side ..." continued Daniel.

Whack! John caught the ball centimetres from his left temple with his right hand.

In shock, Edward uttered a belated, "Fore!"

Daniel was impressed as John looked at the ball and raised his eyebrows in mock surprise. They laughed.

Daniel launched into a wrestling attack as John, defending weakly, threw the ball and what remained of the string back to a pale-faced Edward.

The heat of the day was now at it's highest, the humidity suffocating. The baked hardness of the sisal ropes had rubbed John's wrists almost raw. Still unconscious his body folded like a marionette when unceremoniously cut down. The pain from the impact and collapse of his arms caused an involuntary and agonised scream.

Dragged by his feet along the ground, John was manhandled over tree roots and loose bracken until being clumsily lifted and squeezed back into his small cell. Once secured, two small bowls, one each of rice and water were precariously placed in the corner near his head. Satisfied that all orders had been followed, the chattering guards left John to himself.

Silent and alone, his body battered and broken, John Landau opened an eye, and willing his consciousness into action, slowly resumed the gathering of information for his military mind.

Chapter Eleven

Melbourne, Australia
October 2000.

The lake in the middle of the Melbourne's Botanical Gardens at sunset was a beautiful sight. The large English oaks threw long shadows across still water that reflected the distant orange of a city skyline.

Wandering along its banks, Ilya Chemenko, threw breadcrumbs from a paper bag as the happy recipients of his generosity: a family of eight grey ducks and two red-billed swans, squabbled noisily over the free meal. Nearby, small children played with an inflatable beach ball as their parents gathered together the remains of a picnic and packed for the trip home.

Australian's had beautiful weather Ilya thought. Dry and low in humidity, it was a pleasant change from the growing cold in Europe, but it was a long way to come for such a short meeting and. Glancing at his watch with some discomfort, he knew it would be some time before he recovered from the effects of the flight.

"Good evening Ilya."

Ilya turned toward the voice behind him.

"Ah Harold, good evening to you too."

Harold Lassiter smiled warmly as the two shook hands and embraced. "I'm sorry we had to meet under such circumstances."

"And so far away," Ilya added with a broad smile.

"Yes, I'm sorry about that. How are Nadya and the family?"

"Nadya's well thank you. Anatolii is married and selling BMW's to the new bourgeoisie and Khristin will finish her degree next year. She hopes of all things to go to America on exchange, but we'll see. And Penny?"

"Marvellous as always. She never changes. Like Gibraltar my Penny." The two men settled into a comfortable walk as Ilya continued to feed the wildlife that followed.

"How are things in Paris?"

"Now there's a situation ..." Ilya answered, shaking his head. "You wonder why they bother to go there at all, apart from the food of course. Secretary of State Albright would have her time better spent teaching Putin to crochet. Neither Barak nor Arafat would dare make meaningful concessions. It's difficult listening to the lies while knowing the truth. We are all to blame for the whole thing and I include you and I in that Harold ... guilt by association."

He seemed genuinely down beat about the state of things as Harold guided him to a seat overlooking the lake.

Ilya sighed, "I don't mean to blame you personally Harold, you understand." He continued to feed the ducks and looked at his old friend. Harold closed his eyes momentarily and nodded. He knew exactly what Ilya meant and he was right.

The 1978 defection of Romanian espionage chief Ion Pacepa had confirmed long held suspicions of Soviet involvement in the PLO. It was a complicity that surprised many with its degree of deception over such a long period of time. The duplicitous nature of both sides in the Middle East, at the expense of millions, would always be a black mark against all of them.

Ilya Chemenko was Harold's opposite number in the SVR and was an extremely astute and intelligent man. They had worked several International 'situations' over the years and as the last bastions of hope, had managed to steer their respective sides away from what seemed, at the time, unavoidable confrontation. Their successful relationship was built on a firm belief in the greater good, which at times far exceeded job description or employer intent. Patriotism and ideology did not always serve a just or intelligent outcome. The trilateral talks in Paris were a sham. Regardless of the public statements, both sides were too heavily committed to separate agendas, allegiances, and secret manipulations.

For a time both men contemplated the wanton stupidity until Ilya broke the silence. "Is that the MCG?" He asked.

Harold looked over to the distant and daunting facade of the great arena visible beyond the water lilies through the Canadian Maples.

"It is," he answered. "Home of the Melbourne Cricket Club and site of England's last glorious victory over Australia for the 'Ashes'."

"Such a little urn and so much fuss. Did you win it back?"

"Sadly no."

"Why do you English invent games you're not good at?"

"It's not whether you win or lose Ilya, its how you play the game. You should catch one next time you're in England. Many a world problem has been solved amid the soporific resonance of ball on bat."

"Thank you but no." He raised his bushy eyebrows and laughed, "I'm afraid death by a thousand cuts has far greater appeal."

Harold smiled as Ilya enjoyed his dig at the empire.

Reaching into his jacket the man from SVR brought out an envelope and handed it over. He spoke in eloquent Russian: His power and authority clearly evident in the comfortable use of his own language.

"These are for your general information. They are copies of situation reports from our military. He has been located, your man, but it has been difficult diplomatically."

Harold pocketed the reports and answered in kind, his own Russian flawless, "They do appreciate it was 'their' Intelligence that screwed up in the first place? It was a disaster, good men."

"We did lose sixteen of our own." Ilya countered, "And I might add that it would be much better if I were here negotiating for the return of six men rather than one."

"Yes of course."

"Why doesn't MI6 align itself with a less destructive ally? Personally I don't know a single person who hasn't been shot at by an American at least once."

"We wouldn't be here at all, Ilya, if somebody had simply made an effort to go and look. It is standard procedure and the least a host could do when given the responsibility of two foreign nationals. What did they expect, requests have been ignored for years. Four years to be precise."

"It is true"

"Is he alive?" Harold pressed.

"Mixed reports I'm afraid. How is Vladimir?"

"I'm told he's doing very well. How long?"

Ilya paused and his face softened. "I understand the urgency my friend, we all fear not coming home." He broke into English, "We will do our best."

"Thank you I do appreciate it."

"I'll be in touch. Dazavtra."

Ilya Chemenko extended his hand, and smiled.

"Till tomorrow," said Harold shaking it.

Chapter Twelve

Laos
February 20th 2001.

Captain Uli Gregori rose from a fitful sleep and carefully prepared himself for the coming day. It had been hectic since his arrival at the jungle encampment and he still wasn't used to the humidity of the tropics. The sweat rash around his groin, the first sign of his intolerance, seemed to be going from bad to worse. Today he would follow the advice of the MO and not wear underpants. Already sweating profusely he donned the new camouflage fatigues and hoped their pristine appearance would fade quickly. He had not served in a combat post before and it showed.

Placing his hat upon his head he looked at himself in the small mirror that hung on the pole near his bed. A recent graduate of the Malinovskiy Tank Academy he hoped this tour of duty would enhance his application for further courses and more illustrious military qualifications. Since youth he had studied the strategists Suvoron and Clausewitz and felt sure he was worthy of at least a low-grade entry into higher command. Still he thought, six months as a Field Admin Officer shouldn't present too many problems and he'd be back in Moscow long before the next intake.

Checking his watch he patted his pockets, remembered a pen, and departed.

"Stand at ease Captain, it looks like you're trying to keep your arse from falling off."

Colonel Poytr Melnik sat with his weight on the back of his chair and his feet casually on top of his desk. He took a puff of his American Marlboro cigarette and blew the smoke skywards as his eyes ran up and down his new officer from Moscow.

A veteran of many campaigns, Melnik was battle hardened and tough: the antithesis of the man standing before him.

"Yes Colonel," said Uli trying to relax.

Melnik rolled his cigarette back and forth in his fingers. His manner was cool. "Your first tour?" He asked.

"Yes Colonel."

"You've never been in a jungle?"

"No Colonel, never."

Melnik stubbed the cigarette in the ashtray and quietly blew the last of his smoke. "Have you ever been under fire?"

"No Colonel."

"You've never been involved in a mission on any level against a hostile enemy?"

"No Colonel."

Rising from his desk, the colonel opened his filing cabinet and searched for a file.

"Have you ever seen a man lose a limb? He asked.

"Sir?"

"You know, a car accident or work incident ... a playground mishap perhaps?" Having found what he wanted he slammed the drawer and turned back.

"There were films at the academy but no sir."

Melnik was unimpressed. With complete indifference he sat, turned his attention to the file, and read. Awkwardly Uli waited until the Colonel signed a document, placed it in the out tray, slowly put down his pen, and looked up.

"Then what of fear?"

"I don't follow sir."

"Have you known it? Been physically sick in the face of it?"

"I ... no sir."

"I see. Then given your answers, I must ask how you arrive at feeling worthy of the responsibility?"

"Sir?"

"The responsibility that comes with being a combat officer in charge of men Captain Gregori. A combat officer responsible for others - more likely than not - in fucking combat."

"Sir ... my ..."

"Yes Captain?"

"My papers ... my record is clearly ..."

"No point going there Captain, I don't care for papers," said Melnik standing to reach for a bottle of vodka and glasses. "The question is, do you think, while under fire and faced with possible death when surrounded by bits of stomach, brains and body parts, that you could think clearly enough to lead others to victory or at least keep them safe? Terrified men in terrifying circumstances, trusting 'you' Captain Gregori, not only with their salvation but also with the hopes of their parents, their wives and their sons."

Uli's mouth moved but nothing came out.

Melnik sighed, "I didn't think so."

He poured vodka into two glasses. "So, it appears I have been given an administration officer fresh from his mother's teat!" He gave a wry grin, "Care to tell me how you think this meeting is going so far?"

"Not very well Colonel."

Melnik extended his arm and offered a glass. "Here, drink this."

Uli took the glass and with shaking hands followed the colonel's salute, "Za vashe zdorovye!"

They both downed the contents. "Do you need another?" Asked Melnik.

"No ... actually yes, thank you."

The colonel poured again and watched as this one went the way of the last.

"Sit down." He pointed to a chair and resumed his own seat as the captain complied.

"You're mistaken. The meeting is going well. I know that you haven't lied to me. I know that you are very inexperienced, and I now know, that you drink vodka." He smiled, "Personally I am not unhappy that you are here Captain Gregori, but I think you should be." He leaned forward to add emphasis to his advice.

"This is a very dangerous place, and you will do well to remember it. Your papers, which I did read by the way, show that you have much to be proud of, but it will amount to nothing if you end up dead." Melnik held up the bottle and pointed it, "And you will be, if you haven't heard what I've said."

"Yes sir."

"If you are to lead men under my command, you will never assume anything is as it seems. You will learn from those around you, and until I give you leave, you will ask before you act. Have I made myself clear?"

"Yes Colonel."

Melnik smiled. He returned the bottle to its home and looked to his desk. "Now for your first lesson." He shuffled some papers to find the one he wanted. Locating it, he looked up, "Can you read a map?"

Uli sat in the front passenger seat of the modified 469B. The Russian four-wheel drive had no front windscreen and the back canvas supports had been removed. With him were three seasoned Russian regulars each armed with Kalashnikov assault rifles. One drove while the other two sat in the back. Although they had no radio the vehicle had a ten-foot whip antenna mounted on its side. Flapping noisily on the end was a small red flag.

The new Admin Officer sat nervously looking at the dirt road and the growing density of the surrounding jungle. He wore a side arm and a briefcase was handcuffed to his left wrist.

As they drove he contemplated the mission. A meeting had been organised with a group of guerrillas. He was charged with the responsibility of negotiating the release of a POW. It had been mentioned that a successful conclusion would be looked upon as a major boost to his career. This however, did little to quell his anxiety of it being on enemy controlled land and that his fear, if noticed, would damage his chance of holding firm should negotiations turn fierce. Bargaining with the enemy he had been taught, was about being in control. They had promised no one would be harmed. The flag: a signal that granted them safe passage to and from the site seemed reasonable. Looking at the vastness of wild land before him, he hoped it was all true.

After two and half hours of constant driving the vehicle negotiated a sharp bend in the narrow road and was brought to an abrupt halt. In front, and in the middle of the road, stood another red flag. This one, on a makeshift pole, had small boulders around its base. The driver looked to the captain and with his consent, turned off the engine. They waited.

Half an hour later nothing had happened. They had followed the precise instruction of once arriving not to move. The tension intensified. The driver looked in his rear-view mirror mounted centrally on a post from the dash. Through habit he reached across to fiddle with its adjustment then mumbled impatiently "This is bullshit, I have to piss," and pulled on the door handle. Suddenly a shot rang out and his head exploded backwards spraying the soldiers in the back with blood. He had been hit right between the eyes.

A mocking voice, seemingly from everywhere, boomed out.

"You were asked not to move, Captain."

The men stunned, looked to their leader. Uli racked with fear and in shock, forced himself to respond.

"The terms of the agreement were that we would not be harmed," he yelled, not knowing where to look.

"Are you hurt?"

Surprised by the question he replied simply, "No I'm not but ..."

"Would you like us to forget the agreement Captain?"

"No."

Again there was silence. Nobody dared move.

Just as the tension became almost unbearable the voice boomed again, "Do you have something for us?"

Uli raised his hand attached to the brief case, "I have this," he called.

Immediately a second shot exploded from another direction and this time, the man behind the driver was hit in the back of the head. Blood spattered across the side of the Captain's face. He quickly lowered his arm and closed his eyes in anticipation of his own death.

"I repeat, you were asked not to move, Captain." Again the voice asked the mocking question, "Are you hurt?"

He answered, "No."

"I must point out that we like to kill government soldiers Captain. Do not make any more mistakes, you don't have many men left. Exit the vehicle."

Petrified his legs wouldn't work, the young captain tried the door and opened it. Tensing for another shot he paused momentarily before forcing himself out and onto the road. Standing alongside the vehicle he slowly closed the door and waited.

"I would ask that you advise your man not to move until you return. Do I need to clarify the definition of 'move' Captain?"

Uli looked to the remaining soldier in the back. He was taut, tense and rigidly still.

"No," he called out.

"Please walk into the jungle."

Without looking back he took a deep breath, and trying to look in control, did as he was told.

Walking into the jungle he stumbled over loose bracken and vines. The damp and shadowy closeness enveloped him as he descended deeper into the vegetation. The dark and eerie silence added to his fear. Well out of sight of the vehicle, he forced his way through a dense clump of leaves and was confronted by several heavily armed men.

The surprise at coming face to face with the enemy left him cold and somewhat separated from the reality of the moment. Hit by the stench of human uncleanliness, the guerrillas were like hungry pack dogs keen to be fed.

Hastily they removed his side arm and patted him down. Seemingly from everywhere their number rapidly increased. In the scurry of activity a particularly ugly character grabbed at the briefcase and impatiently tugged. The captain's arm, still attached with the handcuffs, moved with it. Unaffected by the inconvenience, the man reached behind his back and unsheathed a sword. With little ceremony he motioned to sever the impediment.

Shocked out of his stupor Uli quickly jerked his arm back and cried "No! Wait!" The swordsman unimpressed at the interruption again grabbed the arm but this time, with more authority. He raised his sword to continue. Horrified the captain began to struggle fervently.

"No wait, wait, I have a key," he called, "I have a key."

The man holding the sword looked to a compatriot with querying eyes. A nod of assent was given and the arm was let free.

Captain Gregori frantically went through his pockets and produced the key. Relieved and shaking, he undid the briefcase. The ugly man sheathed his sword, snatched the case, and hurried away.

Surrounded by hostile faces, Uli tried to smile. Roughly threatened he was grabbed and manhandled as the key was taken from his grasp and calmly tossed aside. Quickly they used the open cuff to secure his hands together in front of his body. Hastily he was propelled deeper into the jungle to stop where the swordsman had delivered the briefcase.

Tobacqui Khan sat legs apart on a log. A manila file marked 'Gecko' was in his hands. Huge and intimidating, his blood-stained club was in easy reach. His eyes scanned the papers.

Pausing, he thought for a moment then stood quickly and issued his command, "Cover his eyes." Complying, the men firmly applied a red blindfold to the head of the hapless Russian.

Physically propelled through the jungle, Uli tripped and stumbled his way over a distance of varying directions and speed. He recognised climbs and descents and wading through shallow water. Unceremoniously pushed and pulled until eventually they came to a halt.

Tobacqui pointed, "Tie him."

They threw a rope over a tree branch and secured his arms above his head. They then dropped his pants and used his belt to wrap around the bulk of material at his ankles and tied the tail to roots on the ground. Because of his boots, his feet were secure. The men departed.

Uli shrouded in red darkness, stood immobilised. With bare buttocks, he was vulnerable and still. His legs involuntarily shook and his stomach felt sick. The pounding of his heart was loud and painful. Around him it became very quiet.

Scared to move, he waited ... and waited.

Meanwhile the silence spread back to the four-wheel drive. The lone soldier left in the back seat, also waited. He had not heard a sound for a long time. The perspiration flowed freely from his forehead into his eyes and down his neck. Around him, flies had begun to buzz over his dead comrades. It was hot. Sticky. He remained motionless and still, his vacant stare fixed firmly ahead.

Uli turned his head to allow his ears to detect the slightest sound. Not hearing anything he tugged gently on his hands to see if he could budge the rope. He could not. He increased his strain until he had given it all he had. He could not move. He wiggled his feet but they were also secure. He tried lifting his head and looking under his blindfold. He motioned his head against his arm and began prizing it up. A little give in the cloth enabled him to see the faint shape of light and shade when he tilted his head fully back.

Suddenly he heard the distinct snap of a twig. He quickly turned and tried to see. Frustrated, he motioned at the blindfold with more furtive movements of his head. From another direction another twig snapped.

"Who's there?" He called turning in the direction of the sound. He remained still and strained to hear. Another twig snapped, closer but from behind.

"Who is it?" He spoke. "Who's there?" He began to move his head with more urgency as the panic rose within.

A giggle.

Desperately he forced his head hard into his arm and managed to partially clear an eye, more movement and effort cleared the other. With vision he spun his head.

Inches from his face stood Mae Lin. She stared unblinking, bathing herself in his torment. His shock was immediate.

"Are you the negotiator?" She asked with her gaze unrelenting.

Feeling sick, Uli nodded.

"It seems I have something you want." She ran her eyes over his face as if taking it all in. Looking into his eyes she smiled.

Uli was petrified.

"It must be quite valuable for you ... " she breathed over him, "to go to such lengths."

Mae dropped her gaze and gave a little girl smirk.

"Tell me ..." she began.

The captain took in a sudden breath as Mae Lin grabbed his genitals gently and looked up.

"What have you to offer?"

With her intensity unwavering, she slowly began to move her hand rhythmically up and down. She pressed closer still and playfully blew gently across his face. He was frozen.

"Hmm?" She asked provocatively.

Moving her mouth around to his ear she made snapping sounds as she bit the air with her teeth. "Don't disappoint me," she whispered.

Pulling her head back she raised her eyebrows expectantly. The rhythmic masturbation was unrelenting. The captain forced himself to speak.

"I am Captain Uli Gregori of the Russian Army." He paused to gulp air as the motion continued, "I have been given ... authority to offer you one ... hundred thousand dollars for the ... safe return of the one they call Gecko."

Mae Lin persisted with her teasing and squinted, "Which part of him do you want?"

"Part?" Asked Uli confused.

The motion stopped. Mae Lin's eyes turned cold, "A part, for part payment."

A distant shot rang out. Theirs heads turned in unison toward the sound. He looked back at Mae Lin who swung her head to his. Matter-of-factly she asked.

"Do you have a license?"

Uli sadly realising what had happened slowly nodded. With one hand still on his groin, Mae Lin produced a knife in her other. Expecting the worst he closed his eyes as she prepared to strike. Instead, Mae Lin drove the blade powerfully into his arm. He screamed in agony. She put her hand gently over his mouth to suppress the noise.

"Hush now ... shh ... shh baby ... shh."

The motion resumed, this time more lustful and driven, powerful and hard. She uttered a guttural moan and giggled.

"I think you had best offer me all the money at your disposal. Don't you?" She asked giggling again.

The captain was near tears, "One million dollars."

"U.S. Dollars?"

He nodded. Mae Lin leaned in and whispered, "Say it baby."

"Yes ... yes U.S. dollars."

The motion slowed to a stop. Mae Lin touched his wound and with eerie attentiveness smeared blood on his lips. She stayed entranced by his lips for what seemed a long time.

Suddenly her eyes snapped up to his, and with a violent movement, her hand smashed into his groin. She squeezed with all her force as her face hideously contorted. He screamed long and loud, almost fainting with the pain. Mae Lin's breathing was strong as she bit her lip and exhaled heavily. Watching intently she relaxed her grip. The screaming became a whimper. The captain was openly frightened and in agony as tears streamed down his face.

Mae Lin smiled a little girl smile, "The passports and safe passage?"

"All arranged," he gasped.

She pervertedly licked at the moisture on his cheek. "Hmm. Good, good," she uttered.

"You will be contacted," she smiled and pulled the knife. Exhausted, he moaned softly as the blood oozed freely from his wound. Mae Lin spoke with mock innocence, "Are you hurt?"

The captain whispered, "No."

Standing on the roadside with his hands cuffed and eyes covered. Uli Gregori stood tired and bleeding. Removing his blindfold he was shocked as he faced the carnage and what remained of his men. Their bodies, hacked and brutalised, had been stripped of their clothing and weapons ... even their boots had gone.

Gingerly he moved to the driver's door and assisted the remains of the deceased to fall from his path. Stepping in he forced back the urge to panic when the vehicle took several attempts to start. With heightening anxiety he struggled with the cuffs to control the vehicle. Agonising minutes passed as he clumsily took ten points to turn. When he finally managed to depart, his chin quivered with relief. As the speed increased, he convulsively sobbed. A thousand metres down the road he pulled over, hung his head over the side and vomited until there was nothing more to give.

Chapter Thirteen

I t was morning, the Australian summer was in full swing and the heat had pushed the temperature soaring beyond thirty degrees. Rachel's small suburban home lay in a cul-de-sac lush with vegetation and ringed by native blue gums, acacias and yellow wattle. The lyrical bird-song of a magpie travelled whimsically over air that was dry and breathless. Beneath the kitchen window a large flowering Banksia hummed with the relentless drone of bush bees, already at work in the sun.

Inside, Rachel and Daniel were having breakfast. Over the years that had passed since John's disappearance, Daniel had grown into a tall and muscular man. His once long sun-bleached hair was now shorter and more sculptured. His boyish features had made way for chiselled definition and a strong jaw. Like all young men in their early twenties, he enjoyed his 'in-your-face' clothing and masculine presence. However, his eyes disclosed the full extent of the compassion and serenity of the real man within.

Eating his cereal, Daniel secretly observed his sister as her eyes aimlessly wandered the room. Worried for her, he had come to see if he could help. She hadn't coped well with the loss of her partner and her tears and constant depression were of major concern. Sitting in a daze, her heavy eyes were now firmly fixed on the dresser and a framed eight by four photograph of John.

Since her loss, Rachel had become more and more despondent. Locked in personal desolation she remained helpless and overwhelmed by sadness. Shrouded in loneliness and withdrawn, the familiar sparkle in her eyes had gone.

Aware of the enormous gap in his own life since John had not returned, Daniel wondered if any of them, himself, Rachel, or their father, would ever be at peace again.

He put down his spoon and sighed, "Rache?"

She didn't hear at first so he tried again. This time speaking louder, "Rachel?"

Shaken from her daydream, she looked up, "Hmm?"

"You can't keep doing this to yourself. It's been five years."

Rachel stared at her brother. The instant warmth of his aura washed over her. In the sudden touch she felt the strength of John's spirit beating inside him. "He's alive Daniel. I can feel it. I can." Her eyes went to the photo, "He can't get back to us yet. But he will." Turning back to her brother she refused to yield or give in, "He will. You of all people should know how strong he is."

Daniel held his sister's look as a tear slowly rolled down her cheek. Taken back by the depth of her emotion he answered softly, "Yeah I know sis, I know."

In the quiet darkness of the night, John slept. Pale and very thin, his beard and hair were long and matted. His unwashed skin was now covered in tropical sores and his weakened body was cut and bruised.

The beatings had become regular: A program of systematic torture designed to keep him on the edge. Agony followed by recovery followed by agony again, was relentless and unforgiving. The evening battles had become harder and more desperate as he plunged new depths of depravity to survive and win. More frequently his mind wandered toward death as an alternative, as his memories, once his strength, had become distant and obscure. Now, the only emotion driving him to hang on, was hate.

A female voice began to sing. The familiar words permeated the silence and their evil aroused the darkest of fears within.

"This ... little cow ... eats grass ..."

The slow and menacing incantation was followed by the loud and deliberate scrape of metal on metal. John, immediately aware of the arrival of his tormentor, snapped open his eyes. Frantically his mind gathered the tattered remnants of his resistance to control his panic as his body braced for the inevitable pain.

"This ... little cow ... eats hay ..."

Again the words echoed, followed by a long methodical scrape.

Mae Lin stood at the end of John's cell. He could see her torso framed by the rectangular shape of its opening. As she progressed toward him with her song she slid her knife along the length of each bar like a butcher sharpening an edge before cutting.

"This little cow drinks water ..." she sang as Tobacqui Khan followed dutifully alongside.

John watched the hypnotic motion of the blade as it intimidated and moved closer to him.

"This little cow runs away ..."

The knifepoint now played across his face. Willing himself not to scream, John prayed that the imminent cuts would not be as deep as the last.

"This little cow does nothing ..."

Mae Lin's torso reached the end of the cell and with a sudden movement she lowered her face into the opening of the cage and glared. John involuntarily edged back from the pervasive cold of her closeness.

"Except lie down each day ..." she sang.

Mae Lin pushed her bottom back against Tobacqui's groin and began to writhe and swing against him. She stared unblinking at John and moaned lewdly. The sexual perversity unfolded with macabre theatre and intensity.

"Let's whip her ..." she teased with exaggerated breathing and flaunting of her cleavage.

Aroused, Tobacqui began to rhythmically grind for himself. He grabbed Mae Lin's hips and pushed her to the bars. She accentuated the movement with more groans, panting and squeezing of her breasts. All the while, never taking her eyes from John.

"Let's whip her ..."

"Let's whip her."

Her song finished, Mae Lin giggled like a little girl as she made grotesque noises and mock stabbing gestures with her knife. Looking into the tortured soul of her captive she gave the air a seductive lick and spoke as if scolding a child.

"Oh baby, its alright, Mummy doesn't always have to cut you. I can do it anytime ... anytime I want." She giggled again.

Standing, Mae Lin turned into Tobacqui. Her breathing was powerful and hot. With his hands still on her hips she allowed him to press himself against her. Holding his gaze for a moment she suddenly turned and walked off. Tobacqui followed.

John, huddled and trapped without hope, remained lost in his torment.

At a vantage point some distance from the cages, a match struck in the darkness. The glow illuminated the silhouette of an observer as he lit a cigarette. Extinguishing the match by tossing it aside, the spy drew a long inhalation, blew smoke into the air, and quietly departed.

Chapter Fourteen

February 4th 2002.

In the hills that surrounded the guerrilla stronghold, a small wooden sauna stood isolated amongst the trees. Originally imported from North America and made of Canadian Hemlock 'The House of Tao' as it was called, was forbidden to all others but Xiang. The shrunken head of its previous owner hung as a warning above the door.

The possession of the sauna marked a significant moment for Xiang. Twenty years ago, the rich and extensive poppy fields now inside his northern borders had been under the rule of a rival warlord named Tao.

Historical adversaries, the two had fought skirmishes over land rights for years. Tao was a superstitious man who decapitated his enemies and shrunk their heads. He believed that their souls gave him strength and power over other men. A belief that held sway with some, but not with Xiang.

In a day of decisive battle Xiang exploited Tao's arrogance to deliver a resounding victory and his enemy's head. The defeat yielded control of the entire province and marked Xiang's arrival as the most powerful warlord of the region.

The loss on that day of a thousand warriors played heavily on Xiang. Using Tao's sauna provoked thought on the memory and reminded him that arrogance toward an enemy would never deliver a win.

Accompanied by a flurry of steam Xiang emerged from the door beneath Tao's head. With his skin pink and glowing he planted his feet firmly on the landing overlooking the camp. Dressed only in a towel he sucked in and expelled out satisfying gulps of cool air.

His elderly amah rushed to fuss over him. Handing him a fresh towel she set about drying his back and legs.

Vigorously rubbing at his hair and wiping the sweat from his face, Xiang's efforts slowed as his eyes focused on two people in the distance. The sight of Mae Lin and Tobacqui together was not pleasing.

Having known Xiang since childhood, the amah sensed his mood swing. Seeing the couple for herself she spat over the railing and unconsciously rubbed harder at her master's back.

Never a fan of Mae Lin, she'd always wondered at the warlord's interest in the disturbed girl without flesh. After all, he had many eager consorts and they all knew how to please. It was a common joke amongst the women that Mae Lin believed her jade gate was lined with gold. Angered by the rumours the amah couldn't help but mutter out loud.

"The more the wings of a young eagle grow the further they fly from the nest. People are talking."

Xiang turned angrily and pushed the old woman away. Unable to hold her footing she fell heavily backwards onto her rump. Throwing his towel after her Xiang exuded displeasure.

"Be silent before I sew your loose tongue to your foot." He looked at the head of Tao and his voice hardened, "Wings can be clipped old woman. Get my boots."

Delighted with her influence, she scurried away.

Mae Lin approached a large group of men gathered around the covered area known as the Planning Hut. Led by one of Xiang's henchmen, she was accompanied by a small group of her faithful. On her arrival the henchman ushered her through the throng. The crowd of men parted way to allow her entry. Behind her, the faithful were impeded from following.

Xiang was seated. Eating ravenously he talked loudly and demonstrably to those close by. Remnants of the food stuck to his jowls and his manner smacked of a danger. As Mae Lin neared him, his intensity heightened and he began to bait.

"Ah, Mae Lin how kind of you to honour us with your presence."

Xiang's comment was accompanied by a collective of derisive laughter. Mae Lin's senses were immediately alight. She looked about for a friendly face but seeing none she returned her attention to Xiang.

"You wished to see me?"

"I have taken the liberty of assigning Tobacqui Khan a mission in the foothills."

"Lord?"

Xiang looked around mocking. "You don't mind? No complaints regarding his compliance with my wishes?"

Mae Lin shook her head slowly. Her mind was racing to find Xiang's objective.

"I would like to proceed with the transfer of the unfortunate one," he said.

Mae Lin was shocked, "But Lord, you said yourself that it is unwise to deal with the enemy. The negotiation, a mere distraction, you said."

"Well, I have changed my mind." His eyes narrowed, "Effective immediately."

On the outer of the large group, two young members of Mae Lin's faithful swapped concerned looks and hurried away. Mae Lin hastily tried to reason.

"But Lord ..."

"But?" Xiang interrupted loudly.

"My prisoner does not ..."

"Your prisoner?" He pushed harder.

"So sorry, our prisoner does not deserve ..."

Xiang leapt to his feet and quickly closed the gap between them.

"Our prisoner? Did I miss a coup?"

His eyes widened and he bared his rotten teeth in a vicious smile. More laughter followed.

Mae Lin quickly changed tack and under pressure played her main card. With a little girl smile she talked softly.

"Of course he is your prisoner my king of beasts ..."

Xiang was still. He watched and waited.

"But he killed my brother and I have a right to him. He cannot be freed. You see that don't you? He must not be free, ever! Please lion cub, please."

Xiang's face was momentarily unreadable. Suddenly, and without warning, he hit his consort powerfully across the face with the back of his hand. Her head jarred violently from the force of the blow. Xiang screamed his outrage.

"Your insolence is beyond belief! To bring pillow talk to the ears of my subordinates! Your family is of no concern to me. I am Lord here!"

He hit her again and again. Mae Lin knew that she was in serious trouble and to struggle would mean the end. Grabbing her hair, Xiang twisted her head and pulled his knife to threaten her.

"You are fortunate I don't have you impaled on more than Khan's member."

Efficiently he cut off her long plait. Mae Lin expelled a cry of horror.

"You are banished from my province."

He tore her shirt and grabbed at a breast. She winced in pain, but Xiang was merciless and full of anger.

"If I see you again I will flatten you with my blade."

He pushed her back.

Falling to the ground Mae Lin was shaken. Grabbing her shirt together she tried desperately to understand what had gone wrong. With all the dignity she could muster, she stood and came to terms with her options. Her eyes hardened as she searched the faces of the surrounding circle. Finally she settled on Xiang. Mockingly he raised his eyebrows and waited.

Mae Lin accepting, slowly turned and walked out. The group parted to allow her exit. There were leering eyes but a quiet few were silently angry.

Xiang, keen on a final insult, called out matter-of-factly.

"Chap Cheng," he yelled.

Amused, he laughed raucously and was joined loudly by his men.

Chapter Fifteen

I n the rugged stone cliffs that fell dramatically to parched and ancient riverbeds, there existed a series of caves. These caves had been used for shelter by the Hmong on their way to the mountains at the end of the Vietnam War.

A mass exodus of an entire people, the Hmong fled retribution from a government that wanted them dead. Used by the CIA to interrupt supply lines on the Ho Chi Min trail, those who couldn't get to the United States after Saigon fell were left to fend for themselves. Historically harmless and simple farmers, almost a hundred thousand men, women, and children had been exterminated since.

It was ironic that Mae Lin learned of the existence of the caves from Xiang himself. Now, it was she who used them.

It was night. Crouched beside a small campfire she was locked in thought. The amber lick of the little flames paled against the fire that burned fiercely in her eye. Suddenly there was a noise in the outlying jungle. Alert to the intrusion she looked up.

From the darkness the intimidating frame of Tobacqui Khan emerged into the light. Around him, thirty guerrillas also appeared. They were her faithful and they were dressed for a fight. Expressionless, Tobacqui casually swung his hammer onto his shoulder and waited.

It was a few minutes till dawn. Xiang's guerrilla encampment was quiet. Some had stirred but nobody had yet risen. The dark blue rim on the horizon began to lighten in anticipation of the sun.

A dog with a torn ear stretched and scratched while two others tussled over possession of a fleshless bone. A lone guard sat mesmerised by the dying flicker of his fire as he waited for his shift to end. Along the wall of the incarcerated, John's cage was empty and the bars remained open. Strangely, it seemed smaller with him gone.

On the other side of the encampment the exterior woodwork of Xiang's personal quarters changed colour with the soft ambience of first light.

It was an unobtrusive building, with no electricity and a single small window boarded from inside. The interior had just enough room for a desk, some personal items, and a map on the wall. The sleeping area was a bed to one side divided from the main room by a black curtain that was drawn.

Above the sounds of waking wildlife, a staccato tapping noise could be heard.

Suddenly the door banged open. Xiang's amah struggled in with the morning rinse-bowl of hot water. Muttering to herself she placed the bowl down on the desk. Wiping sleep from her eyes she addressed her master in her habitual manner.

"Good morning Lord," she said.

Reaching over the desk she opened the board on the window to the morning light. Straightening the frayed elastic around her bosom whilst looking at the day, the amah spoke loudly so that he could hear.

"Cook says it's dim sum day. So I suppose you'll be happy about that."

In the silence that followed the old woman became aware of the tapping. Curious she turned to the curtain drawn across the bed.

"Lord Xiang?" She asked.

As she approached the noise grew louder. She hesitated.

"Lord?" She whispered, "Is that you?"

Moving closer still, she stepped in something unfamiliar. Lifting her foot to check, she felt a sticky resistance and heard a sucking noise, as it broke free. Dark red fingers of coagulating blood stretched from her sandal to a large pool of blood on the floor. Panicked she wrenched open the curtain.

Xiang was dead. Grotesquely impaled with his sword, his head and neck hung above the mattress as if he'd died attempting to sit up. The sword had entered his mouth and pierced the lower part of his brain causing his head to be arched back at a contorted angle. The hilt had stopped at his bad teeth which, induced by nerves, chattered loudly against the steel. His glasses still on, the bed was awash with red.

Horrified the amah stifled a scream with her hands and slowly edged back in shock. Realising the magnitude of her discovery she turned for the door ...

The heavy smack of soft flesh against unforgiving hardness was loud and final. The vicious strike of Tobacqui's hammer killed her instantly.

"Are we done?" He asked.

Mae Lin emerged from the shadows covered in blood. Her face glowed with satisfaction. She smiled a little girl smile at Tobacqui.

"Not yet, Lion Cub ..." she whispered. She lifted up the manila file marked 'Gecko' and her face darkened. "Not yet."

Chapter Sixteen

It was Monday, 9.15 a.m. in the suburb of Manly. A million miles away from anything resembling a war zone, Sydney held its populace captive in a seemingly perpetual race against time. The congestion of city traffic frustrated those trapped in it. The cars along Pittwater Road were still bumper-to-bumper. It had rained earlier and as always this affected the traffic's efficiency as it wormed slowly toward Spit Bridge and the city proper.

Horns tooted as impatient drivers swooped into the slightest opening of a faster lane. Post weekend shoppers competed with employees for space along crowded footpaths while patrons queued for coffee in cafes, and mothers struggled from buses with their strollers.

Amongst the many retail outlets that adorned Pittwater road was the ancient and austere 'Walker's Fabric and Haberdashery Emporium'. It had been there for as long as anyone could remember. Established in 1898 by English spinsters Martha and Agatha Walker (deceased), it was famous for having at least one of every coloured button ever made.

Occupying the space above Walker's were the ramshackle offices of the accountancy firm, Stanley and Stanley. The surviving partner of a father and son business, Ian Stanley had known Edward Roberts and his family for years. As such he had jumped at the chance to help Rachel with a job as his Receptionist/Secretary.

Ian was close to retirement and his offices had a well-worn mix of the old interspersed with the new. Rachel's desk backed onto a window overlooking the outside traffic, and was conveniently placed between the brown 'visitor's couch' and her employer's office.

Typically, Rachel's desktop was a jumble of papers and files. This morning was no exception. Sitting behind a computer that displayed images of weather patterns from around the world, she swivelled her chair to the window and waited on the end of the phone.

Doing what she had done every Monday since John's disappearance. Rachel rang his originating Unit CO, for news. While waiting, she unconsciously followed the practiced ritual of closing down all expectation of good news and minimising the dread of bad.

The phone answered. A man spoke. His was voice calm and his manner polite.

"Colonel Haig's office."

Rachel put on her phone voice and swung back toward her desk. "Hello, may I speak with Colonel Robert Haig please?"

"I'm sorry the Colonel is out for the moment."

"Oh ..." said Rachel, her disappointment evident.

"Is that you Miss Roberts?" The voice enquired.

"Yes it is."

"This is Sergeant Gardia, Miss Roberts, how are you this morning?"

"Fine, thank you."

"I'm not sure when he'll be back but I'll let him know you called the moment he steps in. Is it the same number as last week?"

"Yes, yes it is, thank you."

"You're welcome Miss Roberts. Have a nice day."

"You too Sergeant."

The line went dead. Rachel feeling empty, slowly cradled the handset. Just then, Mr Stanley's door swung open and Rachel's attention was drawn to her employer's head sticking round it and his querying look.

"Rachel?" He asked.

Rachel was blank, "Yes Mr Stanley?"

"Mr Beaumont's file?" He reminded.

Immediately jolted, Rachel remembered his client. "Oh shit!" She blurted, "Coming Mr Stanley."

As the door closed behind him, Rachel went into a panic and rushed to the filing cabinet. Unsuccessfully looking along the B's for Beaumont she abandoned the cabinet and hastily rummaged through the mass of papers on her desk. Finding it, she thankfully clutched the file to her chest. By chance she noticed a relevant document and grabbed it. Then noticing another she grabbed at that too.

Mr Stanley reappeared and Rachel, piling the papers together, rushed them over to him with outstretched hands. Acutely aware of the untidy presentation she helpfully poked at the bits sticking out as she passed it to him.

"It's all here," she added guiltily.

The phone rang. Rachel's attention was torn between it and Mr Stanley's futile attempts to straighten his file. The phone kept ringing with growing urgency. Distracted, she noticed a piece of paper on the floor.

"Oh!" She said. Rushing to it she snapped it up and thrust it into his hands. Breathlessly she added, "Here, this too. Sorry Mr Stanley."

Feeling uncomfortably useless she smiled apologetically and retreated for the phone. Mr Stanley, giving up on the papers whispered after her.

"Rachel."

She didn't hear.

Frustrated, he leaned forward in an animated attempt to throw his voice, "Rachel!" He whispered, almost shouting.

With her hand paused over the receiver she looked up, "Yes Mr Stanley?"

Trying to remain calm he held up two fingers and mouthed the word 'coffee'. Rachel nodded her understanding as she picked up the phone.

"Good morning Stanley and Stanley."

The calm deep voice of John's Commanding Officer brought an immediate shift in her emotional state.

"Hello Rachel its Robert."

Slowly lowering herself into her chair she fought the rise of expectation and desire to cry all at once.

"Hello Colonel."

"How are you?"

"Good … good," Rachel, in need of movement, swung her chair toward the view.

"I'm afraid I have no news as yet," he offered.

"Oh ..."

"But that's not to say that we're any worse off than this time yesterday or the day before for that matter."

"No news is good news. Right?"

"Exactly."

A tear ran down Rachel's face.

"Is there anything else?" The Colonel enquired, sensing there was.

"It's just that... you may think me silly ..."

"Not at all. Go on."

With the loss of her soul mate, Rachel was desolate. Trying to remain calm she turned to the maps on her computer and suddenly her cup overflowed.

"It's just that I was looking at the weather patterns and ... I'm sure you know ... but it's the monsoons in Indo China and ... well there's a very large hurricane and it says ... to expect winds of up to 150km per hour." She began sobbing.

"I was just going to say ... I wanted to ask ... And I know that you would tell me if you could ... because you're nice ... but do you think that with such bad weather and winds ... that he ... that John will be safe? I mean ... "

Her sobbing became uncontrollable. Behind her, Mr Stanley silently ushered Mr Beaumont to the door.

"I'm sorry ... but I don't even know what he was wearing ... if he'll be warm ... He doesn't like the cold ..."

Haig interrupted, "Rachel."

Taking a deep breath she answered, "Yes?"

Robert Haig was a hardened military man but Rachel had been ringing every week for so long that he couldn't help being drawn. He had great empathy for her and wished there was more he could do. He tried his best.

"Of course he'll be warm. Our kit is the finest in the world. We wouldn't let him go anywhere without the right kit. Do you hear me?"

Rachel nodded.

"Now don't you worry any more about it. John is the best, a little storm won't bother him. Okay?"

Rachel whimpered, "Yes."

"Call me anytime Rachel."

"Yes ... thank you."

Haig hung up. The volume of the continuous dial tone dominated as Rachel clung to the handset and wept.

Ian Stanley stood on the other side of the desk not knowing what to do. Helpless in the wake of her immense suffering, he quietly withdrew.

Across the harbour, in the inner suburb of Glebe, Rachel's father, Edward, was hard at work in the small nursery at the rear of his florist shop. With the advent of autumn he was preparing seedling punnets of Canterbury Bells for sale.

Pausing to stretch the ache in his back, Edward took in his surroundings. For more than thirty years 'Robert's Nursery' had been his life. From small beginnings he and his wife had built a business that had been the bedrock of their existence. Through the tough times, the struggles, the birth of their children, their schooling, and sadly her death.

Looking into the glass confines of the office, Edward could see Daniel moving around the room. Remembering mother and son together, he knew Elizabeth would have liked the person he had become.

Inside, the office was well worn and practical. A painted cement floor held a faded welcome mat across the threshold. A large square desk was covered in orders and invoices and the comfortable chair squeaked when you leaned back. The glass partitions of the walls were decorated with out-of-date calendars and brochures from hawkers and local business. All over the room, tucked in corners and clustered on shelves, a myriad of fight trophies bore Daniel's name and gathered dust.

Wearing blue jeans and a white T-shirt Daniel paced as he spoke. Holding his mobile in his right hand his sleeve revealed the dark blue ink of a Celtic symbol tattooed inside his bicep: a triquetra of interlocking circles representing the holy trinity.

"Yeah, of course I'm interested. But full contact is not what I'm used to. It's not a matter of courage, Vinnie, it's a matter of physical management. Three fights a month seems fine if you don't get hurt."

While Daniel listened to Vinnie's reply he saw his father strain to lift another box.

"How much? Hang on Vinnie." Daniel dropped the phone and banged on the glass. "Dad!" He yelled, "I'll do that, hold on."

Returning to his conversation he went out to help.

"Shit, that's not bad. Look I'll call you later okay. Yeah, yeah before five. Bye."

Daniel hung up and pocketed the phone in one easy movement. Joining his father he reached out, took the box from his grasp and shelved it.

Edward sighed his gratitude and went back to his bench.

Daniel looked at the array of planter boxes laid out in front of him and sorted into groups. "Which ones are which?" He asked.

Edward pointed to various sections, "Campanula Medium. These blue, those white, and over there pink. You can separate the pink if you like."

Setting about dividing punnets with his hands, Edward noticed Daniel was distracted and deep in thought. He knew exactly what about.

"Was that Vinnie again?" He asked.

"Yeah."

Edward stopped working and looked at his son, "You're not actually thinking about it are you?"

Daniel raised his eyebrows, "Dad the Colosseum seems like an opportunity to really get somewhere. It's a pretty good deal."

"It's a dumb deal." Daniel's father was resolute and continued sorting, "Fighting for money is a mug's game."

"Only if you lose."

Edward knew where this was heading and straightened himself up. "Everybody loses son." He pointed a parental finger, "Forget it and pass me that box."

Daniel did as he was asked.

Silently the pair worked side by side until the young man, unable to contain his frustration any longer decided to have it out. "I can't stay here all my life you know."

"Nobody's saying you have to Daniel," Edward responded, "But surely it will do until other things fall into place."

"Look I'm twenty-two, I haven't been beaten in a tournament in four years. I'm my strongest now. What's the harm in building a nest egg?"

"What's the harm? Didn't John teach you anything? In tournaments you don't brain them, and they don't brain you!

"Oh come on."

"Don't 'Oh come on' me! How are you going to feel Daniel when you cause serious injury to an opponent? You break bricks with a single punch for Christ sake. How's the pay cheque going to feel then?"

"It won't come to that."

"If there's money involved ... It will. It's blood money. It goes against everything John stood for and you know it."

Daniel had had enough, "John's gone!" He shouted, "He's not coming back! Doesn't anybody here understand that?"

Edward tried to calm him down, "Look son."

"No! Don't! I can't do what Rachel does, I can't! So don't ask me to. For Christ sake it's exactly the same crap I had to deal with after mum died." Daniel saw the sudden pain in his father's eye, "Shit!" Daniel stood stricken, "Dad I didn't mean ..."

Edward raised his hand to stop him.

Dominated by concern for his daughter he had not fully understood the effect of John's disappearance on his son. Instinctively moving forward he took hold of Daniel in a paternal embrace, "I didn't realise Daniel. I sometimes forget how much you've lost. I'm very sorry."

Edward pulled back and held Daniel at arms length. His chest puffed with pride, "Look at you with the strength of ten men." Taking time to collect his thoughts Edward sighed heavily, "I never intended to influence your life in such a way. As parents we all tell ourselves that we won't, but we do. Perhaps without realising it I have fooled myself into thinking that by hanging on to you, I will somehow hold on to those I have already lost. But always, always Daniel, my concern is for you and your welfare. It is because you are my son. Your mother's son."

Daniel squeezed his father's shoulders, "I know Dad. But I need to make my own way. Please."

Edward knew he had to let go, "Yes of course you must." Pulling his son into him to mask his fear, Edward resolutely patted his back, "Of course you must."

Darkness had fallen. There was a chill in the air and the rolling clap of distant thunder warned of coming rain. In the lamp-lit street the flow of traffic had slowed to an occasional car as the lights from Robert's Flowers began sequentially going out.

The small welcoming bell jingled as Edward emerged from his shop and closed the door. Tired and emotionally drained, he raised his collar against the cold and engaged the lock.

Pocketing his keys he was surprised at the hastening approach in his direction of Ian Stanley.

"Hello Ian what brings you out here?" Edward called.

Wearing a large overcoat and scarf Mr Stanley was outwardly tense, "I'm sorry to call so late Ed but can I have a word?"

Edward sensed trouble and withdrew his keys. Accompanied by a louder clap of thunder he took his friend's arm and answered, "You'd better come inside."

Chapter Seventeen

Later that evening, Rachel sat in the semi-dark, drinking red wine. The hallway lamp was on and music played softly from her stereo. Still wearing her work clothes, she had discarded her shoes and tucked her stockinged feet up into the sofa. Holding her glass by her cheek she sat motionless and gazed through the window at the rain.

She had been fired. Not wanting to think, she had watched the entire storm rise and fall with each cascading wave after wave of its subliminal beauty.

The doorbell rang. Roused from her solitude, Rachel checked her watch and went to answer.

"Dad!" She said surprised, "Do you know what time it is?"

Edward shook his saturated brolly and looked at his daughter with a twinkle in his eye, "It might be time for you to ask me in, but I don't know, what do you think?"

Rachel smiled for the first time in ages and was suddenly reacquainted with how good it felt, "Yes of course. Come in."

Edward entered and she took his coat. Turning to face each other in the hallway, he opened his arms and Rachel fell in. It was a long hug and just what she needed.

"Oh it's good to see you Dad," she said buried deep in his chest.

"So I gather." Edward kissed her gently on top of her head, "You were never like this when I gave you chores."

"I've mellowed," she said looking up, "What are you doing here?"

"I'm visiting!" He said as if it was obvious.

"At midnight in the rain?" She asked suspiciously.

"Correct." Edward's face was deadpan.

Rachel smiled again, "That's nice. Come on then."

Leading him inside she left him to his life-long habit of turning down the stereo to a point where it wasn't worth having, and went to the kitchen. "Daniel rang," she called while looking for a glass. Locating one, she added, "You approve?"

"Not really. But he needs to find himself."

"I guess," she mused. Holding up the wine glass, she asked, "Can I offer you one?"

"What are you having?"

"Red."

"That'll do nicely thank you."

Pouring the wine, Rachel felt the weight of her father's silence. Moving around the counter she tested her suspicion, "You know don't you?"

Edward nodded dutifully and confessed, "Ian dropped by earlier."

He sat on the sofa and accepted the glass as he patted the cushion beside him, "Here, come and sit."

Rachel did and he draped his arm about her as she snuggled in with her head in his lap.

"I'm sorry Dad."

"Oh hush now. Ian is a good man. He's very worried about you. He thinks he'll retire long before he can find a better replacement."

"Liar."

Edward took a sip of wine, "How's my Princess?"

"A mess," she sighed. "I can't hang on to a job. And I think I'll go insane if this waiting goes on much longer."

Edward began to stroke her hair. Rachel enjoyed the pampering. Content with the familiarity of her father's smell and warm protection, she nuzzled in closer.

"You're very like your mother," he said

Loving him, she grabbed his hand and squeezed it.

"I was thinking," he went on.

"Hmm?"

"Perhaps we might be able to help each other. I'm not a young man, and it does get a bit quiet at home. I could certainly use some help in the shop," adding as an afterthought, "part time of course."

Rachel waited before she responded, "He is coming home Dad."

"We can wait together."

Edward took another sip of his wine and loudly sighed his appreciation as he let the idea take shape.

"I cry a lot," she said.

"I've got hankies."

"Do I have to wash those enormous underpants?"

"Only if you're cheeky."

They both sat quietly in thought as Edward continued to stroke her hair.

After some time, "Dad?"

"Hmm."

"Can I sleep here?"

"Two words. Enlarged and Prostate."

Rachel smiled. Edward sipped his wine. The rain continued. Neither moved.

Chapter Eighteen

Thailand
June 10, 2002.

It was 2.45 a.m. A storm raged. Huge winds bent palm trees to breaking point as the sea, white with anger, tore savagely at the Thai island of Koh Chang. Descending from the hills, a black Mercedes traversed the debris-ridden road blanketed in torrential rain.

With its windscreen wipers moving at maximum speed the car swerved wildly into the deserted car park of the island's only disco. Screeching to a halt next to a public telephone, the driver extinguished his cigarette and checked his watch. It was one minute to three.

Leaving the vehicle he battled the elements and waited. Exactly at three the phone rang.

Moving his head inside the small wind shelter, he lifted the receiver and listened. A female voice spoke precise English.

"Hello. Who is speaking please?"

The driver answered with a heavy accent. His gravely voice, deep and direct. "My name is Gdansk"

"Go ahead, Mr Brown is listening."

"We have Gecko."

Chapter Nineteen

June 12th 2002.

She came out of the Pacific along the fifteenth parallel and into the South China Sea. Hugging the reefs that skirted the shipping lanes, her sleek grey body moved undetected at five hundred metres below. Reaching her mission staging area she rapidly began to climb. Breaching the surface the water erupted under powerful pressure from her awesome displacement of twelve and a half thousand ton.

Armed with twelve long-range Granat cruise missiles, an array of anti-air and anti-ship missiles plus an arsenal of torpedoes: The Russian Akula 11 Attack Submarine was a formidable military craft.

One hundred and ten metres long it glistened in the sun. With distinctive high rear fin and massive double hull, the nuclear vessel glided through the water steadily at ten knots.

Inside, scores of sailors manned their stations as operators punched codes into computers and watched sophisticated satellite imagery of their target.

Eight hundred miles due west of the Akula, a United States E-3 Sentry AWAC cruised in a holding pattern of three hundred miles an hour and thirty thousand feet.

Eleven feet above its fuselage a huge thirty-foot rotating radar dome gathered and disseminated information. Inside, a nine-member surveillance crew received their own satellite imagery of the identical target.

The deserted quarry was ideally located within a neutral zone 'somewhere' in Indo China. It provided the perfect environment for an exchange scheduled for precisely ten o'clock.

Surrounded by dense jungle there were only two access roads. Beginning at opposite sides of the quarry each road was open and wound down three hundred metres to the bottom. The quarry's stony base was a circle two hundred metres in diameter. Importantly it was devoid of both vegetation and obstruction.

Centrally located within the circle stood a one hundred metre straight line of five flags. On six-foot poles, each flag had been placed at twenty-five metre intervals. On either end of the line were two white flags. Twenty-five metres in from these were two blue flags. A red flag marked the middle.

Harold Lassiter and Ilya Chemenko stood on top of the quarry. Each wore short-range communication earpieces with a microphone. Each man had binoculars. Each knew the other was armed.

In front of them on a table were two large secure radio transceivers. One Russian. One American. Ilya looked to Harold who was plainly not happy with the arrangements. "It is done, Harold, there is nothing either of us can do now."

"Yet," Harold sighed, "all manner of things can go wrong!"

"It can't be helped. Since you were seen entering the Royal Orchard on the night Vladamir was taken, it can only be assumed you played a part."

"You know I'm not a field agent."

"So do they Harold. But only a fool would risk feeding the tiger twice. It is prudent to do things this way. "

Harold could not argue with Ilya's logic, if anything happened that remotely resembled a double-cross, then all future exchanges would be in jeopardy.

"All is ready," Ilya urged.

Harold nodded and the process began. Speaking into their respective mouthpieces, the two gave identical instruction.

First Ilya, "Proceed."

Then Harold, "Proceed."

Movement began as a small cavalcade of three vehicles entered the quarry via one of the roads. Led by a dark sedan an enclosed white van with two rear doors followed while another dark sedan brought up the rear. Two men were visible in each of the vehicles.

Moments later a similar cavalcade entered from the other side. Both groups descended to complete a predetermined procedure that ended with their simultaneous arrival at respective ends of the line.

As the two vans reversed toward the white flags, a marksman from each group alighted their vehicles. Carrying weapon cases, they both headed for the same point seventy-five metres perpendicular and central to the line of flags.

Coming together, each man gave a curt nod to acknowledge the presence of the other. With calm precision they unpacked their weapons, fitted sights, loaded a single round, and locked. As they took to the ground they each produced a service pistol, which was placed comfortably within reach. Each marksman's pistol symbolically pointed at the other.

In firing readiness they spoke into their ear-mounted two-ways.

"Ready," said the Russian.

"Ready," said the American.

Ilya immediately picked up the handset to the Russian radio. He spoke Russian.

"Mission launch. Confirm secure," he said.

On the Akula, a high definition picture of the quarry and surrounding area was being beamed in via satellite. On several screens, different variations were being observed. One in infrared, displayed the heat emissions of all the men on the ground. The operator, satisfied with the numbers, spoke into his handset.

"Roger, Confirmed secure. Code word 'WALRUS'"

Picking up the handset to the other transceiver, Ilya spoke in English.

"Mission launch. Confirm secure."

On the E-3 Sentry, similarly accurate vision was being observed. Pictures had been assessed and digitally enhanced to give a thorough analysis. The operator acknowledged the call.

"Roger, Confirmed secure. Code word 'ALBATROSS'"

Ilya looked to Harold for confirmation of the code. Harold nodded. Ilya then spoke into his mouthpiece. "Proceed," he said in Russian.

Harold mimicked through his own headset. "Proceed," he said in English.

The back doors of the two vans opened on cue. Each rifle immediately swung to cover their respective target.

Into the sights of the American rifle stepped Vladamir Dravich. Hopping out of the van he looked to the sky to adjust his eyes and take in his surroundings. Accompanied by a CIA field agent he appeared healthy and eagerly proceeded toward the white flag while watching his countrymen on the other side. The cross-hairs remained on his head the entire way.

The field agent placed his hand on Vladamir's shoulder and spoke.

"Mr Dravich please listen carefully. Do not proceed past any coloured flag until both of you have reached the same colour. If at any point you do this you will be shot. Do you understand?"

Dravich nodded.

"You must answer Mr Dravich," insisted the agent.

"Yes I understand," said Vladamir complying.

"Please stand next to the flag."

Vladamir did as he was told. Through the sights of the American rifle his head remained in the crosshairs and as he moved into position, the flag appeared alongside.

Over the radio the American marksman immediately acknowledged, "White Flag."

From the white van at the Russian end, John Landau was assisted to his feet. Standing awkwardly upright, his eyes struggled for a long time with the light. Wearing a pale blue hospital gown and slippers, he vacantly listened to the SVR agent giving repeated instruction and warning.

John's condition was plainly serious. Quite at odds with his clean gown, his dirt matted hair coupled with his long and straggly beard made him look like a wild man. His exposed body was covered in sores, cuts and contusions. But the most jarring aspect was his weight. He was critically thin and wasted. Almost skeletal, the gaunt and pale man was barely a shadow of his former self.

Under assistance he limped with short steps toward the white flag.

Followed in the crosshairs of the Russian rifle the marksman was moved to speak. "He does not look well your man."

As John reached the white flag the Russian immediately advised over the radio.

"White flag."

Vladamir pleased that at last it was beginning, stepped off on the order to begin and moved towards the blue flag. The marksman followed.

John shuffled forward. It was a desperate struggle as he fought the pain that came with every step.

Through the sights of the American rifle, Dravich reached the blue flag and stopped.

"Blue flag," the marksman signalled.

Dravich nervously waited for John to reach his flag. Finally he got there.

"Blue flag," said the Russian marksman.

Dravich took off for the red flag.

Watching through his binoculars Harold Lassiter was alarmed. He had been made aware of a 'physical decline' but what he was seeing went way beyond that. Keeping his eyes on John's progress he called to Ilya.

"Why are his hands bound?"

Ilya, also affected replied, "This is unfortunate. But I am told whenever they release him he takes it as a signal to fight."

Harold stiffened in silent acknowledgement of what this meant.

"It is better this way," Ilya quietly noted in Russian.

Vladamir nearing the red flag, closed in on John. The condition of the man they were using for his exchange had an immediate impact. He had imagined that as he was the head of an entire region, the CIA would have sought somebody like himself for exchange. This was a complete surprise.

He had been a field agent for years, and although he had faced death many times in his life, his greatest fear had always been ending up like the man coming toward him. He made the red flag.

"Red Flag," came from the American rifle.

White-faced, Dravich watched as John struggled toward him. Blood from wounds hidden beneath his gown had begun to seep through. Trying to get his bearings, John stopped and turned his head back and then forward. Slowly he placed one agonising foot in front of the other. Dravich sympathetically edged forward to will him on.

Watching in the sights the American marksman steadied his breathing as Dravich came close to violating the rule.

John was almost there. Looking up he saw Dravich who stretched out an arm and inched passed the flag a bit further.

The rifle's safety was disengaged.

Under the weight of the effort John's eyes rolled and his body reeled in imminent collapse. Dravich instinctively darted forward to catch him.

A squeeze was applied to the trigger.

John swung forward and fell into Vladamir's arms. The momentum of the fall carried him back 'behind', and John 'to' the flag. In the sights of the rifle, it was a close call.

Immediately the Russian marksman said, "Red Flag."

John tried to catch his breath as Dravich held him steady. Overwhelmed with compassion Vladamir wondered how on earth this crumpled man would ever make it on his own. Reaching a decision he turned, lifted John in his arms, and proceeded to carry him.

"Holy Shit!" Said the Russian marksman immediately placing the crosshairs of his own sight on Dravich. He talked into his two-way.

"Instruction?"

The order came back quickly.

"Hold till blue flag. Activate on breech," said Ilya.

Dravich was no fool and stopped at the blue flag. Both sights were on him. He placed John carefully so that he could support himself with the flagpole. John was hurting but turned his head to look at Dravich.

Vladamir spoke in English. "I must go no further. Wait here until I make it back to the blue flag. When I am there, take one step and they will come and get you."

He searched John's eyes for recognition. Seeing the tiniest glint he added reassuringly, "Just one step." John opened his mouth in an effort to speak, but nothing came out.

"You are welcome comrade," said Dravich.

Glancing up into the sights he quickly made his way back and beyond the red flag. The Russian rifle swung back onto John as Dravich still in the sights of the American rifle reached the blue flag.

They all waited. John slowly turned his head toward Dravich and then back toward the agents waiting. Willing himself for one last effort John let go of the flag, stepped forward and collapsed. Dravich quickly joined his countrymen at the other end.

CIA agents rushed to John's assistance and gathered him up. Quickly they carried him to paramedics waiting inside the van.

Ilya spoke into the Russian radio. "Mission Complete. Code word 'Russian Bear'"

Confirmation came back, "Roger 'Russian Bear'."

Ilya looked to Harold as he picked up the American handset.

"'White Dove'," said Harold giving him the code.

Ilya confirmed to the Americans. "Mission Complete. Code word 'White Dove'"

"Roger 'White Dove'."

The E-3 Sentry banked away as the Akula slipped easily into the ocean and out of sight.

Harold Lassiter shook hands with Ilya Chemenko. "I hope he makes it Harold," said the Russian.

"Thank you Ilya, and also for your help." Looking at the van as it climbed from the quarry he added, "He's home."

Chapter Twenty

I n the dying rays of the evening sun the backlit shimmering discharge from huge jet engines dominated the runway of Amberley air base in Queensland. The noise of the RAAF F-111's practising running takeoffs and landings was deafening.

Affectionately referred to as 'Pigs' the Australian F-111's were a unique hybrid with an unmatched strike rate of battle success.

Fully upgraded digital avionics and modern weapons versatility, coupled with state-of-the-art electronic counter measures and radar pods, meant no other aircraft in existence offered its payload capacity, radius and penetration performance. The swing-wing F-111 provided 'first pass' precision land and maritime strike capability in all weather conditions. In short, it remained the most potent conventional tactical strike aircraft in the Western alliance.

Answering the control tower's call to abort the runway, the planes from 82 Wing's 1 Squadron climbed at incredible speed until they were out of sight.

In the sudden quiet, a civilian ambulance pulled up alongside the runway and waited with its engines running. Into the wind and from the west a contracted Lear jet 'air ambulance' hit the tarmac at speed. On board a U.S. Air Force Critical Care Aero Medical Transport (CCAT) Team attended John.

As the jet taxied to a stop, the ambulance kicked into gear and approached for the patient hand-over. Accompanied by his team, a sedated John was then driven fifty kilometres to a private medical facility in Brisbane and admitted to a trauma wing used exclusively by the military.

Several hours later Force Delta's Australian Liaison Officer, Colonel Robert Haig sat in his staff car as it pulled away from Brisbane's domestic terminal. His RAAF VIP aircraft was already back in the air. Alongside him sat his assistant Sergeant William Gardia on attachment from Fort Benning USA. Having flown across the country from their Campbell Barracks office in Swanbourne, Western Australia, the two men had had a full day.

Sergeant Gardia finished his mobile phone call, "... thank you Sister, yes we'll be there in half an hour."

Hanging up, he addressed his Colonel, "That was the triage nurse. Major Landau is stable and is presently under observation in intensive care. He doesn't sound too good sir."

Colonel Haig nodded and quietly looked out of his window at the passing city.

Sergeant Gardia, aware of his superior's need for thought, reached for one of the magazines kept in the pouch at the back of the front seat. Opting for a year old 'Bulletin' he turned on the travel light and settled back searching for something of interest.

Flicking through the magazine he eventually found an article and began to read. It was about the Blunn Report on the controversial suicide of Australian DIO (Defence Intelligence Office) officer Merv Jenkins in Washington June 1999.

It was a tragedy of massive proportions. Accusations of treason by vindictive associates coupled with an insatiable CIA desperate for information on events surrounding East Timor, left the Intelligence Officer standing on his own to fend off three government departments ... each with their own agenda and interpretation of the rules. Caught between duck shoving, political posturing, excessive interrogation and his own proud sense of duty, he very sadly ended his own life at the young age of forty-eight.

The Blunn Report diplomatically arrived at all the significant points required of its charter, yet could not identify a single fault other than policy interpretation and hazy regulation.

Sergeant Gardia lowered the magazine and sighed heavily. Looking over at Colonel Haig his eyes fell into the officer's intense gaze.

"Sergeant?"

"I was just reading about the Blunn Report. It's always a worry for those of us who deal with secret documents on a daily basis isn't it?"

"Yes it is. But we can thank our lucky stars that within the military we have less interference in our job. Especially units on active duty."

"Meaning?"

"We are measured by our success. Politically it would be counterproductive to fuck with our allegiances because then we wouldn't win and that wouldn't look good. Merv was from the military and he probably expected the same allegiance to follow him to DIO. But sadly they're a mob that will never truly understand the consequences of deceit to a front-line. Merv knew and he cared, ergo a square peg in a round hole."

"You knew him?"

Haig nodded, "From Lieutenant to Captain, he was a Lt. Colonel when he left."

"And what's your judgement?"

"Men like Merv Jenkins come along once in a blue moon. He was a beacon of common sense the day he was born. If you're asking me if I think he was guilty of anything, I would say not seeing the 'enemy within' was his only mistake. I don't know anybody in the military, and that includes me, who wouldn't have given him their last drop. He was a true patriot. Plainly and simply a decent and honourable man."

"But the AUSTEO (Australian eyes only) documents he passed on?"

"The passing of information to our allies, and I repeat 'allies', was his job. How many AUSTEO documents have you seen?"

Sergeant Gardia shrugged his shoulders, "Lots."

"I gave you most of them didn't I?"

"Yes."

"Would you say that they were 'leaked'?"

"Not really. You threw them at me from across the room."

"I rest my case. We are both from different armies but how can I rely on you on a battlefield if I never tell you the whole truth. We are on the same side. The power play at the top of the tree does nothing to help the man on the ground. Yet he is the one who takes all the risk. Politics, Trade, Diplomatic missions are all self-gorging hypocrisies based on bent truths, self-promotion and accumulation of wealth. I'm not saying they don't have a place, I just wish they valued the man on the ground as much as they did themselves."

"Don't you think that's a bit harsh sir?"

"No I bloody don't. The bludgers change the rules every five minutes. Its all a matter of controlled plumbing. A 'leak' is only shocking when they haven't instigated it themselves. Its okay to leak information to discredit some poor bugger that speaks out against them, or for political gain, but if it embarrasses them, then look out. How can anybody be expected to adhere to a rule that only applies sometimes, to certain people, when they deem fit? It's obscene. And a damned tragedy if their treachery causes the loss of life."

The release of pent up emotion was typical of the colonel's method. The pressure of Major Landau's circumstance had been felt by all. Sergeant Gardia knew very well that there'd be more to come, and it soon followed as the CO vented his spleen.

"Take the ridiculous nature of 'Rules of Engagement'. How can you send a young man whose scared shitless into a hot spot and ask that he doesn't fire first? Are they mad? Do they have any idea of the danger they place him in? Do they even care? If it's a war, it's a war, they aren't nice and you can't sanitize them by enforcing 'a rule' that helps the people who aren't there feel better about themselves. Armies kill, that's what we train for. If you use them, you get blood on your hands. If some people were honest about that, then maybe there'd be fewer wars altogether."

Colonel Haig looked once more out of his window.

"It's a difficult job when you care," the sergeant offered.

"It's a job that demands care and don't you forget it. We have a responsibility Sergeant. It is not a casual responsibility because inevitably somebody dies. There is an enormous amount of damage done to everybody in war, your own men, their family, the enemy, the enemy's family and a host of innocent people in between. It affects us all for a long time, just ask Major Landau. A leader should do nothing but care."

"Luckily I'm just a clerk."

"Being a clerk doesn't alter your contribution. It takes many men to keep one man in the field. His support is his lifeline. His victory is yours, but just as equally, so are his mistakes."

Colonel Haig sighed, "I chose you, you know, because you do care. The 3/75 Rangers is a battalion that has great and fearless historical standing. They don't make just anybody sergeant in that unit, especially 'just a clerk'."

Sergeant Gardia smiled. "No I guess they don't. Will we be staying in Brisbane long?"

"I don't know. I shouldn't think so. We'll make sure Major Landau is getting everything he needs, then we'll decide."

The hospital smell hit the nostrils of Haig as soon as he entered. The sterile blend of disinfectants and floor polish combined with starched linen and modified air, gave him a headache. Already he wanted to leave.

Sergeant Gardia had gone to the administration area to sign forms and had left him to find his own way down the shining corridors. Nurses in white uniforms walked busily back and forth, as patients in gurneys and wheelchairs were wheeled along large coloured lines that led to elevators or wards. Visitors bearing gifts for loved ones scanned complex signs for clues to their elusive whereabouts. The odd mix of suffering, compassion, hope and despair, fuelled anxiety in the Colonel's stomach of what John's condition would truly be like.

He had been the officer who had recommended him for trial with Force Delta. It had been the right decision, he knew that, but along with the decisions always came a duty of care.

As he moved closer to the trauma wing a greater abundance of military personnel became evident. Occasionally saluting he made his way to I.C.U. and an observation window into the Major's room.

Standing in his camouflaged greens and sandy beret he placed his strong hands behind his back and took in the state of his soldier.

Had it not been for the name on the door he wouldn't have recognised him. Lying unconscious under a light blue sheet, John's battered body was attached to a bank of monitors that read his vital signs while he received drips of blood and saline. A nurse was attending and beside her a doctor stood reading charts. Alert to the Colonel's presence the doctor left his patient to join Haig at the observation window and introduce himself. "Colonel Haig?" He said, "I'm doctor King."

Haig nodded, "Doctor." And got straight to the point, "Well?"

Doctor King settled in beside him, "It's amazing he's alive at all."

"The question is will he stay that way?"

"Yes, I believe he will."

Haig was relieved, "Tell me everything ... broken bones?"

"It would be easier to list the unbroken ones. He has sustained more breaks and fractures than I would expect from a major accident victim. But his have occurred over time. Unfortunately some have healed incorrectly. We'll attempt to reset the fresh breaks if necessary, but where the bones have withered there is not a lot we can do other than repair the surface. In a macabre twist of fate it's a bonus that only his smaller bones were targeted. Apparently pain was of greater motivation than death. This one has been kept alive."

Colonel Haig winced, "And?" He pressed.

Doctor King continued, "Severe malnutrition. Anaemia. Although the tests aren't back, I suspect he has Malaria. His left shoulder has suffered subluxation, and has been partially dislocated for what looks like months. I can't imagine the pain it must have caused. How long has he been enduring this punishment?"

Quietly Haig answered, "We lost contact with Major Landau in November 1996."

Doing the math the doctor was alarmed. "Well there's our biggest hurdle right there I'm afraid," he said frankly.

"Meaning?" Said Haig turning toward him.

"Mental scarring. Six years of beating doesn't sit well on the mind - and who's to know what unmentionable things he had to do in order to survive. Nightmares, anxiety distress, all play their part in slowing recovery."

Haig turned back to John, "Dare to give me an estimate?"

"Absolutely not. Major Landau may never fully recover. He will require everything we have and quite possibly more."

"Well he's earned it," said Haig "And I'll tell you something for free doctor. This man's name and the word 'never' shouldn't be used in the same sentence."

Doctor King never doubted it for a minute, "I'll advise your office when I've fixed the body, then you can begin the debriefing. Anything else Colonel?"

"One thing. Keep his hands secure for a few days after he comes to."

The doctor looked quizzically for an explanation.

"It will save on staff. It should be okay when he realises he's in no danger. I will send somebody over to help on that score."

The doctor nodded.

"That'll do for now," said the colonel dismissing him.

He watched as doctor King returned to his station. Spending a brief moment at the window he decided he wanted to leave. Walking briskly away he was joined by his sergeant.

"Colonel?"

"Yep."

"How is he?"

"Alive. Just."

"I was wondering about his family. Should we ..."

"No. It's way too early for that one. We don't even know if he'll recognise them. No, keep everything as it is in that department. The right time will come."

Sergeant Gardia thought about Rachel, "That'll be a tough one, Miss Roberts calls every week without exception."

Colonel Haig breathed a sigh of admiration, "She's the exception. I hope like hell this works out, she never once gave up on him. The both of them are a lot alike."

The sergeant noticed the colonel's thoughts were still with the major, "He was one of our best wasn't he?" he asked.

"Is one of our best. He didn't come all this way back home for us to wave a white flag."

Haig returned a salute from a passing soldier and quickened his pace desperately wanting to leave.

"Is everything in place?"

"Yes sir."

"Did you find Colonel Masterson?"

"He retired to Hawaii, but yes, we found him."

"Any problems?"

"None. When I mentioned John Landau he offered to fly himself, which I thought was a nice gesture."

Haig laughed out loud, "Nice? Masterson isn't nice, he's the scariest bastard I've ever met. You better watch yourself when he gets here, I think he eats clerks."

"Who is he?"

"Colonel Philip Masterson trains people to be like him. Major Landau was his student."

They came outside and waited for the car.

"He mentioned a shack," continued the sergeant as the colonel thankfully breathed the night air.

Haig nodded, "Thought he might. Get on to Special Operations and tell them we need it. I'll take the car and send it back for you."

The vehicle pulled up and the colonel got in. He lowered the window down to hear any last questions.

"I just say 'the shack'?" Asked the sergeant.

"Exactly."

"How long for?"

Haig paused for a moments thought and then offered, "Start with a year."

Speechless, Sergeant Gardia watched as the car sped away.

Chapter Twenty-one

For as long as can be remembered, man has challenged himself in the field of unarmed combat. No-rules-fighting has existed in various forms for thousands of years. Long before the cable pay-per-view phenomena of Ultimate Fighting or the ninety-year-old traditional bouts of Brazilian Jiu Jitsu, men and women fought in classic tests of skill, strength and courage and many had fought to their death.

Thought to have been practised as early as the fourth dynasty of the old Kingdom of Ancient Egypt, artefacts and philosophers such as Plato and Demonax have documented the unarmed combat 'Pankration' as flourishing during Olympia. Records have dated its official existence as far back as the Olympic games in 648BC.

From the Greek words 'Pan' meaning 'everything' and 'Kratos' meaning 'strength' Pankration was a style of fighting that permitted any activity other than eye gouging, nose gouging, and biting. Kicking, groin punching, head butting and choking were all legitimate tactics. There were no weight divisions and occasionally even women fought men. Nude contestants covered themselves in sand to allow easy grip on the skin and fought until one of the combatants either admitted defeat, lost consciousness or died. If none of the above eventuated, a 'Klimax' similar to a tiebreak or penalty shoot-out came into effect to finalise a contest before night.

In a 'Klimax' opponents were allowed to take turns in delivering a free hit. They could even request a certain stance be adopted by their opponent to maximise the effect of the blow.

Intentional killing of an adversary was forbidden, but accidental death by choking was commonplace and many died from injuries days after the fighting had taken place.

Pankration was in essence the forebear of Mixed Martial Arts fighting, a platform that allowed fighters from all disciplines to pit their skills against each other on a neutral stage. From underground seventeenth century French street fighting styles of Chausson Marseillais and Savate, to more definitive mixed styles like Brancaille, one single element kept the ancient combat sport alive. Popularity.

After the entrepreneurial exploits of Ultimate Fighting in the nineteen nineties, derivatives of Pankration resurfaced everywhere. All attracted crowds, all produced frenzy, and marketed correctly; all spawned a great deal of wealth.

In a paradox of social morality a thousand kilometres south of John's hospital bed in Brisbane, the 'Colosseum' had struck gold.

Backing onto the cornering arc of Sydney's elevated monorail, the 'Colosseum' sat in the centre of Australia's busiest city. Behind its huge Gothic six storey facade was a purpose-built arena for a gladiatorial style of fighting. Four nights a week spectators were packed to the rafters.

The enterprise managed a lucrative turnover based on high priced admission and in-house gambling. For their money, the crowd were entertained with semi-clad girls, live bands, dancers, specialty acts and of course, fighting.

No amount of money had been spared in creating the 'feel' of the spectacle. The main arena was a large twenty by thirty foot sand based oval bordered by a linear designed clear glass wall that stood seven feet high. At each end of the enclosure was a glass entrance doorway and matching glass tunnel: used to shield fighters from the crowd. Spectators sat in seats that circled the arena and climbed at a steep angle to allow for uninterrupted viewing. Picked up by effects microphones, each blow recorded was amplified through the sound system to heighten the experience of the night.

Behind each section of seats, rows of grilled betting windows offered odds that unashamedly favoured the house. Roving girls armed with portable scanners and cash, targeted tardy gamblers and pressured them for running wagers before each bout.

A high-roller section catered for the well-heeled. Large comfortable leather chairs came with complimentary drinks served by attentive and scantily dressed pretty girls. Patrons could insert credit cards directly into a terminal located on their armrest to back the fighters they thought best placed to win.

The ambient feel was predominantly dark, except for areas intentionally accentuated by the lights. Although the name 'Colosseum' reflected the nature of the fighting, the decoration of the arena changed weekly to varying themes of entertainment. This work ethic made each visit to the Colosseum an experience worth remembering and ensured that customers would always return.

At predetermined intervals a large stage occupied by the band descended from the roof on huge hydraulic arms and hung at an optimum level for the crowd. Topless girls danced in columns of light that emanated down from above. This night, like all nights, the band played loudly and the room was dominated by the rhythm of its thumping bass. The arena was surrounded with mobile scan lighting and their beams rose and dipped with the beat, while hi-tech lasers scattered patterns in smoke across the room.

From an overlooking mezzanine, stage managers and announcers operated from Close Circuit Camera images, while bouncers dressed in clothing to accentuate their muscle, watched attentively from every entry and exit point.

Colosseum dancing girls worked the crowd to fever pitch. In local parlance, the place was rocking and everybody in it was pumped.

Outside in the corridors that fed the main arena, Vincenzo Montorelli waited for Daniel to show up. This was his big night, and in honour of the occasion he had donned his best black vinyl jacket to go with his favourite red shirt.

Vinnie and Daniel met during a misunderstanding in the eighth grade. New to the school, Vinnie had convinced a host of students to gamble their lunch money on his pyramid investment scheme. Failing to adequately explain their eventual losses were part of a downturn in market confidence, he was summarily pummelled until a previously unknown Daniel extracted him from the angry mob. They had been close friends ever since.

Vinnie nervously paced up and down while keeping his eyes on the entrance. Agitated, he checked his watch and stood on his toes to see above the throngs of people surging passed. The music was deafening and the mass of human traffic hampered his sight. Finally and thankfully he recognised Daniel's blonde hair as it came bobbing into view.

Vinnie quickly became animated and with his arm extended in the air, jumped vigorously up and down on the spot. "Daniel," he yelled, "Hey Daniel, over here!"

Waving his recognition, Daniel fought through the crowd and eventually made it to Vinnie's side.

Vinnie held his hands up in disbelief, "Shit man where have you been? I told you eight it's almost bloody nine for fuck sake."

Daniel was wide eyed, "Sorry Vinnie I couldn't get a park ... the crowd ... is this place for real or what?"

Vinnie didn't have time to answer, "C'mon, we've got to run."

Moving off at a brisk pace they fought to stay together through the throng. Daniel's head swung backwards and forwards in an attempt to take everything in. Awed by the music, the crowd and the excitement, his mind was racing until Vinnie grabbed him by the shirtsleeve and refocused his attention on the job.

"Listen Daniel you're up against a guy who's also a newcomer. They say he's in the same weight category. I don't know much about him but I haven't heard of him so he can't be too good. Hey, have you got your stuff?"

Daniel nodded and lifted his bag. Vinnie kept up the tempo.

"Good. You need to get ready. The Room Manager will call your name when it's time. You've got," he checked his watch, "twenty minutes."

Daniel's eyes widened appreciatively, "Whoa! Wait a minute. What about the system, referees, codes of conduct, 'Rules' Vinnie?

"There aren't any," said Vinnie blankly.

"What?"

"No referee. No rounds. No rules. If you submit, you let your opponent know."

Daniel was incredulous, "That's it?"

Vinnie tried to think if he'd forgotten anything, but nothing came to mind. "Pretty much," he said with his eyebrows raised. "But if you submit, you lose and we get no money. Get it?"

The crowd had thinned and they arrived outside a wide metal door guarded by an equally wide bouncer.

Daniel suddenly confronted with reality stopped and turned, "Shit Vinnie, I didn't think ..."

Vinnie also stopped. "Don't think," he said placing a security card around Daniel's neck. Reaching up he tapped him reassuringly on the cheek, "You're the best. Just win. You'll get the hang of it, now go!"

Vinnie turned and spoke with authority to the man on the door, "Fighter."

Then to Daniel, "Change quickly Pal, and hey!" He added with a smile, "Relax!"

Vinnie gave a quick thumbs up and turned to cross himself. Mumbling a hurried prayer he disappeared back the way they'd come. Daniel completely unsettled, awkwardly nodded at the bouncer who in turn opened the door to allow him in.

A huge roar went up just as Vinnie hastily moved into to his reserved seat. Nervously he wiped his sweaty palms across his knees and waited.

A fight had just been decided. Down in the Fighter's Preparation Room, Daniel had been ushered to the tunnel entrance by the Room Manager. His body tingled with electricity at the closeness of the crowd and the volume of the music. He'd never known anything like it before. As he waited, the recently defeated fighter was dragged bleeding and unconscious along the ground and back inside the room. Indifferently the Room Manager ticked his schedule and without looking up uttered an insincere 'Good luck," then closed the door.

Suddenly the lights went out and the arena was filled with the theatrical ceremony of beating drums. Daniel moved into the tunnel proper as a near naked girl quickly wiped blood from the glass door. Looking up at Daniel she gave him a quick wink and disappeared. Wearing his white uniform and black belt he focused on his bearings and tried to look unflustered.

Vinnie spotted Daniel in the tunnel and called out.

"Go 'Danny Boy'. You can do it," he screamed.

Daniel looked up through the glass and waved at his excited friend. He wondered at being called 'Danny Boy' but had no time to give it any thought.

The drums stopped and the mass of scanning lights ringing the arena dipped dramatically up and down. The announcer's voice came over the sound system and drawled in typical fight 'speak'.

"Ladies and Gentlemen. In line with the Colosseum's commitment to you the fans, the management proudly present the first newcomers' bout of the evening."

Daniel listened to the whoops and whistles of the crowd.

"In the Southern Pen ..." continued the announcer.

A spotlight suddenly illuminated Daniel.

"The Colosseum presents an overseas fighter who was orphaned at the age of seven. A nomad of the high seas. A holder of six amateur titles, and a fifth Dan black belt. Tonight, here at the Colosseum, he makes his professional fighting debut. Put your hands together for Ireland's Dancing 'Danny Boy' D'Angelo."

The crowd cheered. Daniel slightly bewildered looked up to Vinnie who motioned that it was actually him the announcer was referring to. Vinnie started to clap wildly.

"Go Danny Boy," he yelled.

Daniel totally confused advanced through the open door and raised his hand to acknowledge the applause.

The announcer drawled on, "In the Northern Pen."

Another spotlight flicked on and illuminated Daniel's opponent standing at the opposite entrance.

"Another newcomer. Recently a guest of Her Majesty's Correctional institution ..."

The crowd cheered, delighted.

"And holder of our nation's most prestigious underground bare knuckle title 'Golden Fist'."

Daniel was unimpressed as the crowd roared their approval. Hastily he shielded his eyes and looked for Vinnie. Guiltily, Vinnie slumped into his chair in an effort to look small.

"Put your hands together and give a warm Colosseum welcome, to the 'Fabulous Fighting Inferno', Vincent North."

Vincent North entered and acknowledged the crowd. With his bare top showing a mass of tattoos and wearing tight leather pants the muscular man was the complete opposite of Daniel's fresh and clean-cut look. North energetically launched into a rapid display of shadow boxing to loud applause and whistles.

The scans dipped upwards and the main arena lights snapped on. Suddenly the fighters were bathed in bright light and the crowd, eager for the contest, began to chant.

"Fight, Fight, Fight."

Daniel walked forward looking for the line. Of course there was no line and North charged in like a mad man. The crowd roared. At the last second Daniel dropped to the ground and deftly using his feet, upended him.

Springing back into position like a cat he waited for his opponent to get up. The crowd unanimously began to boo. North got to his feet and in fighting crouch edged toward Daniel who had adopted his defensive stance.

North attacked fervently throwing lefts and rights. Daniel controlled the momentum as he absorbed and competently blocked each blow. He was good and the crowd sensed it. Seeing a small opening Daniel countered with several short sharp body punches that sent North backwards. Again Daniel waited for him. Again the crowd booed.

North resumed his attack and launched a flurry of blows until one connected. He grabbed at Daniel's top and wrenched and pulled frantically to gain further advantage. Daniel, unaccustomed to the messy form of combat soon became unsettled. His loose top now misshapen, hampered his movement and restricted his arms. North relentlessly attacked the groin, head butted, scratched, bit and punched. One big swinging right hand finally landed and Daniel was sent reeling.

Getting up he tried desperately to adjust himself but North seized his chance and was on top of him in a second. The rugged fighter hit Daniel with a flurry of brutal blows.

Vinnie suddenly felt decidedly sick and looked away. In doing so, he noticed for the first time money being exchanged directly between patrons. Buoyed by the amounts of cash he was seeing, he turned back to the fight and yelled at the top of his voice.

"Come on Danny Boy. Come on!"

On the ground and being beaten, Daniel knew he had to do something quickly or lose. Launching a counter attack he targeted pressure points and in the ensuing weight shift, used his legs to tip North off him. Jumping to his feet he landed a clean hit and quickly ran to put distance between them. Now with time to address his wardrobe he ripped off his jacket and flung it to the ground. The crowd roared their approval at his physique. North dashed in for another assault and Daniel responded with the speed of lightning. Effortlessly he released explosive power that lifted his opponent off the ground. This time North knew that he'd been hit. Unlike before, Daniel didn't wait for his recovery and followed his attack with elegant and decisive combinations. He was angry and he wanted it to end. Daniel's dominance was profound and unerringly conclusive. North unable to counter in the face of the onslaught, unceremoniously hit the deck and stayed down.

The crowd immediately went berserk cheering wildly for the new boy on the block.

"Danny Boy. Danny Boy," they chanted.

The music began, the scan lights came on, but Daniel was anything but happy.

In the Fighter's preparation room, Vinnie's body slammed heavily against a locker as Daniel vented his anger.

"Danny Boy D'Angelo?" He screamed.

He pushed the protesting Vinnie once again, causing him to stumble over a seat.

"Easy Daniel," Vinnie said trying to regain his balance.

"Orphaned at six?" Daniel persisted heading toward him.

Vinnie got to his feet and corrected him as he held his hands up to ward off another attack, "Seven, it was seven. So? What's the problem?"

"My name is Roberts you moron and I'm not friggin' Irish, so I'd say that there's an identity problem for a start."

"Okay, okay I'll see if we can change it," Vinnie looked at odds as to what to do.

Daniel wasn't about to let him off the hook, "How come you didn't tell me Vinnie? You let me walk into a no rules street fight. I felt like a caged animal. You lied the whole time."

He raised his fist to intimidate and Vinnie immediately caved in.

"Alright, I'm sorry, but I didn't lie ... I didn't, I just avoided telling the whole truth."

"You didn't tell me anything!"

"But if I had you wouldn't have done it, would you?"

"Not in a pink fit."

"See!" Vinnie added feeling vindicated "... so I was right."

Daniel could never be angry with Vinnie for long. He became less threatening, and motioned to the noise outside.

"Go tell them Vinnie," he said with finality.

Vinnie was shocked and desperate to dissuade him from chucking it in.

"Oh no wait Daniel, you can't back out on me now. Sure I should have been more up front but look."

Vinnie produced a wad of cash and held it up.

"See? Two thousand dollars. Where the hell else are we going to make this sort of money? Eight minutes work, huh?

He gave the money to Daniel to hold as he pressed on.

"And that's just the newcomer money. If you become a draw card, Jesus the sky's the limit."

Daniel eyed Vinnie cautiously.

"I had better plans for myself Vinnie. This is just one side of beef beating up another."

"Yes, it is. But I wouldn't ask you if you couldn't do it. I think you're good enough to win. And if you could hold out for a while, we could do anything we want."

Daniel walked away to think. He weighed the money and the thought. He turned back to Vinnie.

"You're not getting out of this the way you always do. If I do my part then you have to do yours."

"Of course," Vinnie said immediately adding quickly, "I think ... What do you mean ... exactly?"

"That guy tonight was a 'Golden Fist'. I should have known. If you want me to fight professionally then you're going to have to manage professionally. If you don't know about my next opponent, then get off your arse and find out. If you don't have the information, I don't fight. Got it?"

Vinnie was the smiling face of reason, "That seems fair."

"So?" Said Daniel.

"So, um, what?" Vinnie replied slightly bewildered.

Daniel raised the level of his voice to spell it out, "So go and find out."

Vinnie quickly raised a finger of understanding, "I'm on to it," he said.

He reached for the wad of money but Daniel pulled it back.

"I'll hold it," he said firmly.

Vinnie realised he shouldn't push it, and reluctantly left.

Daniel looked himself up and down in the floor to ceiling mirror on the other side of the room. "I need a new wardrobe," he whispered to himself.

Chapter Twenty-two

The sterile room was surprisingly big and several degrees colder than outside. Beneath the eight shadowless beams of the strong overhead light, a clean-shaven John lay pallid and inert. The sound of the ventilator dominated the room as each rise and fall of its enclosed membrane sucked and pushed noisily, along with the mechanical beeps of his monitored heart. Under the watchful eye of the anaesthetist, surgeons carefully repaired damage to his injured shoulder. The operation occasionally interrupted by the metal clang of deposited shrapnel discovered randomly floating along the way.

In the month that had passed since his arrival, John's improving condition had permitted two operations to date. Assuming the success of this one, a further four would be required.

The steady pace of physical recovery however, was not matched by the mind. Any meaningful debriefing to this point had proven an impossibility. John spoke only cursory words and refused to participate in any form of conversation at all, preferring instead, solitude and long periods of isolation. It had been noted by staff that he took any opportunity, regardless of pain or circumstance, to exercise muscles with the determination of a man obsessed. Nothing it seemed could dissuade him.

Immediately above the operating theatre, the door to the overlooking observatory quietly swung open and a lone figure moved in to sit down. Dressed in jeans and customary braces over a white T-shirt, Colonel Phillip Masterson (Ret) sat silently looking on. A strong man, his weathered face held kind eyes that sparkled with wisdom and an alert mind.

He carried a blue folder from which he now read. John's medical report had been prepared for him by Doctor King and contained all relevant medical diagnoses and detailed analysis of behaviour. Carefully Masterson absorbed the information without movement. Slowly and methodically he turned each page, assembling a jigsaw of horrific images. Quelling his own inner demons, the retired veteran of many campaigns looked down at his former student. Closing the file, he knew that the most important person in Major Landau's life now ... was him.

The two had met years ago at the beginning of selection trials for Force Delta.

In the early summer of 1990 military experts, analysts and diplomats from five separate nations attended a top-secret meeting in Geneva Switzerland. The nations represented were: Britain, the United States, Australia, France, and Germany. The agenda concerned mounting intelligence that pointed to a future of significant growth in global terror.

1990 like many others was a year of contradictions. Nelson Mandela, arguably the world's greatest living statesman, was finally released from prison. Soviet president, Mikhail Gorbachev, architect of 'Perestroika', was awarded the Nobel Peace Prize. The Berlin Wall was symbolically dismantled sparking spontaneous mass celebration and Germany's reunification. The Russian Federation declared its sovereignty and people's hero Lech Walesa, already a Nobel laureate, became president of Poland.

In contrasts of the same year, radical group Jamaat al Muslimeen attempted a Coup d'état in Trinidad and Tobago. Tamil Tigers killed one hundred and sixty-eight Muslims in Colombo Sri Lanka. An IRA car bomb killed British MP Ian Gow in one of eighteen attacks on English soil. Muslim extremists threw grenades into a tourist bus in Cairo, Egypt, killing eleven people and wounding nineteen. And in South America, a continent under siege, more than a thousand terrorist-related deaths occurred in Peru alone.

Numbers from the two preceding decades indicated a rising trend from localised nationalistic and politically motivated terror groups, to far reaching religious and ethnically motivated extremists. These extremists in the seventies were responsible for less than twelve percent of all terror attacks recorded. But predictions into the nineties, would see this statistic rise to an alarming fifty three percent.

Of increasing concern was the effect of the market economy's current push toward globalisation. Such expansions benefited terrorists by providing faster and more secure networks of communication. This markedly increased their ability to raise funds and plan future attacks, while improving access to modern technology and advanced weapons of greater versatility and impact.

Precipitated by major incidents such as Libya's bombing of Pan Am flight 103 in Scotland, which killed two hundred and seventy people: the bombing of La Belle Disco in Berlin which killed three people and injured two hundred and fifty: and the bombing of Korean Airlines flight 858 by North Korean agents which killed one hundred and fourteen. The worrying trend toward larger public targets was disturbing.

The rapidly expanding list of groups thrusting themselves into prominence included the Sudanese National Islamic Front. The Organisation of Jihad Brigades in Iraq. The Algerian Armed Islamic Group (GRN). The Red Army in Germany. The Liberation Tigers of Tamil Eelam (LTTE) in Sri Lanka. Jemaah Islamiah in Indonesia. Al-Qaida in Afghanistan, South Asia, Southeast Asia, the Middle East and Africa. The Palestinian Abu Nidal. Hezbollah in Lebanon, Africa and South America. The Irish Republican Army (IRA). The New Peoples Army in the Philippines. The Tumac Amaru Revolutionary Movement in Peru. The Tupamaros in Uruguay. The Farabundo Marti National Liberation Front in El Salvador. And the Revolutionary Armed Forces of Colombia (FARC).

Terrorism would soon, if it hadn't already, blanket the world from the Middle East to Europe, Latin America to North America, Africa to Asia and across the South Pacific to the entire South East.

So compelling was the evidence, the five-nation group were unanimous in their opinion that in coming decades, the world would experience violence against civilians rising to unprecedented levels. Without question, the free world was under attack from a dangerous enemy and disturbingly obvious, was that conventional methods of defence could not win.

It was decided that a powerful reactionary force was required with the ability to strike at the heart of terrorism where an army could not. It would be made up of US, British and Australian forces as they already shared an established military alliance, had fought together successfully in both Gulf wars and Afghanistan, and enjoyed a cooperative intelligence network that covered both hemispheres. France and Germany would assist in finance and intelligence where appropriate, but not with men.

The blueprint was formulated: It would be small, based in the U.S., and divided into secure cells. Operated under complete secrecy it would be led entirely by military elite. The force would be given every possible assistance from the combined defence, diplomatic and intelligence arsenals of the five signing nations. The world's first 'International' unit specifically formed to destabilise global terrorist activity through covert counter-insurgency would be called 'Force Delta'.

A major hurdle to its formation however, was the legality of its operation. Unless ratified by the United Nations, in some way, it could not, and would not exist.

Although the US, France and Britain were permanent members of the Security Council, they could only rely on support for such a concept from a conciliatory Russia and elected members Canada, Finland and Romania. Nine votes were needed from the Council of fifteen to ratify a resolution of this nature ... they were two short.

Definite 'No' votes would automatically come from China and Cuba. While Islamic loyalty and suspicion of U.S. motives would lead the remaining countries Ethiopia, Malaysia, Yemen, Zaire and the Ivory Coast to abstain.

Beaten before it began, the notion of a supreme anti-terrorist unit looked lost until several months later, it was fortuitously resurrected by the unlikely intervention of Saddam Hussein.

On August 2nd 1990 Iraqi forces invaded Kuwait. The aggressive action shocked and divided the entire League of Arab States and was condemned by leading Muslim scholars who, in response, issued the 'Holy Makkah Document' describing the action as tyrannical and its justification Islamic heresy.

The surge in Iraqi sponsored terrorism was immense. In a remarkable twist, this was exactly what the five-nation group required. The resulting vote went eleven to four in favour.

Under United Nations Security Council Resolution number 660/1, authorised pre-emptive strikes against active terrorist units, formerly identified by the Council became legitimised.

This gave Force Delta freedom to work anywhere in the world with full diplomatic immunity and the power to eradicate or suppress any element, movement or faction that actively used terror as a weapon against a civilian populace.

By mid 1992 Force Delta was active. Many months earlier, the selection process was already underway.

As their transportation pulled away the new arrivals had assembled together in a group. Masterson had gone outside to welcome them. As Chief Combat Instructor he was the final hurdle in a series of tests designed to find those most suited. His was a critical phase and vital to the success of the program.

Although the book was still being written, he knew that the questions asked of these men would be the hardest he had ever set. He also knew that if he failed to ask such questions, their lives and many others would be lost.

Walking amongst the group he shook hands and introduced himself. They were all fine fmen. Twenty soldiers, all fit and strong, all trained to within an inch of perfection, and the best their country had to offer ... only four would be selected.

Among the nominations two stood out. Anthony Griswald and John Landau. Where all the others had given firm handshakes with a set jaw and purposeful eyes, these two had met his gaze with genuine pleasure and a smile. They weren't standing together and didn't know each other at the time, but Masterson was taken by their peaceful and relaxed manner. It stood out from a group of hard men whose sole reason for being there was a skill for killing.

And so it panned out. The tests Masterson had devised were to weed out weakness. Force Delta could not afford errors of judgement on any level. Each man would have a license to kill. At their disposal would be enormous power to effect change within varying theatres across the world and even the smallest mistake would have serious consequences.

The nominees all possessed impeccable knowledge of firearms and explosives. Each held university degrees and were fluent in at least two languages outside of their native tongue. Their skills in leadership, tactics, navigation and unarmed combat, were beyond reproach and all were counter-terrorism specialists.

What the colonel needed to know, was how this knowledge would be applied under stress. Combat stress.

His first simple test was called a "twelve by" and took several days to complete. It involved sending all the men at staggered intervals on all-night twelve-hour navigational exercises. The terrain was rugged and a series of obstacles and rendezvous ensured they were stretched physically and deprived of sleep. Without rest, food or water they then had to complete a timed twelve-mile run carrying full kit and weapons. The run finished in the gym. Here again without rest, each man would then be evaluated in unarmed combat by Masterson himself. By normal standards this was not a particularly taxing test for these men, but it would provide valuable insight for a man who knew exactly where to look.

John arrived at the gym and was immediately confronted by an aggressive colonel who addressed him with derision.

"Captain Landau, you were damned pathetic. You might get away with that shit in Australia but not here. I've never seen a worse performance. This is an elite unit, Captain, not a weekend outing for a gutless 'down-under' dick. Come on I've got real men to assess."

John dropped his pack and the two faced off. Masterson launched into a determined assault to break his student quickly. The ferocity was intense with each blow delivered at full strength. John, equal to the challenge, met the onslaught with evasion and natural talent. For exactly twelve minutes the two men exchanged combinations of artistry and sublime skill. Throughout the battle Masterson deliberately left a small opening in his defence, which John did not take. At the end of time Colonel Masterson stepped back and raised his hand.

"Stop," he said firmly.

John did. The two waited and watched each other. John, in awe of the colonel's ability, and Masterson aware that nobody had ever lasted past six minutes.

"Assess what just happened Captain."

John took several deep breaths to compose himself and think. "You attempted to destabilise my will by testing my endurance and then by undermining any hope of a bond between student and teacher, you tried to make me angry."

"Why?"

"Tired men rush to a conclusion in combat," he said, "Angry men make mistakes."

"Assess further."

The opening was a trap."

"How did you arrive at that?"

"You possess too many skills to have such loose defence. I could make no other choice. Although I didn't know how to win, I couldn't allow you to dictate the manner in which I lost."

Masterson nodded, "You look tired."

John with hands on hips, expelled air heavily. His face broke into a broad grin, "Frankly Colonel, I'm completely stuffed."

The colonel liked him. In all facets of the evaluation Captain Landau had proven himself the cream of an extremely good crop.

Over the ensuing months the number of nominees were gradually reduced. Risso and John had by this stage developed a strong bond. Their natural abilities and easy humour held them in good stead. The two soldiers took instruction well and excelled in examinations of both tactical and lateral thinking. Their performances under stress were flawless.

John's natural ability continued to impress. His target accuracy during exhaustion was as good as Masterson had ever seen with any weapon, and his prowess at unarmed combat was head and shoulders above the rest. His use of an opponent's energy to advantage, coupled with the power of his attack was spellbinding. But regardless of his dominance John always treated men with humility and respect ... it was the hallmark of his character.

The relationship between Masterson and John grew. One night the colonel had shown him a little known escape move for a famous chokehold invented by a former student of Japanese Master and founder of Judo, Professor Jigoro Kano. After the lesson the two men had time to reflect.

"Why do you do this?" John enquired.

"That's an interesting question," mused Masterson. "Is this to reflect on my answer, or to find yours?"

John broke into a wry grin. "Jesus, that's astute!"

"Not really, its just the real question isn't it? So why do you?" Said Masterson turning the table.

John had always been good at what he did, yet never understood why. It came naturally ... But somehow that seemed insufficient reason for doing the things he did. Inside he knew he wasn't a violent man, but outside? Outside was a completely different story. Why, always eluded him.

"I'm not really sure."

"A few years ago," Masterson counselled, "I met a sergeant from Australia. He had been a sergeant in three armies. First the British Army, then the Canadian, and then, like I said, the Australian. He had been in every military engagement since Korea. When he wasn't part of an army he was a mercenary. When he wasn't in war, he wrote about it for magazines or historical papers. It was his life."

"You asked him the same question?"

Masterson nodded, "He said that it was 'the moment' he chased."

"Did his answer help you?"

Masterson thought for a while, "Nope."

John was quiet.

"An answer to a complex question takes time Captain. Be patient. It will come eventually. A borrowed one ... never quite fits."

In a final series of tests the remaining men were divided into two-man teams. Six elaborately staged terrorist scenarios were set up across various parts of the United States. Designed by leading experts, each scenario involved different political landscapes, changing threat levels and alternate terrain. With U.S. Army members playing the roles of terrorists, realistic situations faced each team as they pursued specific mission objectives. As would be the case in the field, every military option was available for teams to draw on. This included anything from Stealth bombing strikes to electronic counter measures, or from Secret Service imagery to propaganda leaflets if required. Teams had twenty-four hours of preparation and four days on the ground for each mission.

This was a highly expensive and critical examination of prudent decision-making and combat efficiency, which would not only identify the quality of men, but also the future success of Force Delta.

Throughout five of their allotted tasks John and Risso teamed well together, successfully exhibiting cohesive unity and decisive action. Their final mission however, deliberately set less stringent objectives for them to follow.

Set in the Rocky Mountains of Colorado, this scenario involved fourteen tourists held hostage by separatists in a bid for international recognition and independence from an unsympathetic régime. Their mountain stronghold was heavily fortified and the team's mission objective was to do whatever was in the best interests of the hostages and the situation overall.

Of the five previous teams encountering this mission, four had failed and one had achieved mixed results: freeing seven hostages and notionally destroying the camp.

After three days of complete silence and inactivity, plus a vague report about regular soldiers going AWOL, Masterson decided to pay a visit.

Arranging his request via burst transmission, the colonel was given coordinates for a night parachute drop where a small transmitter would guide him to a rendezvous point. On reaching that point, he was to disengage the transmitter and wait. He was advised to wear white as it was snowing.

Following instructions, Masterson hid his parachute and carefully followed the beacon two miles cross-country from the drop. Finding the small pen sized transmitter wedged in a tree, he disengaged it, and waited. It was cold, the wind blew a chill factor of minus ten and cloud cover minimised visibility. One moment the colonel was alone, and suddenly without warning, he was not.

Risso, dressed from head to toe in white and carrying a full compliment of weapons made his presence known. Without speaking he acknowledged the colonel with a nod and passed him a small digital ear and mouth communicator. This allowed them to speak above the wind without shouting.

"Evening Colonel, this way for latté?" Said Risso with his hand over his mouthpiece. "The enemy are close, no feeding or flash photography please."

He led the colonel along a classic arc toward the rear entrance of their camp. Occasionally he stopped to point out trip wires that went to sensors designed to forewarn of possible attack. Masterson noted Risso's attention to detail and careful awareness over every step. Pausing at a discreet vantage point, Risso identified the distant glow of lights from the terrorist encampment, for the colonel to acquaint himself with their mission.

Reaching a sheer cliff face, the two men passed through an opening in the stone wall. Hunched over to avoid the low ceiling of a narrow tunnel, Risso again paused to guide Masterson through infrared beams connected to explosive detonators. Previous teams had based themselves at the skiers lodge on the other hill, the colonel had not been aware this existed.

Walking to a large sound blanket placed over a man-sized entrance, Risso held it open as Masterson climbed through. Another blanket a few feet further on revealed a small chamber lit with lanterns, an array of equipment and John who was watching four monitors displaying green night scope images of the enemy camp.

"Hello Colonel," he said warmly.

"Captain." Masterson suddenly noticed six soldiers bound and gagged sitting against the opposite wall. Their eyes followed the colonel in mute discomfort as he swung toward Risso. Risso met his gaze with a cheeky smile and eyebrows that moved rapidly up and down several times.

"Coffee?" Risso asked.

Masterson nodded and went over to John. "I wasn't aware of prisoners Captain," he said.

"That was intentional Colonel, we needed to make sure that nobody made a fuss about their capture. If word got out to the camp then we ran the risk of reprisals. At this stage the separatists can only assume desertion as we left all their weapons and equipment stacked neatly by the front gate."

Masterson picked up a map of the area marked with different coloured points. "This?" He asked.

"The red are high explosives, the green are anti personnel mines and the blue are TOW missile firing points," explained Risso passing a mug of coffee.

"In the event of a fire-fight we have laid plans for extraction," John said looking at Masterson. "Why are you here Colonel?" He asked.

"I was wondering what the two of you were doing, nobody has seen or heard anything for days."

John smiled as Risso played an imaginary guitar and quietly began singing a Kenny Rogers song with his exaggerated Texan drawl. *"You've got to know when to hold 'em, know when to fold 'em. Know when to walk away, know when to run."*

Masterson looked to John for a sane answer.

"What my weird sidekick is trying to say Colonel is that we can't see a way in. Whatever we do will result in the death of a hostage. Here, take a look at this." John uncovered a small plan of the encampment. "Thanks to our friends input," he said referring to the bound soldiers, "We have quite a detailed picture of what we're up against."

Masterson noted the complex defence and could see what they meant. "Sometimes loss of life is a consequence of war Captain."

"We know that Colonel, but this isn't your average war is it?" John answered. "We are in somebody else's country and therefore our actions need to be precise. The way we see it is that the hostages are only worth killing if we attack. That's precisely what they want us to do. If we do, the resultant deaths will be blamed on our involvement and give kudos to their claims among sympathizers, even though 'they' were the kidnappers in the first place. If they die, they are martyred for the next generation. In this case the only winner from aggressive action is the separatist movement itself. Right now, they can't afford to harm the hostages without justification, because that risks damaging support for the cause, and gives us legitimate grounds to respond."

"So what do you plan to do?" The colonel asked.

"'What use have I for a victory that ultimately brings defeat?'" Risso quoted obliquely.

Masterson looked sternly at the Texan. "When this is over Risso, kindly remind me to have you either court marshalled or shot."

John gave a less obscure response. "Until the situation changes … we plan to do nothing."

Masterson quietly sipped his coffee. Their analysis of the situation was correct. Under pressure from a timetable, a false desire for progress often led to no progress at all. This had been the reason for the test.

Risso peered over the monitors at their mentor. "The situation isn't going to change is it Colonel?" He asked. Both men waited on his response.

Blowing the steam from his cup the colonel replied, "Nope, I don't believe it is." After a long sip and an equally long sigh of appreciation, he smiled.

Realising they had passed, Risso resumed singing, "*You never count your money when you're sittin' at the table.*" He winked at John, "*There'll be time enough for countin' when the dealin's done.*"

He ended with an imitation of Elvis, "Thank you very much."

As the medical procedure drew to a close, Masterson quietly got to his feet and left. It would be many months before he would personally reacquaint himself with Major Landau in the flesh. A lot of preparation was required in readiness of when that time would come.

Chapter Twenty-three

I ntroduced now as Daniel Roberts, Daniel entered the arena with a bare top and tight leather pants that stopped at his calves. This was his eighth bout and he remained undefeated. The new outfit, coupled with growing ringcraft, added to his aura and rising notoriety. Although his name had changed, the original Irish tag had stuck. "Go Danny Boy!" The fans screamed.

His adversary this time, was a toothless and hirsute giant whose trademark move involved stomping on the head of a downed opponent until submission. The fighter was known to the crowd as 'The Meat'.

A concerned Vinnie had given firm instructions prior to the fight.

"This guy is an absolute animal Daniel, whatever you do stay away from him. His weakness is stamina so tire him. Keep out of his reach and run him around.

"Run him around?"

"Yeah. Fifteen minutes should do it."

"Fifteen minutes? This wouldn't have anything to do with gambling would it?"

Vinnie was mortified, "I'm just looking out for you. Trust me pal, this guy is one mean son of a bitch. Stay away for as long as you can. Fifteen minutes should be good, that's all I'm saying."

Placing a concerned hand on Daniel's shoulder Vinnie added, "You got it?"

Daniel smiled reassuringly, "I've got it, don't worry."

As the crowd chanted "Fight, fight, fight." Daniel and 'The Meat' circled each other looking for an opening. Up in the stands, Vinnie excitedly clutched his betting slip that had Daniel winning in the sixteenth minute. Picking both the winner and the time would add considerably to his thousand-dollar wager. Placing all the money on that exact outcome, as he had done, would net him ten times that sum.

Meat's enormous arms looped outwards in long searching arcs trying to grab onto Daniel. Each ape like movement was accompanied by a gum baring snarl and cries of 'Hunt the Meat' from the crowd. Daniel carefully backed away and eluded the probing reaches much to Vinnie's relief.

Without warning and against the flow, Daniel suddenly swept forward. The speed and force of his attack so stunning, the power so intense that under the barrage of blows 'The Meat' immediately lost consciousness and collapsed.

As soon as his large frame shuddered to the floor the crowd leapt to their feet as one and went berserk. "Danny Boy, Danny Boy" they chanted.

"Ladies and gentlemen. Winner by knock out, Daniel 'Danny Boy' Roberts!" Came the announcement as the scan lights dipped up and down and loud thumping music began to rock the stadium.

It was an emphatic victory that arrived in under a minute. Vinnie stood in disbelief. Slowly tearing his ticket in half he waved a weak fist in the air to acknowledge his triumphant fighter.

Back in the preparation room Daniel towelled himself down after a shower. "Are you alright Vinnie?" He asked.

"Course I am! Well done, a good fight Daniel."

Daniel continued to talk as he dressed; "I was having a chat with that bloke with the red hair, y'know the guy Vinnie, the one that looks after the betting rooms?"

"Not the big one with all the muscles?" Said Vinnie feeling nauseous.

"Yeah him. His name's Reg I think, anyway he was saying that a few months ago a fighter called Goliath and his manager tried to stage the outcome of fights so that they could rip off the system with dodgy bets."

Vinnie tried to sound incredulous, "No!"

"Can you believe it? Apparently they were caught and beaten up by the bouncers - big time. Word is the manager is still in hospital." Daniel ran a comb through his hair and picked up his bag. Looking at Vinnie he added, "Bloody stupid eh?"

Vinnie tried to smile, "Totally."

Daniel paused at the door and looked at Vinnie who was now completely white, "Are you sure you're alright?"

"I might have eaten something," Vinnie responded nervously touching his stomach.

Daniel placed a protective arm around him. "Come on," he said smiling inwardly, "I'll buy you a drink."

Several months later Daniel faced his toughest test. As his name progressed toward top billing, the standard of opposition became increasingly better.

Jimmy Chang was a class fighter and a life long devotee of Brazilian Jiu Jitsu, considered by many to be the best ground fighting style of all Martial Arts. His most damaging weapon, apart from a remarkable ability to find leverage from almost any position, was his chokehold.

Daniel possessed a good knowledge of grappling and although he was more potent standing, in most situations his ability held him in good stead. Against an expert however, it was a different story. Chang recognised quickly that he couldn't win unless he forced Daniel to ground, which is precisely what he did.

The crowd were aware of the moment, and fans of both men were entranced by each move and counter move of the fighters as they battled for supremacy with interlocking arms and legs. Daniel held sway with superior body strength but the suppleness of Chang, easily levelled the contest.

Bathed in sweat the two men fought for almost twenty minutes until suddenly Chang stretched himself like a rubber band and swung around to obtain 'back mount' position and secure his hold.

The crowd audibly gasped at the brilliance of the manoeuvre and began clapping wildly believing it to be the end.

The creator of Brazilian Jiu Jitsu was a man called Mitsuo Maeda, who had emigrated from Japan to Brazil in 1914. He had studied under the Master of Judo, Professor Jigoro Kano. Few people knew the secrets of his holds, but fortunately, one of those people had been John. Remembering the lesson of a secret passed down from mentor to mentor, Daniel immediately released his knowledge.

Chang, having never lost from this position, was completely surprised by the destruction of his hold and the resultant dislocation of his elbow. Seizing his opportunity Daniel leapt to his feet and stood over his wounded opponent ready to strike the final blow. The crowd were stunned.

Holding the delivery back Daniel allowed his adversary the chance to submit. Chang realising he was beaten, took it. Helping the injured man to his feet Daniel bowed respectfully to acknowledge the skill of Chang. Chang reciprocated with a lower bow exhibiting great dignity in defeat. The audience launched into sustained applause for both men. It was a rare occurrence in the arena and Daniel, from that moment on, became the toast of the Colosseum.

Vinnie burst into the rooms after the fight and couldn't contain his excitement, "Man that was awesome. Absolutely fucking awesome. They're all saying it was the best fight they've ever seen. Jesus Daniel, I thought you were gone for all money. Where the fuck did you learn that?"

Exhausted, Daniel sat with his head back against his locker. Suddenly his entire being was alive with the memory of John.

Chapter Twenty-four

July 14 2003.

The mountainous terrain of the Special Operation's secret hideaway was simply majestic. Large expanses of Australian gum trees covered the jagged slopes that rose up from deep valleys toward peaks that offered vistas of extraordinary beauty.

From the highest apex the wilderness stretched into the distance for as far as the eye could see in any direction. The horizon blanketed in the distinctive blue haze of evaporating eucalyptus oil that emanated from trees baking in the sun. Huge flocks of silver crested cockatoos screeched noisily as they settled onto the boughs of white ghost gums that bordered streams and watering holes.

Bounding wallabies and fast moving goannas scoured the ground for sustenance as a lone wedge-tailed eagle glided patiently above looking for prey. It was early afternoon, the sun was out and the mountain air was cool.

A small lizard scurried across open ground and stopped. With blood evident from its recently discarded tail, it remained as still as a statue with its senses alert. Straining its neck eastward it picked up the faint approach of a distant sound.

Within moments the powerful downdraft of a military helicopter scattered bits of grass and dust in a swirling cyclone of chaos that sent the creature running for its life.

Touching down for the slightest of moments, the chopper then banked away from its destination and headed back along the ridges from whence it came.

John stood alone on the edge of the mountain watching the helicopter become smaller as it made its way over the treetops into the valleys below.

It was now eighty-five months since the day of his capture. Holding a small pack in his right hand, John was dressed in jeans and white T-shirt. Clean and shaven, he looked almost his old self. His body mass had returned and the only sign of physical injury was the presence of a cast on his left forearm and wrist. What remained however, was the deadpan expression and lack of life in his eyes.

Turning around he focused his attention on the single building atop the hill. 'The Shack' was a log cabin. With an outhouse to one side and a shower on the other, it had a large brick chimney from which now came a steady stream of white smoke.

The door opened and two figures emerged. A large lady with an apron and huge smile, anxiously wiped her hands on a dishcloth as she stopped at the small veranda. The other, was Phillip Masterson. Dressed in pants with braces over his shirt he stepped forward to advance on their guest.

"John!" He called, "It's good to see you."

John stood stock still, his manner cool.

The colonel, unaffected by the diffidence, took hold of the pack and being very careful not to make physical contact, he motioned toward the cabin and smiled.

"Come and meet Hilda. She cooks the best damn food you'll ever eat ... that's for sure."

The large woman waved hospitably. John remained silent and neither moved nor acknowledged her. Instead he turned around and looked out at the now chopper-less vista.

Unfazed, Masterson continued, "I'll put your bag away. Your bed is under the window. Take your time. Do whatever you want."

Turning with John's pack in his hand, he went back to the cabin. Passing a disappointed Hilda he whispered, "Just go about your routine Hilda. He's needs time to assess our intentions. Leave him be."

Looking at John she nodded sadly and went inside.

The interior of the cabin was welcoming. Pots bubbled away on the stove of a well-appointed kitchen filling the air with the heartening smell of home cooking. Large leather chairs on a deep rug encircled the fireplace, and a long dining table dominated the main room.

With the front door remaining wide open, an hour went by without change. Masterson sat in one of the chairs reading a book, while Hilda, unable to control herself, peaked out the window at John.

"He still hasn't moved Phillip," she reported.

Masterson turned a page and continued reading. "He will," he said.

"How can you be so sure?"

"I did."

Hilda looked at the calm man sitting comfortably cross-legged in his chair. Resigned, she lowered the curtain and went about her business.

Later, alone in the kitchen with music playing loudly from her CD player, Hilda danced and sang up a storm to the rhythm of an Aretha Franklin classic.

"R-E-S-P-E-C-T *find out what it means to me ...*"

Wearing oven mitts, and standing with her legs apart, Hilda placed one hand on her hip and pointed with the other to an imaginary audience while moving to the beat. With each wiggle, her entire body shook in percussive waves that ran from head to foot.

"R-E-S-P-E-C-T *take out the TCB oooh ...*"

Reaching into the oven, her bottom swung violently from side to side. Spinning in time to the music she deposited a steaming tray of crisp biscuits onto the bench. "*Sock it to me ...*" she sang.

Standing on the other side of the counter and observing, was John.

Shaking her bosom Hilda continued her exhibition, "*Ooh just a little bit ... Ooh just a little bit ...*"

"I see you have a fine ear for good music John," she said over the volume.

Smiling broadly, but not extending her hand, she offered a jar of cookies, "I'm Hilda ... cookie?" John took one.

Still dancing she added, "Help yourself anytime. Phillip is out back cutting wood I think."

John left without saying a word and Hilda went back to her humming and cooking.

Outside the music of Aretha was replaced with the methodical sound of chopping wood. Masterson wielded the axe with careful ease as John approached and stood at a distance to watch. Quietly he ate his cookie.

"I see you met Hilda," the colonel called without fuss as he split another piece of timber. Looking around at their environment he added, "Beautiful spot isn't it?"

John replied quietly, "I want to go home."

The colonel buried his axe and looked up. Taking a cloth from his back pocket he wiped his forehead and spoke gently, "Soon son, soon."

John repeated his request, "I want to go home, now."

Masterson was aware of the growing tension, but stood his ground, "You're not ready John. I can't let you go, not yet."

John edged closer, "I'm fine."

Masterson casually threw down his cloth and moved in, "Is that a fact? Well, we'll see."

Extending his arms he went to embrace his old student, "Here, come here it's good to see you."

John was immediately resistant and balked at the contact.

"C'mon John," persisted Masterson, "It's good to see you again."

Unable to cope with the closeness John pushed him away.

"What's the matter? You've known me for years. You know me don't you? C'mon!"

The colonel placed his arms around John again. But this time the response was more physical. Like a cornered animal John struck out, again and again. Masterson expertly fended off each blow as it came but the situation quickly built to dangerous levels.

Immediately pulling back, he raised his hands submissively and yelled, "STOP! NOW!"

Mindful of his body language, Masterson carefully backed further away and finally, John desisted.

Seeing the tension ease from John's face he commented with the deliberate assumption of higher rank, "I'd call that a fail Major. You want to argue?"

"I don't like to be touched."

"Really? You want to assess that."

"I hate it."

"Assess further."

John was silent. The colonel became insistent and raised his voice, "I said assess further."

Confronted and uncomfortable, John struggled as his mind searched for an answer, "I ... I can't."

Softening his approach Masterson became compassionate and outwardly caring, "That's okay son. Take your time. There's no hurry."

Confused and feeling awkward, John turned and walked away. Pleased that first contact had been made, the colonel went back to chopping wood.

Later that evening Hilda served dinner. Following instructions, she had kept the place mats at a distance so that John would not feel threatened. As the fire crackled and warmed the room, Hilda proudly brought two huge plates of roast chicken to both men when they sat down.

Masterson beamed his approval, "Mm mm! Smells magnificent. Looks even better."

Hilda smiled at the compliment, "Thank you Phillip. But my mother always used to say the proof was in the eating."

Masterson picked up his red wine and saluted, "Here's to a wise mother."

Hilda finished pouring John's wine and left the two men alone. "Enjoy," she added in parting.

The colonel observed his companion gazing forward in a vacant stare.

"John," he said.

John looked up and spoke directly, "I can't give you what you want Philip."

Masterson smiled, "Sure you can."

John's look was blank.

"I just want the salt," he said with raised eyebrows. John passed the salt and placed it within reach. Masterson took it, salted his food and ate heartily.

It was late. The sound of the singing bush at night permeated the walls of the cabin and comforted those who slept.

The men's bedroom was a stark and simple affair with two lone wrought-iron beds pushed to opposite extremities of the room.

In the darkness John silently rose and carefully moved under the bed. Huddled with his back against the wall and surrounded by the iron frame, his eyes furtively looked out to the rest of the room. Slowly he began exercising his muscles within the confines of a familiar enclosure.

Motionless, Masterson secretly closed his eyes and went back to sleep.

At dawn the following morning, the colonel left everyone asleep and embarked alone on his morning run. An hour later John emerged from the cabin carrying his toilet bag and headed for the shower.

A simple bush construction, the shower consisted of a small wooden vanity enclosure and a 'fill it yourself' canvas bag with a screw-in rose that released the water.

As John approached, he unintentionally saw Phillip drying himself after his own ablution. He couldn't help but notice that the colonel's back was disfigured and covered in a mass of scars. Unaware of John's prolonged presence, Masterson wrapped his towel around his waist, pulled on a T-shirt and hopped out.

Breaking into a whistle he passed John and smiled, "It's all yours."

Later that day John sat on the veranda and watched perplexed as Masterson walked into the bush and reappeared several minutes later carrying a large stone.

At that moment Hilda stuck her head around the front door, "Can I get you some coffee John?" She asked.

John looked up at her smiling face, "No thanks."

"Okay. Holler if you need anything."

She had almost disappeared inside when John called after her, "Hilda?"

"Yes John?" She said sticking her head back out.

"What's he doing?" He asked as Masterson disappeared again.

"Oh, he thinks the place is missing a barbecue. So he's going to build one." Hilda went back inside as the man in question repeated his performance.

An hour later, he emerged yet again, to place another stone on the growing pile. John stood nearby. As the colonel disappeared one more time, John followed. Tagging along for about thirty metres he watched Masterson find a suitable stone, dig it up and head back to the cabin. Seeing one himself, John picked it up and did the same.

Throughout the entire day the two men walked backwards and forwards into the bush bringing back stones of various shapes and sizes. Without speaking a word to each other, it was strangely enjoyable and a fruitful day's work. In fading light the last stone was placed on an enormous pile.

"Dinner in fifteen minutes!" Sang a timely voice from the verandah.

"Thank Christ!" Said Masterson stretching his back and wiping his hands of dirt. "I'm starving." He walked off toward the cabin and John followed.

Hilda, busy as ever, was in the last stages of preparing the meal and cleaning. Quickly sweeping some dirt out of the door a large wasp buzzed past her head lured by the aroma of her cooking.

"Hey, get out you. Go on," she yelled.

Instinctively she waved the broom at the offending insect in an effort to corral it outside. Masterson walked in with John just as she swung the broom from up high and toward the door. Startled by the blur of movement John immediately fell to the ground cringing with his hands shielding his head. Knocking over several bits of furniture he sidled backwards along the ground in a desperate attempt to get away. Whimpering, he curled in a ball for defence.

Hilda in complete shock held her hand over her mouth in horror, "Oh John I'm so sorry."

Masterson quickly grabbed at her and moved her away.

Gradually aware of what had happened, John rose self-consciously to his feet. Keeping his eyes low, he said nothing and walked slowly from the room.

Hilda was beside herself, "Oh my God Phillip, what have I done?"

Masterson put his arm around her to console her, "Shh! It can't be helped. In fact," he added, "it may be a blessing."

That night as Masterson lay asleep John eventually came to the room. On the floor at the head of his bed was a lit candle. A pillow and makeshift sleeping area had been made for him under the iron frame of the bed proper. Next to the candle sat a small plate of cookies.

John stared at the arrangement for a long time, then sitting quietly on the end of the bed, he bowed his head in his hands and sobbed.

The following morning Masterson had deliberately avoided the cabin to give John some space. Instead, he opted to sit cross-legged under a tree that overlooked the mountains and waited. In time, as he knew he would, John approached and sat opposite. They sat quietly: The colonel watching John and John looking to the ground.

Eventually, Masterson spoke, "And?"

John sighed heavily, "I don't know what you want me to say."

"This is not about what I want."

John was silent.

"It's about what you want. You want to go home."

"Yes," John answered softly.

"Why?"

He looked up, "I haven't seen my fiancé in seven years."

"What do you want from your reunion?"

Lowering his eyes again John replied, "To be as we were."

"Is it possible that if I sent you home today, things would be as they were?"

"If I could hold her ... If I could smell her hair ..."

"If?" Masterson interrupted, "Can you hold, John?"

John's eyes implored understanding from his mentor, "Phillip, I have been to hell and back."

"I know that son. But you need to answer the question."

"I ..."

"Take your time."

"Why do you always say that?" John said feeling pressured.

Masterson's voice was calm and logical, "Because we have it."

John absorbed the annoying sense of the statement.

"Yes you've been to hell and back, but hell has returned with you." He waited for this to sink in, "If we can't flush it out, John, you can never go home."

Masterson again waited, this time for John's eyes to meet his. The reality of what was said caused panic.

"Assess."

"I don't know where to start."

"Can - you - hold?" Asked the colonel pushing the tempo.

After a long pause John answered, "No."

"Assess."

"I can't breathe."

"Assess"

"I can't ..."

"I said assess," Masterson repeated.

"I defend against ..." John couldn't go on.

"Against what?"

John stumbled to find the words.

"You defend against what?"

Suddenly John began to crack. His voice was laced with anger. "You know 'what'. Why ask if you already know? I saw your back, you must know."

This was too much for Masterson. "Don't avoid the question and fucking implicate me?" He said raising his voice, "I know you. You have the wisdom to see. I know you have the power to return everything I dish out with interest. You are the student that became the master so why hide in deception? You must sense the importance of this moment. You must."

Masterson reached out and hit John's shoulder, "Look at me. Do not insult your mentor. If we lie to ourselves what is the fucking point of anything. Answer me. What is the point?"

John was beside himself. "There is no point," he answered hiding his head.

Masterson quickly rapped him with his knuckles, "Don't look away?" John looked up.

"We're bound together aren't we?" The colonel continued.

"Yes."

"We share success as well as defeat. It's our code isn't it?"

John was close to breaking, "Yes."

Masterson sensed the need and pushed every button he had. Leaning heavily on each word his attack was relentless.

"What do you defend against? Why do you sleep under the bed? Why do you cower at a raised stick? Why are you ashamed ... yes you've been to hell and back! But why is it that you can't fucking hold someone you love ... Why?"

John suddenly broke. "Because I'm afraid," he screamed.

Shocked by this admission, his next words were immersed in the huge emotion of the lifting weight and mixed with convulsive sobs.

"I ... I can't breathe ... the smell ... the screams ... the pain. Nights, days, weeks ... bloody years. I can't face it any more Phillip. No more beatings no more sticks no more pain no more blood. Please ... for the love of ... I'm fucking scared ..." With his face contorted in anguish John's knuckles were white as he desperately tried to hold himself together. Rocking backward and forwards he wept, "No more no more no more ..."

Masterson wrestled with his own urges to maintain control. Grabbing John's shoulder he spoke with genuine and heartfelt emotion.

"There you go. That's the first step."

Patting him affectionately through his heavy sobs, Masterson added with quiet and assertive affirmation, "We'll do it together son ... step by step until we can run."

John looked up into the eyes of his friend knowing he knew of the horrors from which he'd come. John's gratitude for his being there was beyond all the combined words he had ever spoken. Yet in that instant not a single one needed to be said. Their connection, stronger and clearer than anyone could ever hope to comprehend.

Masterson spoke as he would to a son, "You do me a great honour John. I have more pride in you at this moment than I've ever had. You will have your life back ... I promise."

Together under the tree that shaded them, surrounded by the land of Aboriginal 'dreaming' they firmly held onto each other in a bond that would never be broken.

Chapter Twenty-five

A late Wednesday morning in Glebe was typical of any day midweek. The traffic settled into the relaxed routine of a mild rush through narrow streets and scarce parking. Buyers enjoyed the amiable atmosphere of casual chats and occasional spending that was the attraction of suburban shopping.

As he had done on every second Wednesday for the past twenty years, plant wholesaler, Kevin Summers, double parked outside Robert's Flowers. Dressed in worn overalls and ignoring the imposition of his old Ford flatbed on passing cars, Kevin wound up his delivery. Standing on the tray he began sweeping away the debris and creating a cloud of dust.

In charge of deliveries this week, Rachel arrived back at the truck. Carefully dodging the dust, she loaded the remaining pots onto her trolley. Kevin secured the broom and checked his clipboard.

"That's the lot Rachel."

"Dad wanted me to remind you about the 'Bloody Gardenias'. I'm sorry for the language Mr Summers, but he insisted I quote him exactly."

Kevin studied her. His face was a mass of lines and freckles. "In all the years I've known your father he's never once limited himself to only one expletive, especially a mild one said as sweetly as that. You've cleaned it up, haven't you young lady?"

Rachel went red, "I might have."

He smiled, "Yeah and I 'might have' no 'air,'" he said rubbing his bald scalp. "Tell him to keep his shirt on, Gardenia's especially 'bloody' ones, are harder to get this time of year. It'll be Friday, or Monday if he'd like me to gift wrap 'em."

He winked and passed the clipboard, "Sign here please."

Rachel read the paperwork as Kevin started the truck. Passing the signed forms through the open window of the rattling door she yelled above the noise of the engine, "Thanks Mr Summers, see you Friday." He waved and moved off with the traffic.

The welcome bell sounded on the door as Rachel parked her trolley and placed the pots on the floor with the rest of the order. Edward was behind the counter putting the finishing touches to a display.

"What did he say?" He called.

"He said you swear too much."

"Now don't be like that. It's banter Rachel and it's expected. If we didn't have banter we'd all be dead. What did he say?"

Rachel checked her make-up in the mirror placed behind the roses to make them look fuller. "He said Friday."

"Good."

Looking at all the plants from the truck she felt guilty wanting to leave, "Dad are you sure you're right with all this?"

"Hmm, what? Don't fuss Rachel go and do your shopping. Here!" He added stepping back from his arrangement, "How does this look?"

Rachel was impressed, "Not bad for a stubborn seventy year old male with appalling habits."

"Excuse me, I'm sixty nine," Edward said affronted. Suddenly he went a bit wobbly and reached for the counter to steady himself.

"Dad?" Rachel said concerned, "What's the matter?"

Edward buried his head in his hands and rubbed his face, "Nothing, it's just a turn."

She rushed to the office and grabbed the chair from behind the desk.

"Here, sit," she ordered. Her father obeyed and the chair squeaked its familiar squeak as he leaned back. Not knowing what to do she took off his shoes.

Edward complained, "It's alright Rachel I have them occasionally ... What the hell are you doing?"

Rachel ignored his protests and began massaging his foot. "Can I do anything. What about a drink of water?"

"I'm okay, honestly." Suddenly his eyes twinkled and he moaned some more, "Ooh! Aah!"

Rachel was beside herself, "What? What is it?"

"The foot, the other foot," Edward groaned.

Rachel grabbed his other foot and massaged for her life.

"Does this help?" She asked looking up at her father.

Edward observed her through the open fingers of the hand draped across his face. "No not really. But it does feel rather good. Your not bad at it," he said grinning.

"Oh crap! I thought you were dying or something. Yuk! When was the last time you changed these socks?"

Edward began laughing and Rachel joined in, though she was still slightly suspicious, "Are you sure you're okay?"

"It was a turn not an organ shutdown. I'm old Rachel, these things happen. They come, they go, come on, think of the customers. Pass my shoes."

Rachel stood and checked her watch "The bus is due. Can I go?"

"Unless you'd like to stay and do my nails, I insist you do. I can't take all this excitement at my age. Here give us a kiss."

Rachel made a face, kissed him on the cheek and left.

Standing at the bus stop around the corner she checked her shopping list and smiled. The time with her father had been a boon to her life. His ready humour and caring had kept her sane. She loved him for it.

Back in the shop Edward, now feeling better, was pruning the new arrivals before placing them on the shelves. His practiced use of the secateurs made light work of the task as he snipped quickly and professionally.

The welcome bell tinkled as the door opened and shut.

Hearing the familiar sound of heels on the cement floor he called out from his kneeling position in the middle of the displays. "That was quick! What did you forget?"

There was no answer. The steps came closer.

"Rachel?" Still no answer.

Looking over his shoulder Edward's face suddenly went white.

Chapter Twenty-six

Several hours later, Rachel hopped off the bus feeling quite pleased with herself. She had finally found a store that stocked clothing in colours she liked. It had been years since she'd bought several outfits in one day, and it felt good. With a spring in her step and a rare smile, she was unexpectedly knocked from her reverie by a slight collision with a young man running by. Unaware of Rachel's existence, he kept going. The force of the bump caused her to drop a bag. Slightly annoyed by his rudeness, she picked it up and carried on.

Rounding the corner more people pushed her accidentally as they brushed past chattering excitedly of a big event. Ahead, Rachel could see a large crowd had gathered about flashing lights.

A little confused as to the exact whereabouts of the trouble it took some moments for alarm bells to ring. Still uncertain, Rachel's pace quickened as her adrenaline kicked in. Realising the centre of the commotion was their shop, she was overcome with a sickening sense of foreboding and panicked. Dropping her bags she ran as fast as she could.

Forcing her way through the crowd she overheard Mrs Zimmerman from next-door mentioning her father's name. Reaching the front of the onlookers, Rachel could see two ambulances had driven up onto the footpath, and several police cars had done the same. A uniformed policeman was pushing the crowd back and asking for more room.

Anxiously sobbing, Rachel rushed forward for the entrance only to be grabbed by another policeman, who quickly pulled her to one side.

"Stand back," he said.

Through the door came a stretcher surrounded by ambulance officers working furiously on her father.

"Oh my God, Dad!" She cried.

Edward didn't speak. His face was ashen and he looked near death. Both his hands were wrapped in bloodied bandages and there was blood all over his clothing.

Rachel grabbed hysterically at the stretcher. "Dad what happened ... Dad?"

The officer placed his arm around her with gentle strength and guided her back. "He can't hear you Miss. Please let us get him into the ambulance." Rachel was panic-stricken and didn't know what to do.

"Where are you taking him?" She cried.

"To the nearest Emergency. Is the victim your father?"

"Victim! What are talking about?" She asked helplessly through a mass of tears.

"It appears the gentleman was attacked."

Rachel was beside herself, "Oh Jesus Christ! Why would anybody do that, he's an old man?"

"We're still trying to find that out Miss. Could I have your name please?" The officer asked, using procedure to keep her focused.

"Yes, Rachel, Rachel Roberts. But why is there so much blood?" Rachel watched intently as her father was placed into the back of an ambulance.

"Your father's name?"

"Edward Roberts, will he be alright, what's the matter with his hands?"

"How old is he?"

Rachel tried to stay on in control, "Um, Seventy, no sixty nine."

"Does anybody else work here?"

Rachel shook her head and was trembling, "No. Please tell me he'll be alright."

An ambulance officer ran past Rachel and the policeman to the front door. A small package was handed to him from inside. "Is that all of them?" He asked.

"What's he talking about? All of what?" Asked Rachel.

"All we could find," came the answer from inside.

The policeman grabbed the ambulance officer on his way back. "The victim's name is Edward Roberts, age is sixty nine."

"Thanks mate, got it."

Rachel could tell by the way the bag was carried out in front of the ambulance officer that it was important. "What have you got?" She asked, her bottom lip visibly quivering.

The ambulance officer took one look at Rachel and spoke to the policeman, "I'll get her a blanket, hang on." Quickly he raced off.

In shock and deeply confused Rachel turned for the door, "I'll have to close the shop."

The policeman hastily pulled her back not wanting her to see inside. "Whoa! You can't go in there Rachel. We'll do that. I'll organise a lift to the hospital so that you can be with your dad."

The ambulance officer returned with a blanket and wrapped it around her. She was now shivering all over and had lost all colour. The ambulance loaded with Edward sped away with its siren blaring as the policeman caught the worried eye of the attending medic. "Rachel is there anybody I can ring?"

Looking up she asked, "My brother, Daniel?"

The officer nodded, "That sounds fine."

"Please," she whispered. "You must tell me."

The officer persisted, "Do you have a number we can reach him on Rachel?"

Rachel grabbed the officer's arm, "I have a right to know. I am his next of kin. Please ... what was in the bag?"

The officer looked into her eyes and concluded he would have to tell.

"His fingers."

Chapter Twenty-seven

The interior of the hospital was quiet. The long corridors enhanced the echoes of distant noises from other areas beyond the swinging see-through doors. The clock on the wall read 1:00 a.m. Its slow moving second hand, noisily clunked through each incessant and repetitive cycle.

In a small white alcove of uncomfortable red chairs, Rachel and Daniel sat waiting. Occasionally a nurse would walk past and smile encouragement before disappearing beyond. Rachel rested her head on her brother's shoulder. On her lap was the bunched up blanket given to her by the medic. They were both exhausted.

Finally, they were stirred by the slap of a door and the approach of a man dressed in surgical green. Struggling to their feet, the two siblings clasped hands to give themselves strength.

The surgeon smiled a tired smile. "He's alive," he said. "But there are complications. Your father has had a stroke. This normally causes paralysis to only one side of the body, but he fails to respond to any stimuli at all. I suspect this is symptomatic of age and severe trauma. But I hasten to add it is far too early to be certain of anything."

"What about his hands?" Rachel asked trying to hold back tears.

"We reattached two fingers to his left hand and three to his right. The stroke makes the whole thing a bit of a lottery. But everything is connected."

Rachel's face contorted in anguish and her voice broke as she began to cry.

"What about his other ones?" She sobbed.

"They were severed progressively at each joint. It was best to concentrate on the whole ones. I'm sorry."

Rachel lost whatever composure she had and wept into her brother's chest.

"Can we see him?" Asked Daniel.

"He's being moved to Intensive Care. After he's settled some-one will come and get you."

"What happens next?"

The surgeon was circumspect. "We wait."

Daniel extended his hand, "Thank you Doctor."

Turning to leave he paused for a final question, "Do they know who it was yet?"

"No. Dad is the only witness."

He nodded a silent apology and left. Returning to their seats Rachel sobbed weakly in intermittent and convulsive bursts. Daniel spread the blanket over his sister and drew her into him with a protective arm. Confused yet united, they waited to see their father.

Chapter Twenty-eight

The first rays of sunlight on the mountain marked the start of John's healing and recovery. Masterson led the way as the two men set off on a run. This was not about fitness or stamina but more an exercise in the rebuilding of a life force that had become detached from its purpose.

The oldest inhabitants of Australia, the Aboriginal people have for thousands of years undertaken the spiritual journey of 'walkabout' when faced with a loss of belonging. Their culture so entwined with the land that the desire to maintain their bond with it was overpowering. Throughout our history many cultures have developed similar wisdoms. Ancient beliefs such as Shamanism, Hindu enlightenment, the meditation of Zen, the power of Chi, have all recognised the requirement of 'balance' and 'belonging' as fundamental to the harmony of existence.

Masterson knew of no other way. Physical maintenance was merely the mechanical element of a body. The nurturing bosom of Nature held the very essence of life.

Mountain air, pungent perfumes, lush vegetation, towering forests, running streams, animals and insects ... all provided energy linked to a higher source. Rediscovering his place within this nucleus of creation, was the first step in John's journey toward the restoration of his spirit.

In the ensuing weeks the runs became progressively longer. Not out of demand, but enjoyment. During the day, simple martial art movements of balance and precision were practiced tirelessly. Their goal was to seek inner stillness, flexible rhythm and harmony with the body's centre. Additional exercise and weight training came at John's own request.

Hilda cooked for them, fed them, and refreshed them. She encouraged them with her huge smile and entertained them with songs from her kitchen. She kept tabs on their movements through her window and marvelled daily at their unity of purpose, strength and commitment.

Each night before dinner, the two men added one stone to the barbecue and cemented it in. After dinner they would light a fire overlooking the valley and John would purge himself of his horrors while Masterson sat in silence and listened. Each night, both men openly wept.

Chapter Twenty-nine

It was a Saturday afternoon and Tom Pearson sat in his sitting room watching the Match of the Day on television. Playing, was an Australian Rules football game between the Sydney Swans and North Melbourne. Outside, his wife, Kerry Pearson, impatiently tooted from her car.

Checking his watch he sighed heavily and rose to switch off the set. Whispering to himself he muttered, "Alright, keep your hair on." Then searched the room for his hat.

Finding it, he checked the badge was straight. Not normally fussy about small things, but a crooked emblem proved an exception to the rule. Its design was well known. Underneath the flying eagle carrying nemesis, were four words written in Latin 'Culpam poena premit comes'. They meant 'Punishment follows close on guilt'. It was the emblem of the New South Wales Police.

Blowing off imagined dust the uniformed sergeant tucked his hat under his arm, grabbed his leather jacket from the rack, and closed the front door behind him.

The small three-bedroom house in Bondi had been their home since his mother had passed away eight years earlier. It wasn't on the water but the few blocks between his front gate and the beach, provided an excellent buffer from the summer crowds.

"Come on Tom!" His wife called, "You're as slow as a wet week."

Tom arrived at her open window, "Can I drive?"

"No. You can drive your own car when it gets back from the mechanics."

The police sergeant stood square-jawed at the resumption of their regular battle. Tom disliked her driving and she disliked his. Kerry was resolute.

"Hurry up dear," she added "I've got lots to do and it takes me ages to get the seat back into position once you've played with it."

Defeated, he swung into the other side and secured the door. He looked across at his wife who waited for him to settle. "Promise me," he said, "that today you'll abandon at least one of your annoying habits and move out of the middle lane. Just once Kerry ... is all I ask."

"People without their own cars shouldn't throw stones," she responded.

"Darling, I'm merely concerned that you'll spend your entire life never realising the concept of traffic flow."

Kerry smiled, "Seat belt please, we don't want a ticket."

The green Mazda swung out of the driveway, merged with the traffic, and moved immediately into the middle lane.

Married for nearly thirty years the pair had two children: George the eldest at twenty-eight, was married and lived in

Broome. Gloria was twenty-four, unmarried and occasionally lived at home.

After his national service tour of Vietnam, Tom had joined the Police Force fulfilling his boyhood ambition. He had met Kerry on his first posting as a constable in Albury on the River Murray. After five years in the country, he served long stints in outer suburban Parramatta and Liverpool until finally moving to his current posting of five years with Sydney's City Central. On patrol all his life, the demands were becoming tougher on his aging legs. Soon he would yield to pressure from his superiors and accept a desk, but for the moment, he was content to keep doing what he loved.

"Will you be late?" Kerry asked.

"Depends on the arrests I guess ... probably about one. You haven't seen my other blue shirt have you?"

"Which one of your fourteen blue shirts are we talking about?"

"The one with the collar."

To anybody else this response would have made little sense, but to a spouse it was sufficient information. "Its soaking," she said "Would you like me to pick you up?"

"No thanks, I'll grab a lift with Feggerty. This lane is clear."

Kerry ignored him, "Sylvia rang to thank you for helping Angelo ... I said you hadn't done anything really, but you know what she's like. How's he going by the way?"

"Who?"

"Angelo."

Pearson looked suspiciously at his wife, "Why?"

"I'm simply asking how he's going. Its perfectly natural for an aunt to worry about her nephew."

"Particularly after a phone call from your sister," he noted dryly. After thirty years Tom could read Kerry like a book, "This is leading to something, I can feel it." He looked behind his left shoulder, "Still clear."

"Come on, how's he going?"

Pearson thought for a moment, "He won't last. I've never known anybody to bugger so many things up without trying. Your nephew is a walking disaster just like his mother."

"But he's a crack shot! Sylvia said he could have made the Olympics. You do remember him as a child hanging from the jungle gym and shooting buttons off the fence, don't you? He never missed! Surely that's worth something."

"I can't argue with you there, everybody at SPG says he's a freak. The question is, will they survive working with him?"

The traffic came to a standstill and Pearson could sense his wife's brain ticking over.

"Are you going to tell me what this is all about or do I have to arrest you?"

"Well, and this wasn't why I was asking ..."

"Of course not," he interrupted.

"But remember when Angelo went to America for his holidays?"

The traffic started again, "Vaguely."

"He met a girl."

Pearson laughed, "Is she suing?"

"Please Tom. Apparently they hit it off and Angelo is very smitten. He's invited her to come over here for Christmas."

Tom's head swung toward his wife as she continued talking.

"Gloria will be on the Gold Coast so I thought they could have her room and stay with us."

"What for? Why wouldn't he take her to his own home?"

"Darling, I hardly think she'd want to spend her first visit to Australia in the middle of nowhere. Here we've got the beaches, the harbour, the bridge, museums, theatres …"

"Christ, Kerry, why do you always have to be the tooth fairy? This lane is clear."

"Please Tom it's only for ten days and he's not allowed guests at the Lodge. He's such a sweet boy and he doesn't meet many girls."

"There's a reason for that you know. Would you get into this lane?" She doesn't and he was becoming slightly frustrated. "Do we know anything about her?" He asked.

"Sylvia said she's on a study visa from Russia at UCLA."

"A communist for Christmas, marvellous! There goes the pension."

"Oh stop it, she sounds very nice and quite clever, her name is Khristin Chemenko and she's doing post graduate Fine Arts."

"Well it's just as well you asked me before it was arranged isn't it?

Kerry was silent as she turned into Day Street and headed toward the station. Guilt was written all over her face.

Tom sighed resigned, "When's she coming?"

"The twenty-third. Ooh, can I drop you here while the light's red?"

Pearson was aghast, "No you may not."

His wife winced in protest, "But it'll save me going two blocks out of my way."

"I'm sorry Kerry but it's illegal to alight from a vehicle whilst parked in the middle bloody lane."

Chapter Thirty

Six weeks after the attack, Rachel stood in the car park of St Villiers Repatriation Hospital straightening her skirt and tucking back her hair. Happy that she'd done her best with her appearance, she reached into the back seat and withdrew a large bunch of carnations. They were her father's favourite and she hoped they would brighten his day.

Sadly, Edward's condition had not improved. Although his hands were healing, the shock of what he had gone through had traumatised him considerably.

The effects of 'Acute Stress Reaction' varied with each individual's capacity to cope with a significant trauma. In Edward's case it manifested as a daze involving limited consciousness, disorientation and an inability to respond to stimuli. Coupled with a partial stroke, Edward had succumbed to extreme withdrawal and a condition known as 'Dissociative Stupor'. The unlocking of this complex illness would depend entirely on circumstance and his deep-seated desire to recover.

In his room, Edward sat in a wheelchair on the far side of his bed staring out the window at the surrounding garden. His face was grey and he had aged considerably. Wearing a gown and slippers, his hands were bandaged and he neither moved nor spoke. Sitting with him was a young policeman wearing glasses, holding a sketchpad and using a pencil.

Rachel entered not expecting to see anyone.

"Oh!" She said startled, "Hello."

The visitor equally surprised, clutched at falling papers as he rose politely to his feet. "Miss Roberts? Hi I'm Snr. Constable Forbes." His eyes went to the array of drawings on the floor, "Umm, Sketch Artist."

"Good morning. Nice to meet you," said Rachel smiling at his effort and shaking his outstretched hand.

Stepping over the mess she immediately crossed to her father and kissed him on the cheek, "Morning Dad." Placing her hand on his shoulder she held the flowers so that he could see them, "Look! Carnations." Rachel's eyes searched for a sign of recognition but Edward remained still and expressionless. Determined to keep positive for him, she smiled, "I knew you'd like them. Here, I'll put them in a vase."

Moving to the bedside table she placed the flowers down and noticed more drawings. Picking one up she looked at the various outlines of different shaped noses.

"This is interesting," she said to the policeman, "What are you doing?"

Having stepped back in an attempt not to intrude on their private moment, the young man moved eagerly forward. "I'm trying to get a sketch of your father's attacker." He turned around his current drawing for Rachel to see, "It's a long shot but, anybody you recognise?

The sketch was of an Asian man with fine features.

Rachel studied the drawing, and then shook her head, "I'm sorry, no!" Suddenly her mind grasped at her next question, "But, how can you? Dad can't talk."

The young man looked quite pleased with himself, "Murder stories!" He said.

"I don't follow."

"I read a lot. Mysteries ... detective stories, things like that. Last night I remembered this plot line when one character couldn't talk but could move a finger. I think they made a movie about it, anyway, they all stand around watching this guy slowly tap a finger, once for yes twice for no ... Bingo! They solve the case, catch the killer, and everyone lives happily ever after. I've been here since breakfast."

Rachel's mind slowly worked its way around what he was saying, "Dad can't move a finger though, can he?"

"No he can't," he said dampening her spirits. "When I rushed in this morning I looked and looked but couldn't see anything, and I have to admit to feeling rather stupid. That is, until I saw it."

Rachel's interest quickened, "Saw what?"

He broke into a broad grin, "A squint."

She felt the hairs on the back of her neck stand on end, "You're kidding?"

The young man beckoned her to join him, "Come and see."

She rushed over to her father's side as the policeman continued, "You can't see it unless you look for it, but watch his right eye."

Rachel stared at her father's still gaze as the young man asked a question.

"You can hear us can't you Mr Roberts?" He then pointed to the corner of Edward's eye for Rachel. "Watch here," he said.

Edward's eye slowly squinted, "Oh my God!" Rachel gasped.

"Keep watching," he whispered, "Is it raining outside Mr Roberts?"

This time Edward's eye squinted twice. Rachel was beside herself, "Dad, can you hear me?"

One squint followed. Rachel reached forward and hugged her father, "Oh my God! Oh Dad! Oh thank God!"

The policeman kept talking, "It took me a while to find it. But since then, we've just been going through different drawings. It's been slow but ..."

Rachel looked at the policeman as tears streamed down her face. Suddenly she leaned over and kissed his cheek. "You are a genius!"

"Hey, you're welcome, I just ..."

"Do you know what this means? He's not gone! He can come back. Shit! I have to tell them." Quickly Rachel grabbed for the buzzer lying across the bed and pressed it.

Realising that he might be in the way Snr Constable Forbes decided to withdraw, "Look I'm all done here. I don't think this is too accurate but it's a start. I'll leave this copy and come back, okay?"

Rachel was too excited to pay much attention. Instead she went back to her father.

"Dad would you like some water?"

Two squints. The young man quietly collected his things.

Rachel was sobbing, "Are you warm enough?"

Again two squints. Completely emotional now, she frantically dragged a blanket from the bed and began wrapping it around Edward's legs.

The constable was almost hit by the door as a nurse walked in. She looked around the room and at the dishevelled bed, "Did you push the bell Rachel?"

Rachel voice was strained and excited, "Sarah, Dad can squint!" Seeing the policeman leave, Rachel called after him, "Constable? Thank you."

He smiled and waved, "You're welcome. Good luck!"

Chapter Thirty-one

The loud music came to a dramatic stop. The lights faded to black and the intoxicating beat of the drums enveloped the packed auditorium. The chatter of the crowd slowed to a whisper in anticipation of the coming bout.

Over the loud speakers the familiar drawl of the announcer in his 'fight speak' was heard. "Ladies and gentlemen. The Colosseum proudly presents yet another 'newcomer' event.

The crowd hooted their approval.

"In the Southern Pen."

The spotlight snapped on revealing a strongly built redheaded man with focused eyes and hard exterior. Whistles emanated from the darkness.

"Homeless since youth, he comes from a jungle and was born to rumble. With an amateur boxing record of 18 wins 1 loss - by TKO - put your hands together for Bernie 'The Mule' Salinger."

The crowd went into wild applause as Salinger stepped into the arena and began his warm up. Throwing fast jabs and uppercuts to an imagined opponent he looked sharp and his footwork dazzled.

The announcer continued, "In the Northern Pen."

The other spotlight snapped on to illuminate a man-mountain in a tight fitting mask. Resembling an executioner he wore a sleeveless top and had a distinctive scar that extended upwards from his left armpit. The crowd gasped their collective approval at his size.

"A man with no previous history in this sport. He's either brave or stupid."

The crowd laughed raucously.

"But he's certainly big enough. Lets give a huge Colosseum welcome, fooorrrrr Khan."

The crowd cheered noisily as Khan casually strolled into the arena and waited.

The chant began, "Fight, fight, fight."

In the manager's section Vinnie sat observing. Taking his job more seriously he was on the lookout for potential rivals and Salinger had a big reputation. Leaning toward the person sitting next to him he was moved to comment.

"I've seen this boxer before, he's fast. Where's your boy from?"

Vinnie's head turn brought him face to face with Mae Lin. The intensity of her eyes sent a cold shiver along his spine. In civilian clothing she appeared neat and well groomed. Her demeanour however, hadn't changed. Mae Lin shrugged her shoulders innocently in response to Vinnie's question, but her unrelenting gaze stayed on him. Vinnie feeling slightly uncomfortable, paid her no mind and returned his attention to the fight.

Salinger ran in and began his assault throwing furious combinations of lefts and rights. Unaffected by the onslaught Khan stunned the attacker with a massive counter punch. Reaching out, he grabbed Salinger's hair with one hand and continuously punched him senseless with the other. Each blow reverberated with sickening brutality through the microphones to a stunned crowd. Repeatedly, a defenceless and soon unconscious Salinger was beaten. Not until he was content with his demolition did Khan let go. When he did, the blood covered man fell like a discarded doll. The arena was silent.

Vinnie was shocked, "Holy shit!" He whispered.

The announcer spoke over the speakers, "Winner by knockout. Khan."

The scan lights dipped and the music began. The crowd responded with applause that was sparse and intermittent as each member of the audience struggled with what they had just witnessed. Hit with an idea Vinnie turned to Mae Lin, but her seat was empty.

Hurrying into the fighter's preparation room Vinnie caught sight of Mae Lin and Tobacqui exiting through the door that led to the public area of the Colosseum.

"Hey, wait up!" He called as the door closed between them.

Bursting open the door, he apologised to the startled bouncer and yelled again, "Hey, wait!"

A short distance ahead they heard the call and stopped. Mae Lin turned around.

Vinnie walked toward them smiling, "Sorry. I didn't catch the name?"

"It wasn't thrown," she responded.

"Oh! Yeah," Vinnie stumbled temporarily on a moment of stage fright, but forced himself to continue, "Look I'm Vinnie, I have a fighter here, Daniel Roberts, you may have heard of him?"

Tobacqui lifted his chin and squared his shoulders.

Vinnie was acutely aware of his size, "Hey Khan, great fight. Look my boy is almost a main card. I thought maybe we could talk, you know, do a bit of business?"

Mae Lin raised an eyebrow, which Vinnie took as a cue to continue.

"Khan here is a newcomer," he explained adding importantly "but I've an eye. He shows promise. Perhaps if things go well for him … I thought, if you were keen, we could maybe share a card."

"Why?" Asked Mae Lin.

Vinnie's face broke into a broad grin, "Are you serious? Money!"

"How?"

"Promotion!" Vinnie felt he had the floor and went into his pitch.

"If we spend our own money to promote the fight, the management will give us a percentage of the book. If your man Khan here can string a few wins together, it may be worth it." Trying to act as if it wasn't a big deal he added, "Think about it. There's no hurry."

Mae Lin turned to leave and then swung back. "Vinnie. Right?"

"That's right Vinnie. Vincenzo. Vincenzo Montorelli. Don't forget."

Mae Lin smiled sweetly, "I won't."

Chapter Thirty-two

In the months that followed, Khan defeated all who opposed him. Brutal and unforgiving, his infamy grew with each bout and inevitably the crowd warmed to the allure of his 'bad boy' image. 'Khan, Khan, Khan' went the chant as they urged him on to greater and more decisive wins.

Proving Vinnie's instincts correct, the wave of support soon challenged the appeal of Daniel as Colosseum favourite. The promise of a classic struggle between good and evil set the tone for a 'Main Card' battle of historic proportions. Management backed the idea one hundred percent.

Excitedly Vinnie unfurled a large advertising poster for Mae Lin's approval.

Her eyes ran up and down the glossy promotion. It had a head to toe picture of Tobacqui dressed as Khan on one side, a big V in the middle and Daniel on the other. Underneath each fighter were their printed names. Along the top and written over a storm cloud exploding with lightening was a headline that read 'FIGHT OF THE CENTURY'.

"And you want how much?" She asked.

"Nothing," said a magnanimous Vinnie, "I'll take what you owe me from the book. We split the rest."

Mae Lin smiled sweetly, "You would do that for me? That's very kind Vinnie."

Vinnie had no idea of the type of person he was dealing with and was completely out of his depth. Rolling up the poster he leaned back on his chair and added smoothly, "Hey, we've all got to look out for each other Mae Lin."

Her eyes sparkled, "What percentage did management agree to?"

"Eight percent. Split two ways we could make ten thousand each, and that doesn't include our own bets and winnings."

Mimicking a little girl, Mae Lin was excited, "Goodness!"

"Shall I go ahead then?"

She nodded.

Chapter Thirty-three

It was five in the morning and still dark. Dressed in his underwear, Masterson quietly placed his hand over Hilda's mouth as she lay sound asleep. Startled out of her wits, her eyes opened to the size of saucers. Placing a finger to his mouth he motioned for her to be quiet. Waiting patiently for the colour to return to her face, he then beckoned Hilda to follow him on tiptoe.

Arriving outside his room, he slowly pushed open the door to reveal John lying asleep, under the covers, and on top of the bed. Proudly, Phillip put his arm around an equally impressed Hilda and smiled.

John was now outrunning Masterson every day by several miles. With his cast long gone, his exercises and weight training were impressive. Lean, muscular and athletic, life had finally returned to his eyes.

The martial art routines had been replaced by combat. Backwards and forwards, and with blinding speed the two men sparred for hours on end, displaying masterful ability and control.

Spellbound by their skills and not wanting to miss anything, Hilda had taken to shelling the peas and peeling the daily vegetables on the verandah.

Regaining his form, John met each surge by Masterson with exquisite defence and countered with attacking manoeuvres of his own. Their enjoyment of the sessions was immense, laughing heartily at mishaps and surprises. Often they would stop to correct each other and discuss alternate combinations and their effect. They both worked very hard.

Outside, at the end of the day, Hilda would fan an exhausted Masterson with her apron as John ran once more before dinner.

The barbecue was almost complete.

Chapter Thirty-four

Seven blocks from the Colosseum was Daniel's converted warehouse apartment. It wasn't in a particularly good area, but it suited his new life style and gave him plenty of room.

Feeling lonely, Rachel had come to visit for the day. Sitting at the kitchen table she finalised some paperwork for Edward while Daniel exercised on his home-gym. Distracted, she looked up as he grunted through the pain barrier of his final set.

Watching her brother's face redden she asked, "When's this big fight of yours?"

"Saturday fortnight," he puffed, "Want to come?"

"No thankyou. I don't like your chosen profession."

Daniel finished his straining, "Last one. Vinnie has some secret scheme going. After this I can buy a dojo or something."

Rachel rested her chin in her hand, "John would like that," she said.

Putting down the weights Daniel picked up a towel. Wrapping it around his neck he sat on his bench, lifted his feet up and looked at his sister, "Don't pout Rache! But have you ever considered that John might never come home? Have you? Its a serious question."

Rachel eyed Daniel, "Sometimes, like when Dad was attacked … But he will."

"What about other men? Don't you … y'know?"

"It's not like that for me Daniel. I miss him, but I have him." She placed her hand on her heart, "He's inside."

Daniel nodded his understanding.

"What about you?" She asked, knowing her brother better than anyone.

"I don't know, it's weird. I always have the feeling that if things turn to shit …" Daniel stopped short and wiped the sweat away with his towel.

"Never mind. Perhaps crazy is a family trait." He had noticed the small bag of clothing she'd left standing inside the front door and knew she was struggling without their father, "Are you staying?"

"May I?" She asked wanting to.

Daniel smiled, "Sure. Pick the room with the least laundry on the floor and claim it."

Chapter Thirty-five

Two weeks later, the first steak sizzled noisily as Hilda threw it on the plate of the completed barbecue. Happily she placed another two beside it.

John sat under the shade tree overlooking the valley. Masterson dressed in his jeans and braces came over and sat alongside.

After a period of silence John looked to the colonel who took it as a signal to speak, "I would like to talk about what you expect."

"Yes?"

"It never leaves you. You can compartmentalise until the cows come home but it never fully leaves."

"Fear?"

Masterson nodded, "Acceptance of fear and finding alternatives is our way of survival John. Courage is the measure of how we control it. Anger is the measure of how we don't."

The two men looked out at the vista. "Do you have any questions?"

John slowly shook his head, "No."

Masterson rose to his feet and extended his hand, "I expect you'd like to go home."

The importance of the words were not lost on either man. Accepting the assistance John stood, "Thank you, I'd like that very much."

"A chopper will pick you up tomorrow morning and return you to Colonel Haig. Headquarters require the standard debrief but considering our time here they will go easy on the usual red tape. You'll have a complete medical and if the results are satisfactory, you will be granted indefinite leave until you decide what to do."

"Will I see you again?"

Masterson smiled, "Only if it involves beer and seafood."

Looking at each other they were both moved. John allowed his heart to speak, "I owe you my life Phillip."

As the men embraced, Masterson answered in kind, "You are most truly welcome John."

Hilda yelled, "Dinner!"

Two days later John sat before Colonel Haig in a makeshift office borrowed from the Air Defence Wing at Amberley.

The debriefing was a formality as Masterson had suggested and John passed his physical with flying colours. During his short return to mainstream military life, he had worn his uniform. It was a good combination: The desert pattern camouflage clothing, his single crown epaulets, the parachute wings on his right shoulder and sandy beret with the famous winged dagger against a black shield. It suited him. Yet although it was familiar, he did not feel very comfortable.

Colonel Haig could sense it and understood. Closing the file in front of him he got straight to the point.

"Colonel Masterson's report is very glowing. You know there was a time when we thought you might be lost to us for good.

I'm glad you've pulled through. Very glad!" Haig hit the desk gently with his hands, "Well there doesn't seem much point in procrastinating. I hope we can continue to be of service Major, the Department owes you a huge debt."

The colonel rose to his feet and John joined him. "Don't be a stranger and say hello to that wonder girl of yours. That is," he added smiling, "if she ever recovers from seeing you in the flesh. Are you sure we can't just drop you at the door?"

"No thanks Colonel. I know I've had eight years, but suddenly I need time to think. The train will be perfect."

"Did Sergeant Gardia give you the address where she's staying?"

"Yes I have everything I need."

John extended his hand, "Thanks Colonel. For everything. I know I wouldn't be here at all if it wasn't for you."

Haig shook hands firmly, "It's an honour Major." He then called out beyond the door, "Sergeant?"

The sergeant poked his head into the office, "Yes Colonel?"

"Organise a place for Major Landau to change, and get him a car."

"Right away sir."

Arriving at Brisbane's Roma Street Station John wore simple jeans and T-shirt and carried a duffle bag with his few possessions.

He had booked an overnight sleeper that would get him to Sydney and Daniel's apartment by mid Saturday morning. Feeling very nervous he stopped at a telephone, took two numbers from his pocket, and rang.

As the train pulled away from the platform he sat in a private compartment deep in thought and holding a photo of Rachel.

Chapter Thirty-six

It was the night before the big fight and Rachel had cooked Daniel and Vinnie dinner. Daniel having finished, smiled at Rachel as Vinnie noisily scraped his plate.

"Some more Vinnie?" Rachel asked.

Vinnie jumped at the prospect of more food. "If you've some spare Rachel ..."

She took his plate to the kitchen. "What's it called again?" He asked.

"Boeuf à la Bourguignonne," she answered.

The name was enough. "Yeah," he said blankly, "Don't go to any trouble."

"It's no trouble, there's plenty here. What does Daniel normally cook when you come over?"

Vinnie sounded neglected, "Sandwiches."

"And he's lucky to get those," Daniel interrupted sliding a bowl that once contained the vegetables, "Here Vinnie you left a carrot.

Rachel placed a fresh plate in front of Vinnie and began collecting the dishes.

"Are you going out?" She asked Daniel.

"No. It's a big day tomorrow. You won't see me after lunch. I'm going to the shop and maybe talking to Ian Stanley. I might even catch a movie before the fight."

"Bullshit!" Cried Vinnie with his mouth full.

Daniel immediately glared at Vinnie who suddenly realised he had detoured from the script.

"Um, that is, not without me you're not. I'm coming as well."

Daniel raised his eyes in disbelief. "Are you two alright?" Rachel enquired from the kitchen.

"Vinnie's just nervous about asking you to do something for him," Daniel offered.

"Really? Vinnie nervous! There's a first." Rachel collected more dishes and looked at Vinnie, "What is it?"

"Vinnie?" Daniel prompted.

Vinnie gave Daniel a pained look and tried to remember what he'd been told to say.

"Yes, well, since Daniel has forced my hand, Rachel, I was wondering if you could come over to my place tomorrow and give it the once over."

Rachel was incredulous, "What, clean?" She called from the kitchen.

"No, not clean, just look at it and tell me what I need. What's missing. You know."

"I'm afraid I don't."

"For a girl."

"A girl! Oh Vinnie that's sweet." Vinnie smiled at Daniel. "No way," added Rachel wiping the grin from his face.

"Why not?"

"Because I want no part of luring girls for your lecherous intent."

"Oh come on Rachel it's not like that."

Daniel decided to come to the rescue, "He's keen on this girl Rache, go on give him a hand. Most of them leave after they smell the place."

"They do not," Vinnie said sneaking in another mouthful.

"What's her name?" Rachel asked.

Vinnie tried to think but his mind was blank. Suddenly he thought of his elderly neighbour.

"Gwen."

Daniel nearly lost it and put his hand up to cover his mouth. Vinnie couldn't look at him for fear of giggling.

"She's coming over after the fight. Come on, do it for old Vinnie. I just want a little help getting her to feel comfortable, that's all."

"Just advice, I'm not cleaning, or washing or cooking?"

"Scout's honour."

"As I recall, Vincenzo, you were thrown out of scouts for selling Taiwanese 'Merit' badges written in Chinese to the cubs."

"I remember that," chipped in Daniel.

"How was I to know they could read? Look that was a long time ago, Rachel, surely I've suffered enough." He put on his best sad face.

"Oh for goodness sake." Said Rachel, "What time?"

"Ten?"

"Okay, okay."

"That-a-girl. You won't regret this Rachel. Thanks."

Vinnie winked at Daniel who nodded with smiling approval as Rachel continued cleaning up.

The Colosseum was almost deserted. In the bookies' office, one light remained on as the bookkeeper worked late. There was a soft knock at the door. Surprised, he looked up at the clock.

"Come in," he called.

The door swung open. Mae Lin smiled and entered.

Chapter Thirty-seven

September 11 2004.

An hour south of Taree and three hours from his destination, John joined other passengers in the dining car to order breakfast. Sitting by himself he watched the passing countryside become more and more familiar. Small recollections, previously forgotten until this moment, flooded back to rekindle his sense of belonging. His memory active, his entire body tingled with growing anticipation of finally holding Rachel and at last returning home.

The clatter of Rachel's heels resonated crisply on the wooden floor of Daniel's apartment. Not wanting to be late, she grabbed her keys and jingled them in rhythm with her footsteps as she strode toward the door. Pausing before she opened it, she called out, "I'm off."

Not yet dressed, Daniel stuck his head out from his room and into the open, "You won't be back before twelve will you?"

Rachel eyed her younger brother, "No, probably not," she answered, "Why?"

"No reason. Say hi to Vinnie."

"Okay." Rachel opened the door and exited. Turning to close it she noticed Daniel's head still watching, "Bye."

"Bye."

Inside, Daniel waited a few seconds just in case she'd forgotten something. When he was certain the coast was clear, he quickly raced around the apartment picking up discarded articles and cleaning.

John's train arrived at the Haymarket and pulled into Sydney's Central Railway Station. Amid a cacophony of inaudible platform announcements he threw his duffle bag over his shoulder and zigzagged a path through the busy throng of travellers and their companions.

Comfortable living was not a high priority for Vinnie. His flat was a down-market affair used only for watching televised sport and sleeping. One of fourteen, Vinnie's flat was on the second floor fed by concrete staircases on either end of the building.

The doorbell rang incessantly, filling the darkened dwelling with its annoying low-pitched buzz. Vinnie rushed out of his bedroom donning crumpled pants over youthful purple boxers. Tucking in his singlet he trod on a plastic take-away fork with a bare foot, "Ow, shit!" Kicking the offending fork under the nearby couch he hid random clothes beneath cushions and hastily straightened his magazines as the buzzer persisted.

"I'm coming," he yelled.

Finally opening the door he was surprised to see Tobacqui Khan with Mae Lin.

"Hey. I didn't expect you two. What's up?"

The large Maori smoothly muscled Vinnie inside as Mae Lin followed.

"Come in then," said Vinnie put out by the intrusion.

Mae Lin looked him up and down, "I'm sorry did we wake you?"

Under her intense gaze Vinnie felt decidedly under-dressed, "No."

Mae Lin smiled, "Good."

Tobacqui deliberately closed the door and Vinnie tried to fathom what was happening. Suddenly Mae Lin wheeled into a slick roundhouse kick that sent him flying.

Falling onto his coffee table, it gave way under his weight. Mae Lin was calm, her gaze unrelenting. Tobacqui didn't move. Shocked, Vinnie struggled to his feet and tried to speak.

"I don't know what ..."

Mae Lin kicked him again and followed it with another and another. Vinnie was not a fighter and the blows did considerable damage. Crashing across the room he smashed glasses and toppled chairs. In pain, he wiped at the blood from his mouth and began shaking.

Mae Lin stood over him with deliberate menace. Her eyes cold and threatening, "Could you explain the difference between eight and twenty five percent," she asked.

Vinnie struggled to prop himself up, "It's just a deal for fuck sake. You could have said no. You still win."

Mae Lin flashed a sinister smile, "I always win."

Revealing a vicious double bladed knife she twirled it expertly in one hand, delighting in the fear its sight induced. Vinnie went cold as Mae Lin moved closer.

"I wonder ..." she asked calmly, "could I use your bathroom?"

He painfully pointed a finger. Her gaze followed the direction given and she smiled. Heading off toward it, she issued an instruction in Mandarin, "Bring him."

Tobacqui moved forward and reached for Vinnie. Very afraid now Vinnie kicked out in self-defence. Khan easily pounded the smaller man several times before roughly dragging him toward the bathroom. Vinnie screamed and vainly reached out for objects to stop his momentum.

In the next-door flat, 82 year-old Gwen Saunders sat with her cup of tea listening to Radio Australia. It was her favourite program and she never missed it. Annoyed by the muffled screams, she leaned forward and increased the volume.

Her young neighbour was terribly inconsiderate with his late night music and loud television. Stroking her cat she resolved to complain to the authorities if it continued.

Chapter Thirty-eight

Tired of ringing the bell and not being answered, Rachel placed the patisserie box she was carrying in her other hand and tried the door handle. "Vinnie!" She called as the door swung open. "Vinnie, are you there?" She heard nothing.

Feeling a bit like a burglar, she stepped inside and gingerly called again, "Vinnie, it's Rachel."

It was dark so she crossed to a window and spread the curtain. The resultant light was sufficient to illuminate the chaos.

"Oh bugger, Vinnie, I told you I wasn't cleaning."

Stepping deeper into the flat, she put her bags on the kitchen counter. Treading on a broken glass she bent down to pick up the major pieces. Placing the shards next to her bags, Rachel eyed the strewn furniture and began to feel uncomfortable.

"Vinnie?"

Going into the bedroom she was struck by his stale odour. "Yuk!" She whispered to herself. "I've found your problem," she offered loudly, hoping he would answer.

Having completed a search of everywhere else, Rachel arrived at the closed door of Vinnie's bathroom. She knocked.

"Vinnie it's Rachel, I brought some cakes." She knocked louder. Worried that he may be injured she opened the door slightly to allow her voice to carry, "Vinnie."

Straining her ears she could hear the shower dripping but nothing else. She pushed the door open a little further.

"I'll come in," she threatened. There was no response.

Bracing herself, Rachel strode into the bathroom expecting to see something awful, but instead, found only a vacant shower cubicle with a dripping head. Feeling silly she tightened the taps.

Leaving, she turned headlong into Vinnie's lifeless body hanging on the back of the door. Tied by the neck, his face was covered in blood and severely cut. With his mouth partly open, his blank eyes looked directly at her through the gap remaining between half closed lids.

Rachel reeled back in absolute horror and screamed. Willing herself mobility she scrambled into the adjoining room only to come face to face with the smiling evil of Mae Lin. Not expecting her, a terrified Rachel screamed again and again. Emitting a guttural cry Mae Lin brutally knocked her unconscious with a powerful punch to the head.

Walking with his bag now by his side, John closed in on Daniel's neighbourhood. Crossing opposite the Colosseum he could see on the billboard the one-foot high letters advertising the next big event.

Tonight
11: P.M
DANIEL ROBERTS
V
KHAN.

He had been advised of Daniel's occupation and had noted it with surprise. John figured that changing circumstances, the pressures of manhood plus his own long absence, might all have played a part in Daniel's choice. He would find out for certain soon enough.

Turning left at the next corner, John headed toward the graffiti covered walls that marked the beginning of Daniel's suburb.

The small man, who addressed Daniel, was almost completely obscured by the enormous vase of flowers he was carrying.

"Mr Roberts?" The hidden man asked.

"That's me," said Daniel happily throwing open the entrance and stepping aside. "Come on in," he added.

"There's more downstairs," the man puffed as he entered.

Immediately behind him, a troop of similarly burdened helpers followed.

Hit by the scent of so many flowers, Daniel marvelled at the variety and volume being delivered. With the extravagant surprise taking shape, an excited Daniel was unable to keep the smile from his face.

The street before Daniel's apartment was lined with Victorian terraces on one side, and a large brick factory wall on the other. The wall, twelve feet high was covered in urban paintings from various artists that spanned its entire length. Along the footpath next to the wall, a lone skateboarder slapped noisily from the gutter to the pavement and back again as he made his way down the street.

On the other side, a group of youths, gathered in their usual hangout, were laughing and jeering amongst themselves. An occasional breeze swept a singular sheet of yellowed newspaper on a spiralling journey from one side of the road to the other.

On the furthest corner, stood a small second hand television shop with security mesh over the windows. Parked outside, a van with its rear doors open was being used to deliver old sets. A group of three Muslim women dressed in dark hijabs stood on the pavement watching black and white images of a loud Islamic documentary visible through the mesh. One of the women bounced a small boy on her hip.

As John approached, the little boy tumbled his soft toy along the ground toward him. Bending to pick it up, the two were momentarily separated by workmen carrying a large monitor into the shop. In that instant the Arabic journalist on the television ceased his commentary of an Asian story and the camera focused on a group of schoolgirls dancing around another in the background. The tune was unmistakable. The words, shattering: *'This little cow does nothing,'* they sang, *'except lie down each day.'*

John froze. Panicked, his eyes scanned the window for the source, but the show had moved on. His mind was racing ... images that he had suppressed, raced into vivid reality ... his heart quickened as he struggled to calm the rising sickness in his gut. Beads of sweat appeared on his temples and his skin became cold and clammy.

Using all his will power, John brought himself back to the present and the screams of the little boy straining for the toy which he still held. Under intense scrutiny from the women, John awkwardly returned it and moved on.

Shaken and not thinking, he walked into the path of the skateboarder who had just crossed the street. Flipping his board into his hands the rider struggled to hold his feet and yelled obscenities.

"Fucking dickhead! Why don't you look where you're going? Stupid wanker."

Embarrassed, John accepted the abuse and kept going.

Their interest aroused by the disturbance, the idle youths watched his approach.

A larger group by night, these boys comprised the nucleus of a street gang known as "Hornets" and were identified by the colour red. Ranging in age from seventeen to twenty-five they were typical of the area: lost in an endless cycle of limited opportunity, frustration and anger. Their bond was based on unity, mob rule, and territorial control. Outsiders were not welcome.

One by one their eyes turned to the lone man walking along their street. Armed with a baseball bat, a youth began banging it on the pavement, in time with John's footsteps.

Acutely aware of trouble, John maintained his eye line straight ahead. Two youths jumped out and walked with him. Several followed behind, and soon others joined in.

A large boy with a tattoo on his neck and spiked hair spoke first, "Where are you fucking going?"

John ignored him.

"Looks like the poofter's deaf," said a voice from behind. The comment was followed by derisive laughter. John was pushed in the back, "You deaf poof?"

Several more youths swung ahead to block his path and John was forced to a standstill. Struggling with the whole event, he tried reason, "Look boys I don't want any trouble."

"Trouble?" Laughed the large youth pushing John even harder. "You're no fucking trouble mate."

The boy with the baseball bat forced his way to the front and held it over his shoulders. The image disturbed John immensely and the colour drained from his face.

"What's in the bag gay boy?"

"Shit. I think he's going to piss himself."

They laughed and grabbed at the bag trying to pull it from John's grip, but he held firm.

Annoyed by the resistance the large boy lost patience, "Fuck this!"

With a howling scream the bat descended. John ducked the swinging blow and dropped to his knees with his arm held above his head for protection.

In that instant a loud siren announced the timely arrival of the police. As the cruising patrol car pulled over, the panicked youths ran off in all directions. John still holding his bag remained on one knee as he came to terms with his emotions.

Sergeant Joe Pearson spoke from his open window, "Are you alright?"

Slowly John nodded. Getting to his feet he began to walk as the car followed. Pearson watched intently. Years on the force had his mind searching to explain a sudden instinct for suspicion.

"Can we give you a lift?"

"No. No thanks, I'm only going a little way."

"Sure you're alright?"

John looked across and tried to smile, "Yeah I'm good. Thanks."

The police car left and John rounded the corner toward Daniel's.

Rachel slowly came to. Her right eye was swollen and cut. She tried to move but she couldn't. Bent over Vinnie's kitchen table, her feet were tied to the legs on the long side and her hands were tied to the others.

Hurting and uncomfortable, her eyes focused on the vaguely familiar woman calmly looking straight at her. Mae Lin's manner was maternal.

"Hello dear."

"Who? Who are you?" Rachel began to struggle but couldn't budge. "Let me go!"

Now, like one of the girls, Mae Lin confided in her, "He wasn't much to look at was he?"

Rachel was confused.

"Vinnie," Mae Lin reminded, raising her eyes in mock judgement.

Suddenly Rachel remembered, "Oh my God, Vinnie. You killed Vinnie."

Mae Lin moved in very close and spoke softly, "Shh ... don't cry baby its alright ... It's not like losing a brother."

Mae Lin began to stroke Rachel's hair. Rachel was petrified and started to cry, "But why? Please. I haven't done anything."

"No of course you haven't ... shh." Mae Lin continued to stroke Rachel's hair until a sudden thought came over her and she held up the cakes from the bakery.

"They're very nice," she commented biting into one. Holding up her free hand Mae Lin giggled mischievously and unfurled Rachel's cut panties.

"These are ruined though," she said.

Rachel struggled momentarily to understand what she was talking about, then realised. Suddenly she was more frightened than she'd ever been in her life.

"Why?" She sobbed.

Without warning, Tobacqui's large hand grabbed Rachel's hair and violently pulled her head back from behind. Mae Lin giggled, and with her eyebrows raised, nodded her head at Rachel's worst nightmare.

Mae Lin moved to within inches of Rachel's immobile head and with cold evil oozing from her every pore, slowly and deliberately forced the remainder of the cake into her mouth. Feeling the preliminary signs of violation, Rachel's resultant scream was muted.

Terror turned to agony as the table violently jolted forward with her rape.

Mae Lin giggled playfully.

Chapter Thirty-nine

Daniel and John stood in the doorway looking at each other for the first time in eight years.

Daniel was immediately tearful, "Oh shit." The two men embraced in a hug that lasted for a long time.

"Jesus! I can't believe it. It's true! You're back."

John smiled and looked Daniel up and down, "It's damn good to see you Daniel. You've grown. And strong too."

Both men wiped away tears at the same time and smiled at their mutual reaction.

"I thought ..." admitted Daniel.

"That's ok," John said stopping him, "So did I."

Daniel picked up John's bag and led him in to see the flowers. Bunches and bunches of them created a wall of colour that covered the length of the room. John stood suitably impressed, "Wow!" He said.

Daniel was still smiling, "Pretty awesome aren't they?"

"Great, they look great. Thanks Daniel."

"Hey I did nothing. You're the one who made the phone calls. I'm sorry I'm going to miss the look on her face when she walks in."

John softened considerably with talk of Rachel, "She doesn't know?"

Daniel laughed over his reaction, "Not a clue John. Don't worry. Right now, Vinnie's probably getting her to make curtains."

John's eyes betrayed his yearning, "How is she Daniel? How's my Rache?"

Daniel again became tearful as his thoughts went to his sister, "Not once John, not ever, did she doubt this day would come ... You two are something else."

John became nervous, "How long have I got?"

"Not long, it's nearly twelve. But she's never on time for anything. Would you like some barbecue shapes?"

John laughed, "Pass. How's Edward?"

"You heard about Dad?"

"I'm sorry, yeah. They told me yesterday. How is he?"

"Not good. But he's getting better everyday."

"Nobody caught?"

Daniel shook his head, "Dad's the only one who knows who it was. There's the latest police drawing on my dresser of some bastard ... but it didn't help."

He checked his watch, "Okay five minutes. I'll see you tonight after the fight. Oh, did you know I ..."

John nodded, "I did. And I've seen your name on a billboard. Should I worry?"

"Nah! Anyway this is my last night. Right, I'm off."

They hugged and Daniel grinned, "I can come home can't I?"

John ruffled his hair. "You better."

"Keys are on the fruit bowl, beers are in the fridge." Daniel pointed to each room as he spoke, "Bathroom, Rache's room, my room. Good luck."

Shaking hands, Daniel added, "My castle is your castle."

"Thanks Daniel."

After the door closed John turned, smiled again at all the flowers and let out an expectant sigh.

Gwen Saunders stood in her open doorway with her cat in her arms. Nervously she stroked it and waited for news.

Rachel's inert body remained tied to Vinnie's table. A male hand gently disturbed her hair and felt her pulse.

A radio transmission broke the silence. "Unit two six, please respond."

A policeman lifted his radio, "This is unit two six. We need an ambulance. Code one."

Chapter Forty

The sun's outline of the window pattern slowly increased its momentum as it travelled inexorably upwards toward the painting on Daniel's wall. Sitting at the kitchen table, John checked his watch one more time as the fridge motor kicked in to break the silence with its hum. Rachel was now several hours late, and for John, each additional moment became increasingly difficult.

Finally stirred by noises approaching the door, John leapt up to quickly run his fingers through his hair and straighten his clothing. Waiting for the door to open, he held his breath under the weight of anticipation.

There was a loud knock.

Remembering Rachel's habit of losing her keys, he smiled, braced himself and opened the door.

Constable Feggerty stood in front of Sergeant Pearson and spoke first.

"Mister Roberts?"

John took a moment to get over his disappointment. "No," he said. Recognising Pearson from the morning he added, "Is everything alright?"

Feggerty ignored the question and pressed ahead, "Do you know where we can reach him?"

John was instantly concerned for Daniel, "Yes … actually no, not really. Look what's this about? I'm engaged to his sister, can I help?"

"Miss Rachel Roberts?" Asked Feggerty latching on to the lead.

"Yes, she'll be home soon." Suddenly the penny dropped and John lost all momentum as his heart skipped several beats. His eyes followed the constable's head turn toward his sergeant.

Pearson responded and moved forward, "You'd better come with us."

In the hospital corridor outside Rachel's room, John, was met by a nurse and a policewoman.

"This is Mr Landau, Miss Roberts' fiancé," said Pearson.

The two women looked him up and down. The nurse smiled. "Hello," she offered warmly.

"Is your name John?" The policewoman asked.

"Yes."

"She kept saying your name. 'John' and 'a woman'. Does that mean anything?"

Pearson watched John attentively, unable to shake his nagging suspicion. There was something about the man in front of him that he couldn't yet place.

John shook his head as his eyes darted back and forth between Pearson the nurse and the policewoman. The nurse, sensing his discomfort took him by the arm.

"Would you like to see her?" She asked.

John shuddered in his breath and unable to speak clearly, nodded. Quietly the nurse led him inside.

Standing on the threshold of the semi dark room his eyes instantly found Rachel. She was very still. Her hair fell over the pillow and in the florescent light she looked pale. His heart pounded.

Still holding his arm the nurse held him back and spoke gently. "Now, John, you understand what's happened, don't you?" He nodded. "Rachel was very distraught and has been heavily sedated. If you do speak to her, it is crucial that you don't quiz her. This is very important. She will tell you when she's ready and in her own way."

John's eyes hadn't left Rachel since he entered the room. A tear slowly rolled down his left cheek. The nurse, mindful of the moment reached into her pocket and placed some tissues in his hand. Squeezing them in she added, "Just keep loving her John, that's what she needs. You can sit with her if you like."

"Can she hear me?" He whispered.

"Maybe," she added reassuringly. "There's a chair on the other side."

Letting him go, the nurse left.

Rachel's eye was very swollen and the cut underneath was held closed by a piece of tape. Her wrists were badly bruised, her bottom lip was split and her smeared makeup was evidence of her crying.

For eight years John's memory of Rachel had kept him going ... her smile, her giggle, the way she screwed up her nose ... her softness ... the sweetness of her breath. It had been she that had saved him from the most unimaginable horrors ... through all he had endured, seeing her again had been his only longing.

Sitting by her side, she was the most beautiful creature he could ever imagine. Gently placing his hand on hers, he reached over and kissed her forehead. Running his lips across her, he smelled her hair, closed his eyes and bathed in the moment of them being together at last.

"Oh I've missed you," he whispered, "My beautiful, beautiful Rachel. I love you so much."

Hours passed as he sat and watched her. Never letting go of her hand. Never taking his eyes from her.

Suddenly her fingers came to life in his. He allowed them to run over his hand. Seeing her lips part John edged closer in to hear her whisper.

"Is it really you?" She held his hand, "I knew you'd come back."

"Rache?"

Rachel's eyes opened but she was very groggy.

"John?"

He kissed her hand gently, "I'm here ..."

Rachel turned her face toward his and tried to concentrate, "It is you, isn't it?"

"Yes sweetheart it's me. I'm here ... I love you."

Reaching out Rachel touched his face.

"Kiss me," she said.

He bent down and tenderly kissed her cheek. She held him to her as tears ran down her face.

"Oh I missed you. I was so worried."

"How are you feeling?"

She began crying, "I'm so sorry ... I'm so sorry ... I didn't mean for this to happen ... I'm sorry." She stumbled over her words and began to sob, "It was a woman John ... a woman ..." Rachel was weak and struggled to stay focused.

"Hush now, we're together, that's all that matters. Rest."

She closed her eyes.

"We've got all the time we need," he whispered.

Moments later, a team of medical people arrived with bustling intent and purpose. John stood up still holding onto Rachel's hand. The nurse approached and took his arm. "You'll have to go now," she confided.

Uncomfortable with the idea of leaving, his eyes shifted between the unfolding activity and the nurse, "I'd like to wait if that's alright," he said.

The nurse took Rachel's hand away and led John to the side of the room as the team began their preparation. "I would advise you to go home, John, and come back later. There are certain things we have to do ... after which she'll need rest."

Aware of his dilemma she was sympathetic and tried to think of how to occupy him. "Does her family know?" She asked.

John looked over at the bed still reluctant to let Rachel out of his sight. "Um, I'm not sure. No, Daniel is out. Her father is ..."

"That might be a job to keep you busy then?" She suggested.

Placing her hand on his shoulder she added, "Go on, she won't want you to see her like this."

The curtains closed and John was left outside.

By the time he returned to Daniel's, it was quite late. Placing the keys in the fruit bowl he looked at the mass of flowers and wondered what to do next. He checked the time. It was 10:20 p.m. Sighing heavily, he fetched a beer from the fridge.

Chapter Forty-one

The size of the Colosseum's Saturday night crowd was staggering. Outside in the corridors, lines of people crushed together to surge like ants in search of amenities or friends. Music from the stage, thumped so loudly that Daniel could feel the vibration through his feet.

Waiting for almost an hour, Daniel couldn't believe Vinnie was so late. Leaving yet another voice message, he pocketed his phone, searched the crowd one last time and disappointed, moved off to prepare for his fight.

Not really wanting a beer, John nevertheless sipped it occasionally as he paced. It didn't help. Deciding to clean up, he pushed open the door to the bathroom and approached the basin. Looking at himself in the mirror he wondered if the nightmare that his life had become would ever stop.

Running his hands though the cold water, he lent down to splash his face and enjoyed the refreshing sensation. Behind him, the door closed slowly under its own weight. Stuck on the back of the door was the poster publicising the 'Fight of the

Century'. John grabbed a towel and again stood in the mirror as he wiped his face.

Slowly his eyes focused on the poster. Something about it caught his eye. Suddenly he stopped drying and spun around. Moving swiftly to the door, his eye's snapped to the scar extending from Khan's left armpit. His face hardened and his mind was immediately alert. Throwing the towel away, John wrenched open the door and raced to Daniel's bedroom. At the dresser he frantically threw objects out of his way until he found the drawing. It had been folded. Opening it quickly, John's whole body shivered with the instant recognition of Mae Lin. Now he understood.

Quickly he checked his watch: 10:40 p.m. Realising that Daniel was in dire peril he raced from the apartment as fast as he could run.

John's feet hit the pavement with both speed and purpose. As he weaved in and out of obstacles he thought about Rachel, her dad and her brother. The darkness had followed him home and his family were threatened ... he was the reason for their suffering and it was up to him to make it right. He could feel his rage building. Subconsciously, he relaxed his muscles and the familiar rise of intense calm steeled his emotions. He was the perfect warrior ... this was personal, and God help anybody that got in his way.

Charging round the next street corner, John ran headlong into the Hornets.

Now a much larger group, the majority were gathered outside the terraces watching streetcars and enjoying the rev of their engines. To avoid delay, John slowed to a brisk walk and carefully crossed the street as a car began burning rubber. The squeal of tyres, the loud motor and the approving roar from the onlookers, helped to keep him from being noticed.

Ahead and opposite the television repair shop however, there were others. John recognised them as the youths from the morning. Although they numbered about a dozen he was unable to change course and would have to pass through.

Victory in a street fight usually went to the one who was prepared to reach extremes first. Smart fighters knew when they were beaten before that point arrived. Survival on the street was a stronger motivation than winning. Since confrontation was inevitable, John was prepared to up the ante to a level of violence they would never forget. This time, the man they encountered would be vastly different from the one they expected.

"Well look what we have here," said the spiky haired youth.

Incapable of seeing the danger, his friends spread to block John's path. Confident of their number one solidly built young man put his hand on John's chest, "Where do think you're goi …" Before he could finish, John immediately grabbed his wrist and broke it. With effortless power he spun the boy around and splintered his kneecap with his foot. Then, in a blur of arm movement, struck him so powerfully, his eye-socket collapsed.

Shocked by the severity and speed, the baseball bat was instinctively raised, but before any meaningful attack could be launched John had snapped it cleanly into two pieces. He followed with a flat hand to the solar plexus that pile-drove its owner backwards into his friends. From behind, two youths rushed in to sneak an advantage. Alert, John spun into their assault with crushing force, shattering a collarbone on impact and breaking a jaw. Intent on making a statement he followed with a combination of punches that broke a nose and cheekbone sending sprays of blood through the air. Moving in his intended direction John quickly targeted two more. With unerring accuracy he fractured ribs with his fists and pummelled soft tissue, before sending them unconscious to the floor with his feet. His balanced landing brought him deliberately and abruptly face to face with 'spiky hair'.

John, not even puffing, stared calmly into the boy's shock at having lost half his gang members in the blink of an eye. Lashing out, more from fear than with purpose, he reached for John's torso with his arms and tried to take hold. With frightening speed John swung his own arms inside and up and broke both limbs with ease. Grabbing the boy by the throat, John held him up to abate the screams. Suddenly, none of his friends wanted in.

John's eyes were like raging fire. "Tell them to back off," he ordered.

Spiky hair was petrified. "Let him be," he whimpered.

Those left standing were more than happy to oblige. John, free to continue, immediately resumed running.

Chapter Forty-two

The war drums were playing and Daniel stood in the tunnel waiting to be introduced. Above him laser beams threw creative patterns across the arena through theatrical smoke. The Colosseum was packed and the crowd was buzzing. Redheaded Reg, parked his large frame outside the windows and passed the word to his bookies that the house would take no further bets.

The drums built to a crescendo and stopped. The scan lights dipped and the lasers ceased their activity. The anticipation was electric. Daniel quickly looked up to see Vinnie's vacant seat. He was concerned. In the adjacent chair, Mae Lin smiled sweetly and looked on.

"Ladies and gentlemen," boomed the voice of the announcer in his best 'fight speak'. "Welcome to tonight's Main Card Event. The Colosseum proudly presents the much awaited, the much anticipated, Fight-of-the-Century."

The crowd roared in unison.

"In the Southern Pen. Victorious in all twenty-seven professional bouts here at the Colosseum. Never defeated, ladies and gentlemen. Put your hands together for the destructive, the daunting, the dancing dynamo ... Daniel 'Danny Boy' Roberts!"

The spotlight snapped on to illuminate Daniel who raised his hand to acknowledge the applause and stepped into the arena.

The announcer continued, "In the Northern Pen. A sensational powerhouse with already 24 wins. All by knockout and also undefeated ladies and gentlemen. Give a big Colosseum welcome to the Cantankerous King of Carnage. Khan!"

The other spotlight snapped on and Khan walked in to the Arena to stand with his eyes fixed on Daniel. The crowd went into thunderous applause.

The scan lights dipped up and down for the final time and the arena was bathed in light. The chant went up. 'Fight, fight, fight'.

The two men slowly approached each other and adopted their fighting crouch. The crowd began screaming their partisan support.

John in full flight, converged on an intersection congested with nightlife and traffic. He wove his way through pedestrians and without stopping raced across the busy street. Amidst blaring horns and loud cursing, cars swerved to avoid him. Unable to take evasive action, one screeched to a halt and was immediately rear-ended by another behind it. The offending vehicle was a police car and the driver was Sergeant Joe Pearson.

"Shit!" He screamed, and then spotted John, "Hey you, stop."

John ignored him and ran on. Pearson sounded his siren but to no avail. Infuriated, the policeman rammed his gearbox into reverse and began extricating his car from the other, angrily intent on pursuit.

Khan landed a powerful blow and Daniel reeled back managing to cover his withdrawal with a series of counter punches.

Again they circled, summing each other up. Daniel launched an assault using a combination of kicks … each was blocked but a follow up body punch got through, then another, and another and Khan was driven back. Daniel moved in to take advantage but Khan countered with a massive back-hander. The crowd gasped in response. Khan launched another attack and Daniel again moved backwards covering each blow as it arrived. Hits from both fighters connected during the exchange, and though Khan was driving, Daniel's form was strong. The speed had picked up. The two were evenly matched and the crowd loved it.

In the manager's section, Mae Lin remained calm as those around her were collectively caught up in the excitement. A thin line of perspiration had formed on the top of her lip.

Daniel suddenly launched a ferocious kick to Khan's chest. He followed quickly with a rapid succession of very fast punches to the same region. Khan was stunned by the severity of the attack and forced back. Daniel was relentless and worked hard as his dripping sweat made his torso glisten. A beautiful combination with feet and hands culminated in a superlative spinning high kick that connected, and Khan fell.

The crowd immediately rose to their feet.

The force of the blow opened a large cut on Khan's cheek. Although down, he was definitely not out. Aware and cautious, Daniel carefully circled. Unseen, Khan lowered his mouth to suck in sand then sprang to his feet. Again the two men measured up.

Reaching the Colosseum, John ran in. Hearing the sound of the audience rise and fall, he found his way to the entrance turnstiles where a bouncer lifted his hand to stop him.

"Sorry mate. Full house. You can't come in."

John could now see portions of the crowd and parts of the arena. The crowd volume rose again. His manner was short.

"How do I get to the fighters?" He asked.

The bouncer decided to be smart. "Depends whose asking," he answered.

John didn't have time to play games and flexed every muscle in his body. Holding a look that would peel paint, John spat his response through clenched teeth.

"I fucking am."

The bouncer paled visibly and pointed, "The fighter's entrance is along there, Sir ... but ..."

John instantly ran off in the direction given. The bouncer, more confident with space between them yelled after him, "You can't go in there."

Cursing, he picked up his two way and spoke, "Hey Bruno, there's some nut on his way to see you."

Locked in battle the fighters came together in a flurry of blows. Khan lashing out with his greater reach, grabbed Daniel by the back of the neck. Interlocking their outstretched arms the two became engaged in a battle of strength. With superior power, Khan slowly dragged his opponent in. As their foreheads touched he expelled a stream of sand into Daniel's left eye.

Taken by surprise, Daniel immediately used his feet to bring Khan down and regroup. Withdrawing backwards he tried desperately to clear his sight. The crowd sensed the sudden change. Eager to capitalise, Khan leapt to his feet and charged.

Blind in one eye Daniel blocked for his life, but his defence missed his sight. Khan landed two powerhouse punches and Daniel reeled back. Sensing victory, the ugly aggressor followed with a sickening left right left combination and Daniel, hit hard, went down. Desperate to stay up he tumbled quickly to the side and back to his feet. Anticipating the manoeuvre Khan struck him with a brutal blow to his blind side. The force of the punch sent a stream of blood across the wall of glass.

Shaken and on all fours Daniel knew he was lost. Finding Khan's approach in his good eye, Daniel raised his hand in submission. Ignoring him, Khan kicked viciously breaking the extended arm and propelling Daniel along the floor of the arena. The crowd immediately stood and roared their disapproval.

Silently Mae Lin's face bore a girlish grin.

John finally made the entrance to the Fighter's Preparation Room but the attending Bruno moved into his path. Both men heard the severity of the crowd reaction.

A big man, Bruno stood firm, "You can't ..."

Realising he had very little time John grabbed the man's throat with the force of steel and stopped him speaking.

"Let me in NOW!"

Back at the entrance turnstiles, the previous bouncer pointed happily toward the fighter's door for Pearson and Constable Feggerty. They ran off in pursuit of John.

Another kick and Daniel barely conscious felt his ribs break. Seriously injured, he lay inert and defenceless. Hovering over him, Khan lifted his head by his hair and looked to Mae Lin. She squealed with delight. The crowd were quiet, this was not what they wanted to see. Khan landed a sickening blow that was amplified around the Colosseum.

Outside the Fighter's Preparation Room the police, and the embarrassed Bruno, waited for his supervisor to unlock the entrance. Bursting inside they discovered an unconscious Room Manager splayed across chairs still holding the clipboard to his chest. Pearson arrived at the door that led to the tunnel. Hitting it with his shoulder the door refused to budge.

Breathing heavily and annoyed, the sergeant yelled to the others, "Where does this go?"

"The arena. Shit he's in the arena," Alarmed the supervisor spoke into his mouthpiece.

"Control. Somebody's in the arena ..." Pearson listened and tried to grasp the one sided conversation. "No ..." the bouncer continued "... we can't, we'll have to go through the other end."

Pearson had heard enough. Pointing, he addressed Feggerty, "Feggerty go with him to the control room and wait for my instruction." Then to Bruno, "You, take me to this other entrance, and quick."

The crowd was now in total shock and some were screaming. Khan lifted Daniel's head and readied for the final blow.

Suddenly the door to the Southern Pen was kicked in.

John stood in the arena and yelled, "Tobacqui Khan!"

Khan immediately swung his head as John addressed him in Mandarin.

"Murderer of shackled men," John continued and hit his chest with his fist, "Face me."

The giant momentarily struggled to recognise the man before him.

"I am Gecko! Is it not me you want?" John said.

Khan let Daniel's head go as John walked calmly and deliberately into the centre of the ring. He removed his shirt and the crowd responded to the scars on his chest and back.

This was a John few had seen. Risso had. And Masterson suspected it. Very few had survived it. This was his dark side.

John continued to bait Tobacqui as he waved him forward, "Come let me see the man without his hammer."

Khan rose and removed his mask. He looked to Mae Lin whose eyes narrowed in wariness and calculation.

Following his gaze John saw her. Pointing an accusing finger he yelled in English, "You will be next whore of Xiang."

Those around Mae Lin turned their heads toward her in an effort to fathom what was happening.

Khan rushed at John who flexed to meet his charge with a guttural scream and awesome power. Khan was hit dead centre of his mass and his entire body rocked. John followed with blinding speed and delivered a series of bone crunching missiles that moved Khan in a way no one thought humanly possible.

The crowd gasped collectively at what they were seeing.

After the onslaught Khan's eyes showed a hint of panic. John calm and deliberate, moved into his ready stance.

Through the viewing windows of the long tunnel Pearson observed what he was up against. The crowd was enormous. Summing up the situation he pulled his radio, "Unit one twelve, requesting back-up."

Again Khan attacked and again John responded with force. Dropping momentarily he screamed again and speared two fingers under the left rib cage into Khan. He immediately spun and kicked the giant warrior with such force that he slammed into the wall of the arena.

Sergeant Pearson was busy on his radio, "Feggerty when I go in, tell them to announce that nobody is to move. Tell management we need their men for control. We don't want a riot. Understand?"

"Roger Sarge."

Khan wheeled around and looked down as blood began to flow from his wound. John readied.

Khan attacked with all he had ... with both feet and hands he unleashed everything. John met it all with enormous speed and poise. Again he dropped momentarily and speared two fingers under the right rib cage. Spinning differently and majestically he despatched Khan with another powerful kick. Again he crashed into the wall.

Pearson watched in complete amazement. He had never seen anything like it. Ever!

John's menacing eyes were cold and intense. Khan observed the second wound and looked up to Mae Lin. Standing, she returned the look and left.

This time, John launched his own attack. He was brutal ... clinical ... the speakers picked up the sound of breaking bones as he systematically forced the destruction of his foe. It culminated with a barrage of body blows that left Khan physically incapable of further response.

Pressed against the glass wall, Tobacqui waited knowingly as John closed in with his eyes focused, and unforgiving. "That, was for my comrades," he said, "This, is for Rachel."

He launched a double fisted, thrusting uppercut that caved in Khan's upper teeth and pushed his nose bone into his brain with fatal results.

Khan died instantly.

Chapter Forty-three

After witnessing the carnage, the crowd struggled to understand what was going on. Caught in limbo they waited for the lights to dip or the music to begin ... craving anything that would signal it was all part of a regular performance. When nothing came, they nervously asked questions amongst themselves.

Kneeling at Daniel's side John gently lifted his head. Seeing his friend in such a mess was disturbing.

"Daniel, Daniel," he whispered.

Slowly Daniel's eyes opened and he motioned to speak but the volume was too weak.

Called in from other posts within the Colosseum, bouncers appeared from everywhere and scurried to cover the exits. Over the loud speaker the announcer addressed the crowd in his normal voice.

"Ladies and Gentlemen the management and the Police Department request you remain in your seats. I repeat, please remain in your seats."

In an effort to hear, John placed his head closer to Daniel.

With difficulty Daniel whispered, "I'm okay John ... did I win?"

This was a good sign and pleasing, John smiled and brushed Daniel's cheek. "You won," he said gently.

Several screams from the crowd warned of a change to the situation. Pearson had entered the arena with his gun drawn and aimed at John.

Clearly, the sergeant yelled his instruction, "Put your hands behind your head and move away."

John carefully placed Daniel's head on the ground and slowly stood to face Pearson and his weapon.

With John firmly in his sights the sergeant waved him away from Daniel as he spoke into his radio. "Unit one twelve. We need two ambulances and paramedics at the Colosseum's main arena. Code one."

The radio sparked back, "Roger one twelve."

The sergeant holstered his radio and addressed John. "I knew there was something about you. What the fuck are you, you son of a bitch?"

John quickly assessed. Seeing the war ribbons on Pearson's chest. He assumed his rank.

Speaking clearly John responded with a loud voice and complete authority. "I am Army Major John Landau. A Special Air Service Operative attached to Force Delta."

"What the fuck?"

"A Coalition Counter Terrorist Unit with United Nations Sanctions. I carry level one immunity and would appreciate you lower your weapon Sergeant."

The sergeant was incredulous, "What?"

John would not accept any other option, "There is no time for 'what'. You are wearing Vietnam ribbons and an Infantry Combat Badge."

"What of it?" Pearson asked.

"Think!" John requested, "Weigh it up Sergeant. Tap the memory. Something about me you said. Well, I hunt bad people."

Suddenly Pearson twigged, this was exactly the suspicion he couldn't place, "Have you got ID?"

John reached into his back pocket and threw his wallet. The policeman caught it and read.

The radio sputtered, "Unit one twelve. Cavalry's here Joe what do you need?"

Pearson grabbed at his pressel switch and yelled down to the radio on his hip, "Hang on Mike."

Constable Feggerty arrived in the arena for support. Pearson waved at him to stand at a distance then motioned his weapon at John, "Go on."

"I'm not finished here, there is another one and she will get away."

"She?"

"Asian, (5'6"), black pants, white top. Female and very dangerous."

Pearson's mind was racing to join all the dots, "A woman?"

"Ring any bells?"

Suddenly they heard the report of shots. The two policemen looked at each other. Quickly Pearson pocketed the wallet and lifted his radio.

"Mike?" He called.

Anxiously they waited for a reply but nothing happened. "Unit one seven this is one twelve come in, over". Nothing.

John was alarmed at the new development and his body language portrayed his concern. Sergeant Pearson was equally worried. "I'm sorry but you need to decide 'now' Sergeant," called John.

Pearson nodded and lowered his weapon. John immediately went to his side.

"Come on," he said, "We don't have much time." Turning to Feggerty he issued firm instruction.

"You, stay with him," John pointed to Daniel and Pearson confirmed his support for the request with a curt nod.

Picking up his shirt, John ran out the Southern Pen doorway and Pearson followed.

Racing down the side of the Colosseum they came to the rear of the building and a police car with its lights still spinning.

Two policemen lay on the ground dead and some distance apart. The driver's window had a bullet hole in it.

"Holy shit!" Pearson ran to his friend, "Mike?"

Speaking into his radio he frantically searched for a pulse. "Unit one twelve, Officers down. Repeat Officers down. Shots fired. I repeat shots fired. I need an ambulance and immediate back up ... At the Colosseum fight club ... I need the DDO and attendance by SPG."

Pearson looked to John for confirmation as he continued, "Suspect is Asian female, five six, wearing dark pants and white top. Last seen in vicinity, armed and dangerous."

John nodded as he felt for a pulse on the other policeman.

"Roger one twelve. Units despatched. DDO Leslie assigned. ETA State Protection Group three minutes."

Pearson called out, "Anything?" John shook his head, "His throat's been cut."

The sergeant checked his friend. "Mike's been shot," then noted his empty holster, "And his side arm's missing."

John rolled the other policeman over and called out, "Is your issue a Glock?"

Pearson responded, "Glock 22."

"I found it."

Pearson came over and winced at the gaping wound on his fellow officer's throat. Kneeling, he identified the gun, "That's ours. At least she's not armed."

John corrected him, "You're forgetting the knife." Quickly he began searching the outside of the building.

Pearson moved to the car and switched off the lights. Watching John he picked up the car's radio handset and called in Central.

"Central," said a female voice.

"Margaret this is Joe Pearson can you patch me through to the Comm. Centre."

John found the security door leading back into the building. He pushed it. It tried to move but something blocked its progress. He pushed harder.

The radio responded with a different voice, "Go ahead one twelve."

As the door slowly opened it revealed a smear of blood on the floor.

Pearson held onto John's ID, "I need an immediate check run on an ADF Army Major John Landau. I spell, Lima, alpha, November, delta, alpha, uniform. Serial number five, five seven, two six seven."

"Roger one twelve."

On the other side of the door a bouncer lay dead in a pool of blood. His throat had also been cut. Pearson joined John as he felt for a pulse. They heard the approach of distant sirens.

"Dead?"

John nodded and stood up with his senses alight. "And the wrong side of the door," he added. His eyes searched the dim corridor that led to the bowels of the building. Suddenly he whispered, "She's still here."

He took several steps deeper into the corridor and listened.

Pearson still by the door, was distracted by the radio, "Unit one twelve, Comm. Centre." Quickly he rushed out to take the call.

John was alone. The increasing wail of approaching sirens permeated from all directions. Stepping further in, his heart raced and his skin went cold and clammy. The sirens blended into voices and suddenly he was being beaten.

Over girl's laughter he heard the voices, *"This little cow eats grass ..."*

Again and again he felt the knife pierce his skin and heard the tormenting giggle. Cowering and cringing ... desperate to protect himself from yet another beating ... he was screaming. The loud sirens were almost upon them. Covered in perspiration John could smell his own loathing.

"Unit one twelve," said Pearson.

"Confirm your Major. He's a big one. Government clearance: Level one."

"Roger. Thanks," he replaced the handset.

Outside the sirens had arrived. A police helicopter hovered noisily and flashed it's light over the scene. Sergeant Pearson alighted from the vehicle and began to move toward the action. His two-way sprang to life.

"Pearson this is Leslie, where are you?"

Grabbing his radio the sergeant responded, "Side alley toward the rear. With the vehicle sir."

"Got you."

At that instant, seven police cars and two ambulances screamed around the corner. Two cars screeched their way across the outside street to control traffic, and the remainder sped under the vacant track of the monorail to pull up in the alley with sirens blaring and lights blazing. Both marked and unmarked ... their sirens were silenced as they drew to a halt.

Around the front of the Colosseum more police cars and ambulances pulled up and were joined by the black mobile transport vehicle of SPG.

As soon as the truck came to a stop the back doors flew open and SPG officers dressed in dark flak jackets and armed with assault weapons immediately ran to positions of ready response. In moments, the whole area was under police control.

Captain Leslie, dressed in plain clothes, rapidly approached Pearson as the two converged. Paramedics sped past both men to attend the bodies.

Leslie screamed instructions to a subordinate while on the move, "All exits go."

Rounding on Pearson he immediately wanted to be filled in, "What have you got?" He asked.

"Two down in the main arena. One dead, the other is serious. Constable Feggerty is in attendance. Mike and Lomas were found here. Gunshot and cut throat. And there's a bouncer down behind the door, also with a cut throat."

Leslie nodded, "Suspect?"

"Believe terrorist or similar. Asian female. We think she may still be in the building."

"We? Who's we?" Asked the captain.

"Myself and Major Landau." The sergeant looked around and remembered where he left John. Suddenly he cursed, "Shit!"

Having followed his instincts, John had silently progressed up several flights of stairs and found himself midway along a lit narrow corridor with a single door at the end.

Standing stock still, he waited and listened. In the silence beyond the door he heard the faint sound of jingling metal.

Stealthily he removed the single light globe and edged toward the door.

On the other side was a large expanse that covered the rear of the building and formed a substantial portion of the Colosseum's third storey.

Used for storage in parts, one side, furthest from the windows, held rows of lightweight metal shelving. Large industrial mops and broom heads sat alongside a large bin of heavy hardwood handles. The shelves were stacked with cleansers, myriads of assorted disinfectants and bottles of commercial bleach.

In the centre of the room were signs of recent renovations. Some floor to ceiling glass panels had been installed as dividers to future offices and plastic sheeting hung from the roof where spray painting had taken place. Central to the work in progress, a large wheeled trolley packed with builder's tools and paraphernalia stood idle in the middle.

Huge panelled windows running the length of the room offered just the faintest illumination from the night. The spinning red and blue lights of the vehicles below danced a faint pattern along their bottom.

The door from the corridor was shadowed. It was opened and quickly shut. The room was quiet. John silently waited in the darkness with his back pressed against the adjoining wall. The silence was briefly broken by the giggle of a little girl.

With every muscle on high alert, John knew the nightmare would have to end. Reaching down to the door's handle, he turned the lock.

Chapter Forty-four

Above the Colosseum's fifth floor, an SPG team burst onto the roof. Efficiently fanning out toward the vents and air conditioning motors, the group went into cover and movement as they scoured for an aggressor in hiding. Heavily armed and equipped with night vision, they were uncertain of the level of threat but with two policemen down, nothing was left to chance.

Joining the police chopper, an open door SPG helicopter circled with an aerial marksman.

Slowly John moved through the rows of shelving. Carefully he stopped, listened and then proceeded. It was dark. The silence was deafening.

The soft metallic jingling again drew his attention. It continued rhythmically. Moving toward the sound, the volume grew louder but he couldn't make out the source. Straining his senses he knew he was close to something.

The helicopter outside passed the building. The eerie effect of its light through the windows reflected off the floor and bounced scattered shafts of brilliance about the room.

In the brief moment of light John saw the cause of the jingling. Dog tags hanging on a chain were being blown by a gentle wind. They were Risso's.

Suddenly he felt her presence. Lurching backwards he caught the flash of her blade as it cut a shallow line across his chest.

Emitting a loud guttural screech that shattered the silence, Mae Lin pursued him like a wild animal as he reeled back trying to regain his balance.

Her attack was a blur ... relentless and unforgiving. Slashing wildly she delivered kicks and blows as John slipped and tripped his way backwards over unseen obstructions while anxiously avoiding the knife.

Coming to the edge of the roof, the SPG team leader looked down at the street on the west side of the Colosseum. Activating his mouthpiece he spoke to his commander as the chopper swooped overhead.

"Alpha team, Captain. Nothing here."

Screaming loudly Mae Lin connected with a powerful kick that drove John through a sheet of glass. Shattering on impact, several small shards pierced his skin. Demonic in her pursuit, Mae Lin slashed the air in wild sweeps that missed her target by the smallest of margins. Using his feet John took her legs from under her. As she rolled to regain her ground, John snapped upright in readiness of her next assault. It was delivered in a split second.

Furiously he blocked blow after blow as she tried desperately to cut him. Failing at every turn to cause serious damage Mae Lin was suddenly lifted from the ground by the force of a body kick that propelled her in stunned amazement through a glass panel of her own.

Leaping to her feet the two combatants faced off. Mae Lin was cut and small patches of blood seeped into her white top. Driving forward, she spun into a high kick, which was deftly covered, but her swinging blade caught John on his upper thigh. Despite the damage, John smoothly moved sideways and again lifted Mae Lin with a combination of body hits that sent her reeling.

Bouncing immediately back onto the attack Mae Lin wielded her knife with continuous combinations forcing John on the back foot. Dancing across the debris she delivered a powerful kick to the head. Spinning with the blow to minimise its effect, John landed with balanced recovery but suddenly no foe to face.

From the darkness he was hit without warning by the driving force of the workman's trolley as Mae Lin pushed him toward the windows. She was manic. Avoiding calamity, John just managed to fall to the side as the trolley burst through the glass.

Alerted by the shattering impact, the men below hastily looked up. The loaded trolley, preceded by jagged sheets of glass, smashed onto the parked cars as policemen scurried to safety.

Captain Leslie picked himself off the ground and immediately began yelling, "Get some light up there."

Quickly he spoke into his radio, "Team Alpha. The second level. East side ... Go, go."

Cursing at his dirty suit he turned to a young SPG attachment standing on the outer with a rifle.

"Angelo!"

The young man ran over eager to be involved. "Here's your big chance to make yourself useful." Leslie pointed to the dilapidated building opposite, "Get up there and tell me what you see. Go."

Angelo ran off as Leslie's men used vehicle-mounted spot-lights to illuminate the windows. Sheltered behind their cars they drew their weapons and waited.

The lights from below lit the glass and a section of the ceiling. The ambience played on the room as a heavy broom handle was taken. John regained his feet to hear the sinister hum of the makeshift staff as it whirled threateningly toward him.

Back in familiar territory, Mae Lin now stood in the open. As she began her balletic movement his eyes followed the arms that produced the weapon's arc. He braced himself for the onslaught.

Mae Lin attacked. Controlled and methodical, each blow blindingly swift. John moved with sublime agility as he successfully blocked and countered. Backwards and forwards the battle for supremacy raged as the tempo was lifted.

With furious pace the fight travelled the length of the room. Skillfully using both his feet and hands John continually pressed Mae Lin's attack by forcing her into defence. Pulling out all stops Mae Lin used the reach of her weapon to deliver a shattering barrage of clinical severity that brought John momentarily undone.

Angelo carefully avoided the 'Danger under Repair' signs and rushed into position on his roof. Looking up he waved at the light from the chopper as it fell over him on its way back to the Colosseum. Quickly he took the covers from his sights and scoured the room with his rifle.

John winced in pain as Mae Lin twirled her staff and finished with it pointing at him. Her breathing was laboured and her panting rose and fell with the growing excitement of what she perceived as the coming kill. Their eyes locked.

Smirking with a girlish grin she was confident of her power. John's eyes bore back into her and darkening further, exposed his rage and menace. Shaken by his intensity, her smile faded.

Angelo had the two of them in his sights and spoke into his radio, "One male on the floor. One female standing. They're a long way from the door."

Leslie's voice echoed across the airwaves. "Hit the door."

The door exploded with a loud bang. Mae Lin's eyes travelled instantly to the source. Through the resultant smoke, two weapons penetrated and fired two stun grenades in quick succession. As they cascaded into the room John seized the initiative and launched himself at Mae Lin.

Grabbing her in a rugby tackle he propelled them both toward the window facing the street. His momentum carried them through.

The grenades exploded shattering many of the Colosseum's old windows showering the police in glass.

Free-falling together Mae Lin and John landed on the Monorail as it passed under them in exactly the same moment as they fell. The force of the landing separated them. The inertia of the moving train catapulted them dangerously over the edge. Falling to either side the two hung precariously onto the edge of the roof thirty feet above the street. Aware of their vulnerability each tried desperately to climb back up before the other could take advantage.

Inside, passengers screamed as John's hanging body smeared blood across their window from his leg and chest as he struggled for leverage.

From his vantage point, Angelo was the first to see what had happened. "Shit!" He exclaimed, "They're on the rail."

The eyes of the police watched as the Monorail sped by the alleyway taking Mae Lin with it.

Leslie began yelling, "Clear these vehicles. Quickly!"

Hastily he activated his radio, "Somebody get me a visual," and looking up at the chopper added, "Air Wing, follow the Monorail." Yelling at another subordinate he screamed over the sound of revving engines, "Harvey! Call Transit and tell them to turn the bugger off." Back into the radio, "Team Bravo, follow that bloody train."

Angelo diagonally slung his weapon over his shoulder and dashed toward the other edge of his building. In his rush he forgot the warnings. Under his weight the roof gave way and Angelo fell through to the next level ... and again through to the next level below that. Landing onto the leading edge of plasterer's scaffold it over balanced and tipped, propelling the hapless attachment through a large window facing the street.

Beside the collapsed scaffold and lying amongst the debris Angelo's radio had come adrift.

"Angelo, what do you see? Angelo?" It squelched.

The police chopper followed the Monorail as the SPG helicopter joined in the chase. Swooping low through the light of the helicopter above it, the marksman directed the pilot to get in close.

Below in the alley and connecting street, there was chaos as vehicles accidentally collided with others as the police tried frantically to react. Leslie screamed purple-faced instructions as Sergeant Pearson negotiated a car through the mayhem and headed off after another vehicle already in pursuit.

"Move it ... Get that out of here ..." bellowed Leslie before trying the radio once again, "Angelo? Angelo?"

Several storeys above the ground, Angelo hung precariously by his webbing just below the window that he had broken. Still shaken, his weapon remained slung across his shoulders and he was covered from head to toe in dust. Vainly he reached for a hold but was stranded. Hanging in relative silence, he watched the Monorail turn left.

In pursuit, the two police cars rounded into the heavy traffic with their lights flashing and sirens wailing.

Managing to climb onto the roof of the train first, Mae Lin saw John almost there himself. Trying to get to him she was suddenly caught in the helicopter spotlight and forced to dive under a passing sign that nearly swept her off. John, finally able to make his feet, now stood aggressively at the other end. Up ahead he could see the approaching bend of the rail's horse-shoe track as it resumed its repetitive cycle.

Inside the SPG chopper, the marksman tried valiantly to hold Mae Lin in his sights. Periodically seconded to government culling programs to reduce wild boar herds from the air, his experience was now being tested on a human target.. on a moving train, in a built up area, with irregular turbulence. "Steady ... hold her steady ... I think I've got her," he called to the pilot.

"Commander this is Sniper One we have the target," The pilot transmitted.

Leslie, about to join the chase, glanced at the body bags now being loaded and snapped the radio up to his mouth. "Take the shot," he ordered.

"Green Light" the pilot yelled. The marksman fired. The Monorail swung left and Mae Lin moved laterally out of his sights and immediate danger. The round imbedded harmlessly into the side of a building with a puff of dust.

Leslie tensely waited. "Negative. It's a miss." Cursing he jumped into the car and sped off.

Trying to keep an eye on the train, Sergeant Pearson battled the traffic as he swerved to follow the car in front. In the blink of an eye the lead car was T-boned by a civilian car entering the intersection from the right. Pearson slammed on his brakes and spun his wheel in a frantic effort to avoid collision. Sliding into the parked cars on the side of the street he accelerated through as sparks flew off his rear mudguard from the heavy contact. With his siren screaming and his heart pounding, he continued with the pursuit.

A city block away from the rear of the Colosseum, the Monorail slowed as word to stop reached the driver. Seizing the opportunity Mae Lin leapt onto the landing of an adjacent building. Seconds later, John followed.

As soon as his feet hit the ground she again set upon him with the knife. Cut across the upper arm he repelled with his own aggression. Combinations of lefts and rights, body punches and spectacular kicks flew between the two as they moved progressively toward the building. Both were masters and the skills were breathtaking. John, physically stronger, Mae Lin defended with attack and run.

Circled by the light of the police helicopter they battled at a frenetic pace as John concentrated on avoiding the knife.

Like a rabbit caught in headlights, a stunned window cleaner dropped his bucket as they advanced toward him. Using the distraction John drove Mae Lin backwards with a kick to the chest.

Breathing raggedly, Mae Lin rolled with the blow and withdrew through the cleaner's access to the office inside. The large open plan room contained neat rows of equipment and desks.

Seconds behind her, John was instantly caught in another assault. Wielding her knife like a sabre, Mae Lin screamed savage abuse as she relentlessly slashed after him. John defended with everything he had as they both careered into office furniture and leapt over desks.

Bouncing off a water cooler he blocked furiously. Seizing an opening he stung with a lightning strike to the soft flesh at the bottom of her neck. During her gag reflex, and the split second that she buckled, John kicked her firmly into a bank of computers and their station. Landing solidly, Mae Lin rebounded and spun quickly to cover her defence. They measured each other. Both were panting. Their stamina was being tested. John moved into a slow and deliberate stance.

Sergeant Pearson had stopped his damaged vehicle at the building lit by the helicopter. Finally he had found an entrance and proceeded to run inside. Behind him with screeching tyres and sirens screaming Team Bravo arrived in support.

Again the two engaged in combat. This time, in a slow dance of deadly intent. Desperate to gain an advantage Mae Lin lunged forward, but it was a critical mistake. John out-manoeuvred her and with brilliant combinations and blinding speed knocked the knife across the room and sent her powerfully back. Falling heavily, Mae Lin was severely shaken. Bleeding freely she came angrily to her feet.

Pearson found the stairs and raced up as fast as his legs would carry him. A flight behind him the armed SPG squad followed.

Furious and indignant, Mae Lin launched an avalanche of blows and kicks, but her effect was waning. No longer concerned for a weapon John efficiently despatched her sideways with superior strength. Puffing wildly she struck again, and yet again he parried and sent her back. He sensed his advantage.

Striking again, John easily out pointed her and mockingly slapped her face. He had her. Screaming her venom Mae Lin fought desperately with flailing fists and searching nails that clawed at him while she bared her teeth. Unimpeded, John grabbed her arms and yanked her forward until they were face to face.

With her arms restrained, she lost all control. Lunging forward Mae Lin was manic as she spat streams of saliva and tried desperately to sink her teeth into his flesh. John head butted her. Following strongly, he landed blow after blow until finally Mae Lin collapsed. Her body crumpled and exhausted.

Moving to stand over her he looked down at the broken embodiment of evil. Rolling toward him, she smiled. Angrily, he hit her again.

Reaching down he grabbed her head and lifted her to him. Bleeding heavily himself he spoke carefully so he could be certain she would comprehend. "This, is for Risso," he said quietly, "My friend."

Just as he motioned to strike, Sergeant Pearson burst into the room surrounded by armed men. Struck by the sight of the two bloodied combatants, they lowered their weapons and waited.

John could feel all their eyes were on him. Quietly, they let him decide.

Visions that only moments ago dominated his existence, suddenly became distant and unimportant. With his heart full of love for Rachel, John remembered a friend's advice.

'... It is our way of survival John. Courage is the measure of how we control it. Anger is the measure of how we don't.'

Slowly John released his grip. His tormentor, impotent and grotesque, slipped away from his grasp and finally and forever, his life. It was over.

Standing at his full height he looked across at Pearson who holstered his weapon and nodded. John walked over the broken furniture toward him as SPG moved in.

Much has been written of the time spent between leaving consciousness and approaching death. It is impossible to prove scientifically, yet those who have returned from the brink, all describe the great light and the peacefulness experienced as they witnessed replays of significant moments during life ...

It is the same with the cleansing of a spirit dragged beyond endurance to such depths that its owner prayed for death.

The flash of a single moment can seem like hours as the memories of a friend and his laughter pass unhindered to take the shadow from the light ... to send an evil nursery rhyme to fade eternally unwelcome on the wind.

Badly beaten, Mae Lin looked nothing like a threat as two Team Bravo members reached down to begin her arrest.

Suddenly she sprang to her feet. Hideous with hate and covered in blood she revealed the knife. With a psychotic scream, and all her strength, she slashed the men back to give her room. Launching a last attack with her double bladed missile, she aimed at John.

A city block away, Angelo slowly expelled his breath and gently squeezed the trigger on his long barrelled rifle. The target ... no larger than a distant button from a shirt. The single hand-loaded 7.62 millimetre round exploded from the muzzle with a flash. Through his powerful sights he watched the trajectory as the round travelled at over three thousand feet per second down the service road between two buildings and four hundred and twenty metres toward the lit office a short distance from where the Monorail had come to a halt.

A small ping of cracking glass was heard as Mae Lin's hand was about to release the knife. A microsecond later a dull thud changed her expression of hate to one of surprise as the round violently exploded first into then out from her body. The impact instantly took her life.

Deftly moving to one side John caught the knife mid blades and only inches from the head of a stunned sergeant.

Shocked, Pearson watched John raise his eyebrows in mock surprise and drop the weapon harmlessly into an office bin. Smiling a broad grin, John felt the familiar feeling of being a little more like his old self.

Four hundred and twenty seven metres away a sole marksman swung helpless and happy. It had taken a shot in a million but finally he had done something right.

Chapter Forty-five

Two years later:

It was sunny. The cool sea breeze rose gently with the afternoon tide to move amongst the treetops and softly rustle their leaves. A pair of crimson Rosellas puffed their blue cheeks and preened noisily in the bushes as Daniel aimlessly watched three dusky butterflies flutter from the Boronia to the bottlebrush, and back again.

Tanned and wearing sunglasses he sat in his mother's favourite cane chair surrounded by the native garden of their home on the coast. Sighing contentedly, he leaned forward to replenish his juice. On the back of his T-shirt in large red letters was written 'Vinnie's Gym'.

"Hey Dad," he called, "Would you like a juice?"

Edward stood further along the garden watering his strawberries beside the house. Wearing gardening gloves, he rested the bulk of his weight on a crutch that clipped onto his arm. Aside from a slight droop in the corner of his mouth and a limp in his left leg, he looked as he had always done. His fingers had healed well and although the right index finger remained stiff, it was perfect for drilling holes in the soil and planting seeds. His humour was as keen as ever.

"Juice might be okay for muscle bound idle youth Daniel, but real men drink tea," adding, "With a tiny dash of non fat milk please and half a teaspoon of raw sugar ... and perhaps if the weight isn't beyond you ... one of those little biscuits your sister makes."

Daniel smiled and stood, "In the cup with the flowers on it?"

"Better make that two biscuits ... I need my strength."

A small lizard darted up the wall to stop briefly in the sun. It was a Gecko. Its small pads clung securely as it scanned for danger. Edward gave it a squirt. Immediately it ran along the weatherboards and scampered into the open window of the bathroom.

Sitting in the bath were Rachel and John. Amongst the bubbles, Rachel rested her head in the crook of John's shoulder as he lazily dangled a leg over the side.

"You know I don't think I could ever be happier than I am at this moment," she said.

"Is that because I'm cooking tonight? I warn you it's just a curry."

Moving closer in, Rachel kissed his neck, "I love you."

He squeezed her shoulder, "That's lucky, because I love you ... What's Josh doing?"

"Playing with the bubbles." She lifted their son from her knees and her eyes widened in mock surprise, "Hello beautiful baby! Hello!" Rachel nuzzled into his tummy and the little redheaded Josh squealed in delight.

John held out his arms and wrapped them tenderly around his son and wife.

Thousands of miles away, the English skies were typically grey and the incessant morning rain beat down on the highways that fed greater London. It was cold and the wind gusted as Penny Lassiter pulled off the M1. Sheltering herself from the elements, she moved inside the Moto food Junction to use the public phone. She had just dropped Harold off at Heathrow, bound for Dubai and another insurance calamity.

As the phone dialled she busily tidied her hair.

It answered. "Hello, Burton's Fish," said a young female voice.

Penny responded, "Hello. Look I'm terribly sorry to call so late but could I order a Christmas turkey?"

"Hold the line please."

A familiar male voice came on the line, "Penny."

"Dubai," she said.

"Any idea how long?"

"He took four changes of underwear."

"I see. Have a nice day."

Penny hung up the phone and left.

Ilya Chemenko replaced the receiver and immediately sent his agent to Dubai. On the desk in front of him sat a sealed security report on an Australian police sniper working with SPG. News of his daughter's engagement had been a surprise, but Nadya had given her blessing so now it was up to him. He sighed and opened the report.

Several thousand feet above the cliffs of Dover, Harold Lassiter accepted his scotch from the hostess and leant back to relax in the soft comfort of his wide leather chair. Checking his watch he assumed Penny had already made contact and wondered whom Ilya would send.

Gently sipping his drink he allowed its warmth to wash over him. He knew he hadn't been sighted in Jakarta that night at the Royal Orchard Hotel. It was an interesting predicament having a Russian agent for a wife. Like Gibraltar, his Penny.

Whistling cheerfully, Phillip Masterson walked down the gangway to his boat moored in the Hawaiian archipelago. Wearing his familiar braces over a T-shirt, he removed his weathered baseball cap as he stepped aboard. Sorting his mail he discarded the envelopes, deposited the new parcel on the galley table and reached for a knife.

Cutting the string, he unwrapped the paper from the cardboard box and looked inside. On top, was a hermetically sealed packet of fish fingers. Beneath those, a six-pack of 'Crown Lager' and last but not least, a picture of Rachel, John and Josh. He smiled. On the back was printed 'Thank you' and it was signed ... 'Gecko'.

The end

www.ingramcontent.com/pod-product-compliance
Lightning Source LLC
Chambersburg PA
CBHW070604170726
48291CB00003B/693